Commander's Dilemma

Seven Sailors for Seven Ships

By

Robert Parlier

Historical Fiction

CE 1885-1887

PublishAmerica
Baltimore

First printing

ISBN: 1-4137-9304-5
PUBLISHED BY PUBLISHAMERICA, LLLP
www.publishamerica.com
Baltimore

Printed in the United States of America

Dedicated to my most supportive wife
who has always offered many helpful suggestions
throughout this literary journey.

Many thanks to the following people:

Patricia M. Terrell
James Micklem
Ella Hilton
Rainey Moon
Jacqueline Shepperson
Charlotte Leslie
Ron and Maryanne Freeland

*Since this book is Historical Fiction, the names of actual
people of the past have been changed to protect their privacy.*

PROLOGUE

At Naval Repair Terminal: Leaving, a silent storm swept through his head. His brain kept asking: "WHY? WHY? WHY?"

Every word of the last few minutes blasted through like a runaway blow torch. It was his superior, his commanding officer, who spoke first. "I have a new assignment for you."

The rotund officer returned Lieutenant Commander McDill's salute and ordered, "At ease, Commander." Dennis McDill stood at parade rest, not at ease. For two years his body tensed at the sight of Captain Mort. Always sensing that Mort disliked him, McDill was agitated and uneasy around his commanding officer.

"Commander, I'm transferring you to Virginia, to City Point, Virginia. We have seven of our Civil War ships tied at a pier down there. They need repairing. I want you to take a crew and fix them." Norman Mort gazed out his window rather than face the tall man in front of him.

Shocked into silence, McDill's mouth drained dry as if someone had crammed sand down his throat.

"Take six men, no more." The captain continued to look out his wide window. "Take all the time you need. We'll send your families to join you later, I know that will be a great morale boost for you and your men."

Such an assignment could only mean some kind of demotion or worse, and McDill could not understand why.

⚓

At Navy Prison: Choked semiconscious, the prison guard slumped to the floor. It worked. He snapped the key from the guard's belt. Another guard, hearing the commotion, sped to the cell.

Seeing two escapees, he instinctively blew his whistle. Five uniformed men chased the fleeing convicts into the courtyard. For three months, Gaith Johnson had secretly dug a hole under the fence. Reaching the hole, he uncovered the dry sod and squeezed his body into the narrow tunnel. His accomplice slid through the crumbling sides directly behind him. Soon the fast-darting duo ducked into a nearby thicket. Thorns dug their sharp talons into the skin of each man. Bleeding, panting, the two dropped into a cool stream about two miles from prison. While they enjoyed their brief rest, Gaith heard a familiar sound. A train whistle screamed a mile away. Its boxcars wheeled slowly enough for him to grab an open door and sling himself inside. His inept cell mate reached for the door and missed. Two bloodhounds were seen chewing his friend's leg, with five guards close behind.

An hour later, the train stopped at a water spout. Its boiler gauge registered almost empty. An engineer, lone and in charge, dismounted to pull down the spout and water the thirsty boiler. Finished, he turned to enter the engine room. Gaith saw his chance. Near the track he spied a two foot piece of iron railing. He picked up the weapon and smashed it hard against the back of the engineer's head. The victim tumbled backwards, rolled over in a quiver. Gaith leaped in, shoved in some coal and began to pull levers. A successful lever pull got results. It commanded the train to leap forward. Gaith leaned out the opening to see if he was being pursued. He spotted a body lying in a pool of blood. The quivering had stopped.

Chapter I

Panting hard, Chief Petty Officer Rogers broke from his exercise, trying hard to fill his lungs with the morning's oxygen. It felt like ice was seeping into his pores. "Lieutenant, do you know where we're going?"

"I only know we're to report here and wait for our commander. I'm sure he'll know where we're heading." Lieutenant Dubois checked every crammed duffel. "It looks like we're packed for the duration," he observed. "It could be a long time."

Rogers, still shaking from the cold, chattered, "Sir, I hope it'll be warmer where we're goin'. If our skipper got caught in the hurricane eight weeks ago, he may not make it at all."

Rogers painfully remembered that hurricane seasons were not ideal for crossing the Atlantic. Unfortunate mariners often had to struggle against the roughest stormy weather. Atlantic winds could slam their brutal waves against seagoing vessels producing countless shipwrecks. Towering, choppy waves could tear out the seams of a large vessel, even a durable frigate. Gale winds shredded sails until they flapped around like tattered rags ripped to pieces by cannon balls. Many a sailor was washed overboard into the angry sea that literally pulled him beneath the keel of a floundering vessel. Chief Sam Rogers remembered very well many violent crossings during nature's worst seasons.

Rogers served in three combats. His face, furrowed and bronzed, depicted a face blown by westerlies and burned by the equator's scorching sun. Aged slightly beyond his years, he could be anybody's grandfather. White hair, with streaks of red, poked out from his head, eyebrows, and ears.

Down a nearby street the crew heard the piercing squeal of a police whistle. They caught sight of a young man galloping ahead of a pear-shaped cop with a handlebar moustache that curved to each side of his nose. The old silver-haired policeman was too slow to catch the villain. "Halt," the elder peacekeeper yelled with a voice that wobbled with his steps. The thief sprinted among the tall dark buildings and disappeared.

Rogers caught a vision he witnessed long ago. A similar chase. His mind's ear could hear it clearly. *"Drop that pocketbook right now! You heard me. Drop it. Gaith, I don't care if your Dad's a millionaire. You blasted thief. Drop it now." Youthful feet easily outran the aging lawman. In seconds the boy disappeared, leaving one pudgy policeman to slump down on the sidewalk. The old cop shook his fist. "Boy, if I ever get you, I'll haul you before your father and the nearest justice of the peace."*

Chief Rogers shook his head to pull his mind back to the present. "This harbor town's full of thieving scum. I, for one'll be glad to get outa' here." Rogers fetched his spyglass from his duffel. When he opened it all the way it was almost as long as he was. "This is better than government issue," he bragged. Slowly the super-extended scope panned the harbor several times for some ship bringing a boss bearing good or bad news. "No ship in sight, Lieutenant." His ice-laden whiskers moved with the beat of his lips. "He must be late or we're early."

"Chief, I'm sure we're supposed to report on this dock at this hour, but...."

Ear drums vibrated. Everyone stopped. A whistle blew its screeching notes into the cold morning. It was sharp as a sword slicing through metal armor. Wheels pounded their harsh clacks on parallel irons. Thundering decibels bounced at all angles over the harbor. The squealing whistle offered its plaintiff prayers to heaven. Two giant hisses sneered at nearby pedestrians when the locomotive arrived. Lieutenant DuBois spun around to face the engine's familiar sound. He could see the ancient Iron Horse pulling its cars beside the waiting platform. DuBois shouted above the train's caustic sounds. "It's him!" Puzzled men eyed each other asking the same question, "Our C.O.? On a train?" They moaned. DuBois cheered. He checked his pocket watch and glanced at Rogers. "Our boss is nearly on time."

"Lieutenant, we're going by train?"

"I certainly hope so. I haven't ridden a train for years. I really want...."

"Look, Sir. Coming down here." O'Leary's eyes boggled.

Up the street a starched-backed, quick-stepping figure marched toward the freezing group. The lieutenant called attention immediately, moved forward and saluted. "All present and ready, Sir."

He saluted, then a loud voice bellowed, "I am Lieutenant Commander Dennis McDill of the U.S. Navy. I'll be your C.O. for this assignment. We'll have to go by train. I couldn't secure a ship." His shoulders squared like iron rods and his piercing ice-blue eyes flashed like signal lights. "Prepare for personal inspection." Every man stiffened like ironing boards stuck in concrete. Each seaman snapped a crisp salute when Commander McDill stepped in front of each sailor and asked him his name. Dennis McDill had transparent blue eyes, emphasizing unique clarity. O'Leary, six feet, had to look up to this commander.

Commander Dennis McDill planted his feet firmly in front of each serviceman, gave him a quick inspection. The senior officer turned to his junior officer and smiled. "These men appear to be able-bodied, seafaring men. Are they all experienced, Lieutenant?"

"Yes, Sir. All are experienced and ready for duty."

Commander McDill took two steps backwards and pulled out a sheet of paper. "Men, here we have orders to travel to City Point, Virginia."

At that, vivid images squirted through Chief Roger's mind. "Permission to speak, Sir?"

McDill lowered his paper. "Permission granted."

"Since the war ended that place became a Godforsaken part of the world—just one old mansion, a store, two churches, and a few run down houses. Frankly, Skipper, we were glad to leave that old town and get back home."

McDill felt the same. He lowered his voice and looked down at the chief petty officer. "I know, Chief, but our Navy has a special assignment for us. There are seven war ships tied to a dock down there. Headquarters wants us to check them out and repair them."

Perplexed frowns plowed jagged trenches down the faces of the six bewildered shipwrights standing on the pier. Rogers could not harness his lack of confidence. "Sir, those ships were put out of service long ago. They must be nothin' but rottun' hulls." All the noncommissioned mariners locked on each other's pupils. Despair hung like a cracked ceiling ready to drop at any moment. The crew's silence signaled a double depression. McDill quickly noticed their sagging morale, but continued.

"If we can fix them, we can use them again. That's what Captain Mort figures. The Navy needs to save money." McDill regretted this assignment. Rapid thoughts returned the jolt of a hateful flashback. *What a miserable mission for a faithful officer. I'd give anything to be on some battleship right now. Two battles, a silver star and I wind up with orders to take care of some old barges that haven't sailed in twenty years. Some higher-ups must want to get even with me for something. What do they want? Forced early retirement? Immediate resignation? Or what?"* His thoughts ended abruptly. Commander McDill faced the crew and pointed to the waiting locomotive. "Sailors, follow me."

Some discouraged seamen traveled toward the train station in broken formation with heavy duffels swinging on their backs. They had to trot to keep up with their quick-stepping leader whose agility could match that of a twenty-year-old. His Naval Academy training taught him to walk and march with a posture that any admiral could admire. Of his forty-four years, he spent fifteen of them at sea and five years fighting bloody wars at home and abroad. At least his orders gave him the privilege to choose his own lieutenant whose job it was to interview and to transfer some of the best shipwrights he could muster. Lt. Commander Dennis McDill wanted the best, for he realized they were destined for an almost impossible assignment—salvaging seven decomposing hulks. The moods of the men divided into three categories. Some dreaded the order, a few were eager for a new adventure, and some did not care either way. It was just another job.

Chief Rogers was a typical old salt who had served thirty-one years in the Uncle Sam's Navy. He was old enough to claim a grandfather who fought in the Revolutionary War. Younger seamen often developed a lasting respect for the ancient mariner. Not only did the aging petty officer relay orders from his superiors to enlisted men, he viewed young sailors as adopted sons. He could advise them better than a professional counselor.

A short march up a gentle slope led the group around the shore to the old Iron Horse whispering her steam and waiting for another cargo. Two boxcars were linked behind its engine. The first was designed for passengers and the second was built for freight such as luggage, equipment, medical supplies, and food. McDill wanted his men to be ready to survive anything, anywhere. "Stow your personal gear in the first car. Our tools, equipment, and rations will follow on the car behind us. While we travel, I want all of you to get some rest. You'll need your energy to unload this stuff when we arrive. Lieutenant DuBois and I will ride in the first seats, and the rest of you sit behind us," McDill ordered.

DuBois was a child with a new toy. He stepped up to the engine and fondly rubbed the "ribbed cage" of its hard iron sides. "Old gal, you are a wonderful sight. You look just like my old faithful friend that I had when I was twelve years old."

Commander McDill glanced at his second in command stroking the engine. "You think this old, faithful gal can get us to our destination?"

"Sir, she seems to be in good shape for an old lady. I think she'll make it."

"Good. Now get your things and we'll give these seafaring men a taste of land-lubbering."

"Aye, Sir. I'll be glad to oblige."

After they boarded, the engine gave a grunt, belched a puff of steam, and slowly churned itself down the tracks. Loud clacks accelerated until the old girl gained full speed. Thick sheets of black soot flew past the cars and some sifted into the windows, supposedly shut tight enough to keep out cold air. Passengers attempted to sleep but riding was so rough, it kept everybody open-eyed and angry. Voices jiggled with every vibration of the bouncing train as it rumbled southward to its target.

Passengers had to shout to be heard over the loud clatter of rolling wheels over solid iron. Those who hated their assignment detested the ride just as much. But Lieutenant DuBois was as thrilled as a new angel learning to fly. He paced up and down the aisle peering out every window. One time he opened the door to the engine room and climbed in to talk with the engineer. Both exchanged boyhood adventures with tracks and trains of the past. They talked half the way to the Point's train station. "When I was young, we lived near a train station in a little town. Then, I was a skinny kid. Not much fatter now." DuBois' wavy blonde hair and gray eyes gave him a royal air. He walked erect with the swagger of a Marine general. "Every day I'd jump on my bike and head down to the tracks. I learned to lean down and listen. The louder the sound waves wiggled, the closer my old friend came. I could even calculate the distance the train was by touching my ear to the rail." DuBois gazed wistfully at the control levers when he recalled his past.

"I rode trains to New York with my folks many times. My old man was a conductor on a passenger train. If we rode with him, we could ride free. When I turned twenty-one, his friend taught me how to stoke coal and throttle one of these old ladies." The engineer reminisced with a sigh and stoked the boiler again.

DuBois talked in a fast stream of chatter. The engineer had to butt in when the lieutenants had to pause and refill his lungs.

Rogers squirmed and wiggled his strong oarsman's shoulders. "This old crate's bumpy as an old run-down choo-choo I rode one time. When I was younger my bones could tolerate jolts and jerks much better. Man, I hope this trip don't last much longer. My tail bone can't take many more of these bumps." Rogers groaned loud enough for McDill to hear him grumble.

"Relax, Chief, we'll be there soon." The commander was uncomfortable, but he could not admit it to his subordinates. He closed his eyes pretending to sleep. Enthusiasm kept DuBois wide awake.

Eventually the old horse's wheels cranked slower and slower until they stopped. A drab colored train station came into view. Old Iron Horse humped her way to the platform where the station master stood smiling to greet arrivals. Earlier, his telegraph tapped a message advising him to expect a gang of seven sailors. His curiosity struggled with his placid composure. "Why sailors?" He mumbled and shook his head. "Don't see many Navy guys here since the war."

The old lady had halted to a full stop for the station master to grab the mailbag hold in few letters and parcels for the citizens. A slender bald-headed engineer jumped onto the platform.

"Any trouble, Clyde?" The station master strode over to his boyhood acquaintance.

"Nope. No trouble, but it was colder in Baltimore than wet bathing suits in Greenland when we left. Thank goodness, it's a little warmer down here."

"Yeah, a little. But we have some good and bad. Tell me. What's the Navy doing down here?"

The short, bony engineer looked at the station master blankly and pushed back the remaining dozen hairs on his scalp. "I don't really know. I heard some of 'em talk about our old abandoned ships. Didn't they send you a telegram or something about why they are coming down here?"

"No. Just that they were coming. Reckon it's a secret? Who's in charge?"

"An officer named McDill."

"Is that him?" Comer pointed to the platform. "That young good-looking one standing beside the car giving orders?"

"No. That's his lieutenant. The one you're looking for is a Lt. Commander. You know, more gold on his arms. He's the taller one, about 6'4", I figure. See him? Over there."

"Yeah, I see him walkin' straight over to the platform. Reckon I better salute?"

"Aw, I don' think that'll be necessary."

McDill leaped onto the platform like a leopard hopping on an impala. He requested in his most official voice, "Are you in charge?"

"That'd be me. I'm Horace Comer at your service."

"I'm U.S. Navy Lt. Commander Dennis McDill, and that young officer coming over here is Lieutenant Phillipe DuBois."

"Please to meet you both. Welcome to City Point." Comer shook hands and inspected the cargo. Curiously, he asked. "Do you have a place to stay?"

"No, do you know somewhere we can stay?"

"Well, those folks over at the Ellis House sometime take in roomers."

"Think they'd taken in seven? We have our own food and supplies."

"Can't really say for sure. Want to follow me, Commander? We'll go see."

Comer led McDill up the crest of the hill to the Manor mounted majestically on the very tip of a sharp point of land between two rivers. McDill enjoyed many beautiful harbors in his lifetime, but his eyelids yawned wide at the sight of the Appomattox River and the James River as they tumbled together to carve out a basin a mile wide. One small sailboat slipped up the Appomattox with two fishermen trolling for some elusive fish. Suddenly a flashback rattled around in his cranium. He remembered several naval gunboats stretched across each river. Large cannons mounted in turrets swept their huge muzzles across each river searching for enemy intruders. Each firing created such a recoil it could shove a ship ten feet backwards. Smoke clouds ballooned a bluish haze over the harbor after many volleys were hurled at the enemy. In the midst of one battle, two enemy ships broke in two and turned keel-up. A score of sailors from the sunken ships swam to shore. If they found the right shore, they found security. If they found the wrong shore, they found prison.

McDill walked beside the skinny-necked citizen who smiled gregariously between two bucked teeth. Comer had no education, but was a bright man nonetheless. In Grant's army he learned the telegraph. After the war, Horace Comer was hired to run the local telegraph office. His chief pastime was fishing, fishing for any aquatic denizen.

"You lived here long?" McDill asked.

"I was in the Northern Army during the war and served as a telegrapher. When I was discharged, I decided to stay here. I really like running the telegraph and the train station. My wife and younguns came down and we bought a little house about two blocks west of here."

Looking back at the shore, McDill spotted three small boats and a dinghy. "Those boats I see tied up down there, can they be rented? We might find a need for some."

"All but one of the boats are mine. The dinghy was left here by your Navy. Everyone in town can use it. Sometimes I rent my boats, but you may use them free of charge," Comer offered.

"Thank you, Mr. Comer. Those may come in handy."

"Around here people call me Comer. You can call me that, Commander."

Up close the big house looked huge. "Why I never realized that was so big. During the war we often sailed up and down these rivers some distance from the Manor. We had no time to visit, but I still remember this regal-looking place."

"Commander, many people marvel at the size of the biggest house on our Point."

"Comer. What do you do for entertainment?"

"When I'm not working at the station, I fish, mainly for sturgeons. They're all bone on the outside, but inside we think they're good to eat. And I get a good price for caviar."

"Caviar? The only caviar I ate was in Paris." He stopped to think. "By the way, our men haven't eaten a good home cooked 'steak-and-potatoes' meal in days."

Comer kept talking. "We have the best caviar. But I'm told the sturgeons are running out of food. They won't last long around here." He looked over the hill crest "Oh, here we are. I'll ring the doorbell and introduce you to Mr. Roberts. He's been the occasional caretaker for the last few years. When Miss Josephine Ellis is home, he's her butler, also."

"I'm really impressed with this big house."

"Excuse me a moment. Here's Mr. Roberts now."

Seeing the officer, Roberts nodded making a slight bow.

"Commander McDill, I want you to meet Ralph Roberts."

"My pleasure, Sir. Gentlemen, please come in." Roberts' shiny face, featuring perfect teeth, nodded again. A large parlor near the entrance hall stretched out to receive and welcome visitors. McDill's eyes widened showing white circles encasing their exposed irises. He was thunderstruck! Old Colonial-style furniture glistened with tenderly applied polish. Queen Anne furnishings glowed without sunlight or lamplight. Triple dental crown molding glided gracefully between the walls and ceiling.

"Mr. Roberts, you must be proud of this mansion and these fabulous furnishings."

"I am. I only wish I owned them."

"Mr. Comer told me you are the caretaker. I must say you've done a fine job with this wonderful palace and its furnishings."

"Thank you. I try hard to keep this Manor in good order." Roberts served a round of grape wine while the commander informed Comer and Roberts about his background highlighting his mission to save seven ships. Both

Comer and Roberts wagged their heads with an undertone of undefined depression. "Commander, those ships have been tied up to the dock unattended for almost twenty years. You have a great challenge ahead of you," Roberts warned.

"Why I came to see you, Mr. Roberts, is to seek lodging for my men before we take a look at those old vessels," McDill explained with a silent hope.

Roberts rubbed his chin with his dark brown hands until his fingers itched. Both palms opened in surrender. "Sir, I'm afraid all of your company cannot stay here. This is a treasured building. We allow only distinguished gentry, such as you, to sleep in this most historical structure."

"You mean I can stay, but my men can't?"

"I'm afraid so, Commander."

"Then, where can they stay? I won't leave my men."

"Commander. Lodging is very scarce here. However, you might arrange some meals. Mrs. Ellis, wife of our beloved physician, often feeds many at a time. In fact, during the war she fed groups of soldiers and sailors. At the moment she's housing two civilians that are passing through."

"Where's her house?"

"By your compass, up the lane due west. Take the road behind this house. You'll see a small road as you veer to the left. We call it Brown Lane. Dr. Ellis' home is the fourth one on the left. Mrs. Ellis should be home, but the doctor may be away on a call."

"Mr. Comer, will you take me there?"

"Yeah, I'm glad to help a fellow serviceman."

A half-circled path looped around the rear of the Ellis Manor where a small street, being blurred by a heavy rain, waited to dare any traveler to trespass over its soggy surface. Cedars drooped liked serfs bowing before their overlord. Under the force of an intense gale, tall poplars rocked and swayed like gospel singers. Frequent traffic had carved deep ruts that ran their crooked courses along the entire length of the road. Soft soil became a gummy quagmire. Acrid skunk odors clogged their nasal passages until their eyes watered. Two men plodded, slowly gathering globs of sticky mud that clung to the thick soles of their boots.

Through the haze they saw a clean, small white house, sitting as a statue of serenity by the side of the lane. The smell of lilacs soon replaced the skunk's stinking aroma. White house paint was so bright, it wiped out the atmospheric gloom. Comer knocked the clay-red mud from his boots, walked up the steps of the porch and tapped lightly on the front door. Soon, a pleasant face peered out from under graying hair that sported two dark blue bows. "Good morning," a cheerful voice softly welcomed both as McDill continued to wipe his boots. She adjusted her apron cracking the door wider. "Come in, please." Mrs. Ellis quickly recognized the officer's insignia. "Commander, won't you have a seat?"

Comer introduced the Naval officer. "Mrs. Ellis, this is Lt. Commander Dennis McDill."

"My honor, Sir." She nodded. "Please excuse me a moment while I take my roast out of the oven." The slender lady faded out of the room into the kitchen. A mouth-watering smell of beef cooking in the oven floated into the nostrils of two hungry men.

"That'll be some dish when it's cooked." McDill's tongue licked his lips twice.

"She's one of the best cooks in Virginia," Comer boasted.

"I can believe that," McDill agreed. He pictured her in a neatly pressed dress under her starched white apron. He fancied her cleaning every utensil just after she used it. At the sound of small feet, he looked up to see a prim pepper-white haired lady glide through the threshold and slide into a seat opposite the two salivating males. Her large eyes looked directly into McDill's.

"What brings you here?"

"Seven old Monitor-type ships, Mrs. Ellis."

"So you came to see our small armada languishing beside our old pier?"

"Yes, Ma'am."

"Commander, we haven't seen many ships in our harbor for several days."

"We came by train. Six other seamen and I have been assigned to repair and take care of those ships down at your dock."

She wiggled a feeble smile, her raised eyebrows betrayed her feelings. "You don't say?"

"Yes, Mrs. Ellis, that's our order. I came to see if you're willing to board seven hungry men for a while. We can furnish some dry goods—flour, meal, canned vegetables, some dried meat, and seasoning."

From her seat she waved at a small door. "We've canned a lot of fruits and vegetables this year. Our pantry is filled to the ceiling."

"Naval Headquarters gave us money to pay you a modest sum."

"For regular meals that will be all right, but when we have a special occasion, it's on the house. And this is a special occasion." Two small dimples depressed when she smiled at the officer.

"That's very charitable! I wouldn't have expected such outstanding and friendly generosity." He emphasized "outstanding" with a high pitched note.

"Where are you staying, Commander?" she asked rubbing wrinkles from her apron.

"Do you know any place that can put up seven seamen?" he asked.

"Unfortunately, there isn't much lodging is available in town." The prim lady of the house shrugged.

"Do you have any rooms to rent, Ma'am?"

"We have two tenants. After that, we have no room, but I can cook more food today and treat your men to a free meal."

"That is supreme kindness, Mrs. Ellis."

"I'll have the food ready in an hour. Can you bring your crew over?"

"Yes Ma'am. Gladly. We'll have just enough time to unload our gear from the boxcar. The engineer left one car so we could use it for storage, but we have to unload some items. And I want to inspect those ships soon."

"Good luck, Commander. If I may say, 'It's nice to have you aboard.'"

"Thank you. We'll return soon."

When Comer and McDill left, the rain had stopped and the mud began to dry into hard red clay.

"Mr. Comer, I'll find my way back. My men are waiting."

"If I can help, please let me know. I live a few houses from here."

Commander McDill and Horace Comer separated with a handshake. When he approached the pier, McDill could see six people standing beside the boxcar enjoying the meager warmth provided by a winter sun. They stood at attention when they saw their commanding officer and gave him a brief salute. "Lieutenant, you and the men follow me. We're going down to the dock and see what we have waiting there for us."

Chief Rogers paused and looked at his C.O. "Sir, may I ask a question?"

"Sure, go ahead."

"Is there any lodging in town?"

"We have a place to eat, but no place to sleep. I'll get to that later. On the double, let's go."

Seven sailors walked downhill to a broken-down deserted dock. Seven ships slowly rose and fell with the motion of tidal water from the basin. The sad scene produced several agonized groans. What they saw was unbelievable. Four were half submerged. All flags were shreds. Metal sidings had grown huge blotches of rust an inch thick. Some of the large Dalgreen cannons were heavily loaded with reddish oxidation. Rotten wood could be seen under the metal exteriors of every ship. Sickening squeals reached out in pain at each wave that splashed against the unfortunate vessels. Amid the moans, DuBois shed a tear to behold such stately crafts descending into such a depth of dilapidation. His heart split when he saw so much ruin. He wailed, "My God, why did our government leave these great boats in such horrible shapes?"

McDill announced. "The news is worse. You're looking at your temporary homes."

Rogers sucked in a cubic yard of air. "You mean…those, Skipper?"

"There's nothing else," he admitted. "If we unload our provisions from the boxcar, we'd have these for our homes. Then our rations would suffer from the weather."

"Our train left three hours ago." DuBois observed sadly.

McDill's head nodded toward the ships as though he were counting. "I assign each of you one of those 'little houseboats.' You have rusted cannons for roommates."

"Sir, things can't be any worse, can they?" Rogers cried.

"I certainly hope not, Chief."

McDill felt like crying, but he held back to show a brave front. "Go to the boxcar, get your gear, and I'll assign you to your river boats to sleep in tonight. Understand?"

Unison "Yes, Sirs" meekly responded to their commander's reluctant decision.

Five grumbling non-coms staggered up the hill to get their duffles while Commander McDill stifled his silent anguish. He knew their spirits were plunging into a dark, endless abyss. But the good news might cheer them, he hoped. "Attention men. A nice lady up the street offered us a free meal. Mr. Comer and I could smell a very delicious roast cooking in her kitchen. As soon as we unload, we'll go marching for a good meal."

Every groan changed to applause. For days, every sea dog yearned for a good home-cooked meal. McDill hoped it could salve some of the jabbing shocks his crewmen endured.

"Commander, is she married?" Rogers inquired sheepishly.

"Her name is Mrs. Ellis, wife of a local doctor."

"Too bad. She reminds me of my Missy who died five years ago. She was the best cook on the East Coast." His head dropped in memory of his deceased lover.

Dennis McDill restrained a grin as he inspected all the men before they left. He wanted every gob to be clean and well groomed before meeting the elegant Mrs. Ellis, who dressed well even when she was working. McDill could still picture her sporting a neatly pressed dress under a starched white apron. Again he depicted her checking and washing each kitchen utensil just after she used it. "All right, men. You'll do for this affair, I hope."

"Skipper, river water ain't the best, but our ears are clean." Chief Rogers reamed his ears and bragged.

"Let's go. Left turn. March." Lieutenant DuBois commanded.

Three rows, two abreast, with one leader in front advanced in cadence up the short incline through the village. A late autumn sun supplied more warmth than expected. Thoughts of a good meal and a warm sun cheered the seamen as they paraded in double time toward the little house. They gathered gleefully anticipating a good meal simmering to satisfy their hungry appetites.

A slender man with a solid shock of glacial white hair waved his hand as the crew approached. "Welcome to our home. The Mrs. and I are expecting you. It's not often we see seafaring people these days."

"You're Doctor Ellis, I presume." Commander McDill extended his hand to receive the doctor's welcome. The doctor's hand, buried in the commander's, pumped with enthusiasm. "Mrs. Ellis informed me that you attended to many fighting men during the war. It's a pleasure to meet you."

"Yes. That was a long time ago, but I still take care of the sick and lame in this little village." He bowed slightly. "Please come in. Our humble table is set for all of you."

Each sailor entered, shook hands with his host and introduced himself. Mrs. Ellis rushed in, curtsied, and introduced herself. Her subtle palm signaled each one to sit. As they gazed at her, she glided by and conversed like one of the most graceful women they had ever known. For two people approaching their latter years, they exerted the energy of two happy teenagers at a barn dance. The couple could easily audition for the role of surrogate parents for the younger sailors sitting at their long dining table designed to board a dozen eaters. Cooked beef caressed the noses of every sailor sitting in the flickering candlelight recently lit by the host. Fresh cooked rolls made the servicemen sit at attention for one small bite. Sweet potatoes brightened the room even more. Apple pies lay in neat rows on the adjacent cabinet waiting to be devoured by seven starving men. They could hardly wait for the blessing's amen. After the prayer, rolls were passed, then the meat was served. Afterwards sweet potatoes found their way to each plate. Politely, everybody waited anxiously for the hostess to stab her fork delicately into a slice of beef before they began to eat. Potatoes, steaming with butter, melted into yellow pools over the red underground staples. Knowing mariners' preferences, Dr. Ellis produced a bottle of wine and a bottle of rum. "You may have your choice. Mrs. Ellis will pour, and we'll raise a toast before we eat. I want to toast our guests. Raise your glasses, men. I say, 'Here's a salute to our great United States Navy. Salute to our servicemen.'" Clinking glasses and thankful voices filled each cubit of the Ellis home. Some of the sailors ate with such ravenousness they almost forgot their good manners.

During the feast Dr. Ellis leaned over to Commander McDill and asked, "Why has the Navy sent you folks down here to look at those old ships?"

"They want us to repair them." He sighed, putting down his fork.

"Do you really think those unfortunate vessels can be repaired?" His eyebrows nearly tipped his hairline.

"Doctor, we don't really know. We'll see what we can do. We already know they're in horrible shape."

"Perhaps you can work miracles," Mrs. Ellis drawled with her smooth Southern lilt.

DuBois nodded. "From what we've discovered so far, it'll take a miracle, I'm afraid."

"Yeah, more than that." Rogers' cynical eyes looked like balls of spitfire.

"You men would be welcome to stay here, but we already have a full house," Ellis observed.

"We'll bunk aboard the ships. Each of us will take one and find a safe place on his ship to sleep."

Hearing that, the physician dropped his fork. His mouth gaped as wide as the yawn of a hippopotamus. The shock sent his fork rattling across the floor to bounce under a cabinet. The unflappable Mrs. Ellis picked up her husband's fork and asked, "Won't that be hard on the men?"

"It'll be tough, but seafarers are tough. We can take it. I always expect seamen to be ready for the worst."

All seven sailors savored the hospitality and the food; however, their throat muscles constricted at the thought of an uncertain night's lodging.

Pressing his napkin to his lips and wiping his broad chin, McDill smiled at his hosts. "We've been here for hours. If you two kind people will excuse us, we must get back to the dock before it gets dark."

After a brief farewell, the seven men, with full stomachs, lumbered down to the wharf. Behind them a sharp tailwind picked up speed and stabbed ice cold air between their shoulders. Strong gale winds ushered ominous black rain clouds that lifted over the horizon. Freezing rain splashed down and quickly became black ice on the ground. Tree limbs bent and broke under the pressure of increasing layers of the freezing stuff. Growing waves plowed over each other to reach the shore. All seven ships strained against their moorings so hard their tethers almost broke. They rocked and bucked like mad wildebeests.

"Men, listen up." McDill's bass voice boomed above the howling gale. "Lieutenant, you take the Atlas; O'Leary you take the Canonade; Chief, you have the Catskin; MacEaton you have the Manomac; O'Connell...Mattahorn; Sullivan, you have the Wycoff; I'll take the Leland."

A mantle of ice spread over the entire flooring of the pier. Its treachery caused men to skid at the slightest movements. Under supreme difficulty, they scrambled to stuff their scarce luggage inside their assigned sleeping quarters. Storm-tossed waves shook the dilapidated vessels until they strained to stay afloat. Seven ships found themselves careening carcasses swaying in a maelstrom.

Before boarding the Leland, Commander McDill stared at his floating bedroom, labeled "Leland," almost obliterated by heavy moss and scum. "Nice name for a little lady." He bent his head to duck into the turret. The devoted McDill loved all kinds of water craft, but this one was wretched and falling apart. He crouched to enter cramped quarters, straining to see in the darkness. He lit a match but as he raised up to see, he hit his head on a wooden beam. He rubbed his head in irritation. Then he checked it to see if it was bleeding. No blood, only a bump that was growing bigger and bigger. His match smelled dank from the wisps of light put out by the match. He could see black mold growing along the walls like a creature claiming the ship as its own.

The fire burned his finger and he dropped it, hitting his head again as he fanned his fingers in an attempt to cool them. He knew he'd have to find a candle soon if he wanted to see anything at all in this black hole. He stepped forward, his foot slid on a slimy mess and deposited him with a sharp thud onto the deck. Maybe it was a good thing he was unable to see clearly; otherwise, the slimy muck would have him utterly disgusted. In spite of his distress, he managed to unpack his duffel and shed his wet clothing. Over the high-pitched sound of the moaning gale, he could hear the ceaseless cursing of several disgusted sailors.

There was no competition for the best gunboat, for all were about equally miserable. Only the Leland seemed to have some faint hope of recovery.

Everybody was drenched, cold, and miserable. Even their blankets failed to defend against the numbing dampness. Rogers thought the elements were bad in the Arctic Sea in January. This was even worse.

One time, when he was an ensign, McDill barely survived a capsized ship in the North Atlantic. A wet, grayish cover engulfed his entire body. Salty water flowed into his mouth and nose, choking him. Desperate fear seized his mind. At first, his arms and legs flung helplessly while he was suffocating second by second. His whole life flashed into his memory. Death was getting impatient. Then something pulled at his brain—the will to survive. He had to survive. Directly above him a small shaft of light could be seen, forcing his arms and legs to spring into action. His limbs shouted, "head for the light." Swimming up, he swallowed enough water to make him gasp (the worst thing he should have done). Alongside the light, a small outline of a lifeboat appeared overhead. Encouraged, he held his breath to shut out the water. Suddenly, his mouth shot open for life-giving oxygen when his head burst into the gap where water meets air. An oar reached for him, and with one tremendous motion, he was slung into the boat and landed like a dead flounder.

"Thought you'd gone to Davey Jones' Locker." A crewman tossed him a blanket. "Ensign, our ship is gone. We're the only ones left, just me and the boson's mate."

"Did you see any others?" McDill searched the horizons.

"No, we've looked everywhere. It's real bad, Sir. There're thousands of sharks in these waters. All we found were fins and pools of blood."

McDill gave a silent prayer for the dying, and thanked God for his life and the lives of his rescuers. After two amens, McDill asked, "Any rations stowed away to keep us from starving?"

The boson's mate pulled out a small can. "We have twenty-five cans of this stuff. It ain't very tasty, but it'll keep us alive for a while. Which way, Sir?"

With both eyes shaded from the glaring sun, Ensign McDill calculated. He stroked his square jaw and uttered a slow, definite order. "Due west toward the sun."

Thirty-three cold days and thirty-three freezing nights on a lifeboat, three sailors consumed all their food. Long beards and sunken jaws made them look like whiskered skeletons of death. Finally a frigate, bouncing like a speck on a mosquito, was spotted on the horizon. The bony sailors, even weak from hunger, tore off their shirts and waved frantically. The frigate responded by flashing a signal and blowing its fog horn. A long rope ladder dropped down and each man mustered enough strength to climb up to the deck. McDill's voice almost failed, but managed a feeble pitch, "Permission to come aboard, Sir."

From the tower, the captain gladly returned the request. "Permission granted."

At that recollection, McDill's mind snapped to attention. Again his head bumped hard against the side of the turret. "If this little craft sinks, I wonder if I'd be rescued. I wonder." This night was little better than McDill's unforgettable lifeboat voyage. Storm winds wailed at the heavens until after 5 a.m. Only then could the crew catch a short nap. One of Virginia's fiercest nights finally ended. Ice began to melt when the sun peeked cautiously over the horizon, wondering if it was time to appear.

All of the sailors flew out of their ironclad hovels at dawn.

"O'Leary's hurt!" MacEaton's deafening screams alerted McDill and the entire crew. He howled with his hands cupped on each side of his mouth. Every hand rushed to the bow of O'Leary's ship. His hulk sank down in accelerated agony and folded on the deck His huge body curled as he grabbed his leg. O'Leary was a frightened human moaning in great pain.

"What happened?" McDill hovered over O'Leary.

O'Leary wailed, "Skipper, I think my leg's broken."

"How did this happen?" McDill quickly inspected the leg, not hesitating for an answer.

"That storm rocked my ship so hard it shoved me under the cannon. It got jammed between the cannon and the deck. I pulled as hard as I could to jerk it out from under. When I did, I heard it crack." Wincing in terror, he bit his lips. "My leg's broken!"

McDill ripped off his coat, tore his long shirt in two-inch strips. "This man is bleeding! MacEaton, get a splint. I'll need to tighten this tourniquet. When the blood stops, Sullivan, you tie the splint to his leg. Tie it tight, but not so tight it'll cut off the circulation. Sullivan's medical knowledge was nil, but he was able to twist the strips around the patient's leg enough for the commander's approval. "Sullivan, you and MacEaton carry him to the doctor. Hurry!"

O'Leary once won a 250-pound weight lifting championship. His solid muscular body challenged MacEaton and Sullivan to their limits. They made a human seat by crisscrossing their arms and locking their hands to each other's wrists. The two almost dropped their companion while staggering under their heavy burden. Twice they stumbled, almost to the ground, but again they locked their human bridge in a death grip. Leaning on their gritty determination, the living ambulance reached the steps of the doctor's house. Fortunately, Dr. Ellis was home. "Bring him into my office, first door on the left." Dr. Ellis sliced O'Leary's pants for an unhampered look at the wound. Ellis nodded to his nurse. "It's a compound fracture, and it's a bad one." Quickly, Mrs. Ellis, doubling as the nurse, rushed in and striped away the rest of the sailor's pants for the doctor to get a better look. She ignored the red spots of blood growing from O'Leary's wound, in contrast with her chalk white uniform.

"Someone pull back the curtains, so I can get as much light as possible. This one's going to be delicate." The doctor's head nodded in slow motion.

MacEaton, not familiar with the room, prowled aimlessly hunting for the nearest window. "It's over there. Just pull them apart and tie them," Mrs. Ellis directed.

"Nurse, give him something to ease his pain before we operate," the doctor ordered.

She gently poured several ounces on a cloth and eased it over O'Leary's nose. Soon his moans reduced to quiet, normal breathing. "I think he's ready," she said.

"All right, I'll begin to cut small slits just above and below the fracture to give more room. We'll have a clear view of both halves."

As the doctor's scalpel skillfully cut into O'Leary's skin, blood steadily oozed out of his veins. "Nurse, keep wiping so I can get a better view where to join these jagged edges." Both medics realized it was imperative for the puzzle to match precisely so the patient's leg would heal. Since both halves of the bone were shattered, Dr. Ellis had to muster all the skills he had learned. Mrs. Ellis constantly sponged the wound and wiped her husband's brow. The tiring physician shifted several times to take a second look. He had to be perfect, or O'Leary would never walk again normally. Dr. Ellis worried because his old hands were not as steady as his young hands. The operation lasted for more than two hours. Dr. Ellis was getting weary, each grueling

24

minute. Mrs. Ellis cleared sweat from her husband's forehead again. Twice Ellis was tempted to take a break, but that could mean disaster for his patient. He braced himself and stretched his arms for a brief relief. Eventually the pieces of the broken leg matched.

"There, you can wrap the bandage around the sutures. Pull the gauze tight."

MacEaton and Sullivan recognized the doctor's sigh of success and asked how soon would O'Leary's leg be normal enough for him to walk. "It'll be at least six weeks. I'd like to keep him here for at least one week until he recovers enough to walk a few steps," Ellis advised.

Returning to the dock, Sullivan and MacEaton sadly concluded that they had one less worker to help them with a very difficult job. When they told McDill about O'Leary's injury, McDill's transparent eyes gazed skyward and he groaned. "We'll have to do the best we can without him."

The next day invited a thirty-mile-an-hour wind that plunged thermometers down twenty-five degrees, typical of the area's unpredictable weather. Townspeople had learned to cope with the roller coaster rides of their thermometers. For at least two months they would keep summer and winter clothing unpacked. Summers sizzled with high temperature and soaring humidity. Winters could bring ice storms. Some felt mid-summer and mid-winter were the most miserable parts of the year. Outside labor was often hampered by the uncertain climate. Shipwrights' frozen hands slowed down their work considerably.

To forget their troubles, Chief Rogers and Third Class O'Leary spent short breaks swapping memories as they dangled their feet off the edge of the deck of the largest ship. When they sat side by side, O'Leary towered over Rogers' frame. Both were about the same age, but O'Leary's muscles still rippled like lake water driven by the wind. Rogers tried to relax on the long deck with his corncob pipe that remained unlit. One thing encouraged them. They had heard from the Ellis family that there was little crime in the village, unlike some of the larger cities of the world. Except for some fruit, nothing had been swiped for years. O'Leary stood up and limped around the ship. His accident left its calling card, a crippled leg with a huge scar that sneered at him when he looked at it. He longed for his agility to return. The old seaman could remember in the past seeing a boy snatch a banana and tried to run away with it. At that time he was a young policeman. When he spotted the young hoodlum, he sprang forward with an eight-foot lunge, grabbed the boy and returned the banana. He recalled releasing the boy's collar and pushing him into a corner for the grocer to watch while his helper scurried to get the little thief's parents. Widows of Baltimore quickly learned to depend on the tall, rugged cop to help them with strenuous work and children's discipline. Rogers vividly remembered a similar incident that happened while they were waiting for their C.O. In his mind he could see the boy, the stolen purse, and the old cop. He couldn't remember any names except the name the policeman shouted several times, "Gaith."

Five years ago, back in Baltimore, a wiry policeman led an adolescent up the steps of the Johnson mansion. Being handcuffed was not the young man's idea of a good time. Colonel Johnson already knew by telephone that his son was apprehended. "What's Gaith done this time?"

"Shoplifting, Sir." The dark, side-burned patrolman placed his left hand on the captive's shoulder and unlocked the cuffs with his right hand. "This time we'll leave him in your custody if you or he will pay for the stolen goods."

"What did he steal?"

"A rifle."

"How much?" Colonel Johnson reached inside his coat.

"It's listed for fifty dollars, but I can't take the money. It'll be up to you and the manager to settle this one."

Although Gaith was almost as big as his father, his dad jerked him inside the house. Gaith was lifted off his feet when the old marine pulled him into the parlor. The heavyset ex-serviceman's scolding lasted for more than an hour. It ended with one last paragraph:

"Gaith, I don't understand why you do these things. I can buy you a hundred rifles. We're rich enough to buy half of the town. If you don't stop this, you'll land in jail."

As usual, Gaith promised he would never do it again, but deep down he felt a kind of confusing resentment. Sometimes, even he failed to figure why he stole things. Gaith knew right from wrong, but he was obsessed with an uncontrollable urge to steal. His father, knowing this, often covered up for his son's weakness.

Sitting in front of the store, O'Leary and Rogers remembered their old times. "Yeah, I joined 'cause my folks had no money. I had to find a way to eat and I didn't want to steal it." Rogers recollected. He turned his head seeing that O'Leary was still in pain. To divert O'Leary's attention from his old wound, Rogers yelled, "Hey, remember that young guy back in Baltimore when we were waiting for the Skipper? I think he snatched a pocketbook. An old codger chased him until the old cop had to give up. He even knew the crook 'cause he yelled his name. It was Gaith, I think."

"Chief, your memory's better than mine, but I remember the woman yelling for the young pirate to stop."

"A speedy pirate at that." Rogers stretched, got up and looked directly into his friend's face. "O'Leary, did you chase a lot of thieves?"

"Oh, yes. Many times, but no more." He flashed a frown and held his leg. "This confounded leg's never going to be normal."

Misery shrouding the crew was virtually unbearable. Often they felt like weeping, but that was considered unmanly, especially for brave seamen. Still they wept inside without showing their anguish. Some cursed Headquarters for their despicable assignment. Dennis McDill believed he was being punished for something he couldn't imagine. Analyzing his situation, he could find nothing wrong. He had always obeyed orders and even went beyond the call of duty once. For example, designed ships. He actually created the best designs the shipyard had at that time.

Dennis strolled up and down the pier in front of the outdated and dilapidated monitors. They squatted and sneered at him, "Leave us alone. You can't save us. You're useless. Go home, sailor."

To make it worse, many of the citizens of the city seemed aloof and inhospitable toward the crew. Old wounds of the war opened when strange northern militia arrived. No one could be more despised by the older southern sympathizers than a northern sailor from Baltimore. They remembered the blaring cannons and their sailors slaughtered or captured. It seemed the crew had only three friends: Dr. and Mrs. Ellis, and Comer.

McDill had not met him yet, but Vice Mayor Brewer had heard about the presence of the Navy on the shores of his city. Brewer's crimson face, clenched teeth and fists could convey his wrath without saying words. But he had words—plenty of words. Brewer stumped in front of the country store. "Folks, y'all know where I stand. I'm agin' those gobs coming to town in their uniforms. I found out that most of 'em are Catholics, bad Catholics at that. They're not good like the few we've had here for years. If we don't watch, they'll take over. You hear? They'll just take over. They tell us they're here to do something about them old tubs in the harbor, but they won't stop at that. They'll run the town, and you and I won't have any more say. Let's run 'em out of town and take their old boats with 'em." His obese torso paused to fill his lungs. "Anyone here object?" Over fifty percent of the men and women thought silently. Out of fear, those who disagreed said nothing. They felt helpless because the mayor was in England visiting his sick mother. Many considered their mayor to be more tactful, but Brewer was in power in the meantime.

"So be it. I want twenty volunteers to follow me to the dock down there. We'll get rid of those deck swabbers once and for all."

Fifteen men volunteered to tramp down to the shore to confront McDill and his crew. They carried no weapons. It was a bare-knuckled affair.

Hearing the shouting mob, McDill sent MacEaton to round up the men. "Tell them to be ready to fight, fight with their fists. Go on. Move it!"

MacEaton's "Aye Sir" trailed behind his speeding feet. All the sailors positioned themselves on shore just in front of the gunboats. The tallest sailors, McDill, DuBois, and O'Leary stood in front of the rest. In contrast, Brewer followed behind his constituents. Fifteen belligerents literally flung themselves downhill howling and yelling one word in rhythm, "GOBSGOHOME!" The first attacker swung at McDill's head. Dennis sidestepped the blow, grabbed the aggressor by his britches and tossed him into the river. He struggled ashore, but he was too cold and wet to resume his fight with Dennis. The second attacker aimed to strike DuBois below the belt, but Phillipe parried the blow with a professional fencing motion and punched his attacker on the chin, which spun him around in severe pain. A third man galloped toward O'Leary. When O'Leary's assailant reached his target, the ex-cop grabbed his man in a neck lock. His victim choked, turned purple and fell to his knees when O'Leary's strong arm released him.

Three seamen stood side-by-side with clenched fists. "Next," yelled Skipper McDill. All of the aggressors stood like stones for a minute, then they scattered like rodents running from a forest fire. Three of them stumbled away rubbing their aching bruises.

Dennis, seeing them flee, sighed, "I'm afraid this is not over."

Chapter II

Cold strata clouds parked directly overhead. After winning the confrontation with the city's unsympathetic rabble, Lt. Commander McDill decided to have a short conference with his crew for two reasons: First, he wanted to calm them, and second, he wanted them busy preparing to get to work. "Look, fifteen men do not represent the entire town and you saw we sent those cowards running. Take a short break, calm down and let's get to work."

McDill had to pry his crew's minds loose from the lodging problem, so it was better to get specific. "Lieutenant, Chief, I want you to take a crew member and give every one of these wrecks a thorough inspection. O'Connell, Sullivan, start repairing the Leland right away. Lieutenant, I want a complete written report by tomorrow or sooner. Understood?"

"Yes, Sir, understood." The lieutenant saluted and turned about-face.

"While you're inspecting, I'll look for better quarters."

They had taken a quick look at each ship the day before, but this day revealed more problems. Obviously none of the ships were seaworthy. Every boiler was tortured with rust and falling apart. Seams widened to the breaking point. MacEaton's foot crashed through some rotten planks and fell through the decaying deck down to its keel. Not seriously hurt, but to his embarrassment, his pants ripped from his waist to his ankles. Blushing, he looked around to see if any feminine eyes were spying on him. To his relief, there were no ladies near enough to see him.

Rogers' growls could scare a tiger. "I've seen better in a junkyard. We'll have a devil-of-a-time mending these poor old boats. If I had a vote, I'd say we forget the whole danged thing and go home." His craggy face scowled, revealing tobacco-stained teeth chewing hard on the end of his pipe. Overhearing the Chief, Lieutenant DuBois ordered, "You don't have a vote.

Get back to work. The Skipper wants a complete report by tomorrow, or he'll have everyone of us keel hauled pronto—no court-martial—just keel-hauled immediately. Back to work." He repeated louder. "We wouldn't want to argue with our boss, would we?"

McDill tramped back onto the pier to check. "Lieutenant, I want an accurate estimate of how many metal and wood pieces we'll need. Headquarters might send us a barge with lumber and metal. I want us to be accurate. Can you do that?"

"Aye, Sir. That was one of my jobs at my last port," DuBois answered.

"All right, see to it. Get it done while I take care of some other business."

As Dennis McDill left the dock an idea emerged. He remembered where Comer lived. "*I bet Horace Comer can find a blacksmith for us. Back home the village Smithy knew about metals and how to bend them to suit our needs.*" Dennis oriented from the Ellis house, moved west and spotted Comer sitting on his front steps mending fish nets.

McDill's shadow interrupted Comer. "What brings you to my humble home?"

"We need your help."

"Anything to help our country's military. Name it, Commander."

Dennis looked up and down the street. "Is there a blacksmith around?"

"Sure is. You got any horses to shoe?" He grinned and picked debris from his teeth.

"No, but we've got seven ships to cover." Dennis continued to look up the street.

"There's a blacksmith's shop at the end of this street just before it turns into a country road. I'll be glad to take you there."

Somehow McDill sensed he could depend on the station master. "Is he any good?"

"Yeah, he's very good. He takes care of all the horses in town and county. Some say his nails are so good any carpenter would be glad to use 'em."

Comer and Dennis walked down another road full of ruts, so deep they could measure the amount of traffic from the depth of each furrow to show evidence of how much the Smithy's popularity had grown. About a hundred yards away, the men could see the Smithy's announcements—the clanging of hammer against metal, the acrid smoke above the store, and sparks popping out to meet a few snowflakes. The nearer they came, the more they could see flames fanning out from the anvil. Sparks flew in all directions when the hammer beat the metal into shape to fill the prescription of each hoof the blacksmith encountered. When they arrived, they could see Smithy straddling the leg of a nervous stallion. With a sharp curved knife, he dug out trash from a hoof and filed down its edges so he could properly fit a shoe to the horse's hoof. When he finished, the big stallion stamped his hoof on the clay-hardened ground. Relieved of the inconvenience, the horse pranced around to display his own satisfaction of having one shiny shoe that fit perfectly. Next, the stallion whinnied and offered another hoof.

"Simon, I want you to meet Lt. Commander Dennis McDill of the U.S. Navy."

The blacksmith looked up from the other side of the big horse. "Glad to meet you, but I don't believe the Navy has many horses to shoe."

Dennis answered. "You're right, Simon, but our Navy has some old iron clad ships to shoe. We need sheets of metal to cover those old dilapidated boats tethered to the dock down in the harbor. Can you do sheet metal?"

"Never worked in sheet metal, but I'll give it a try." Simon's dark tanned body moved from the side of the horse. Simon straightened his back, thrust out his massive chest. His flashing brown eyes reflected the pride of accomplishment, for he was the best. Horse owners would always tip a dollar or two when they left with a well-shod animal. Simon was so strong that townspeople believed he feared nothing, living or dead. Long hours of hard work earned him two arms bulging with enormous biceps. He looked at McDill, "When I finish today, I'll go down before dark and take a look, if you want."

"Smithy, if we can get our terminal to get the raw metal down, do you think you could hammer it into the shape of the forms we want? My C.O. agreed before we left Baltimore to send ingots. They don't shape them anymore for these out-of-date vessels, so they left us on our own to find someone down here who would."

"It'll be a big job, Commander. Your men'll have to construct a big table and cover it with bricks held together with concrete to keep the table from burning up. You know I'll have to heat the metal enough to make it bend correctly. "We don't have the facilities down here that you have up there."

"I knew we'd have to improvise. Our terminal was too busy to devote any time, material and labor to decommissioned vessels." Dennis pulled out his watch. "It's getting late. I have to find quarters for my men."

Just arriving, DuBois overheard the part "find quarters." He was bringing the report to McDill.

"Thanks, Lieutenant. You're on time." He quickly scanned the report. "It's worse than I thought."

"Even though it's bad news, I hope it's satisfactory, Sir."

"Lieutenant, we've got to try again to get decent quarters. We'll knock on every door in town again if we have to."

DuBois' chest heaved. "Sir, to get out of having a turret for a roommate, I'll do anything...anything, Sir."

"You take the west side of town. I'll take the east side," McDill ordered.

Despite the cold snow and sleet, the officers approached every home in the village. Some people were sympathetic, but threw up their hands and answered the familiar "No room." Some people who despised the North, slammed their doors in anger. Dejection, frustration and loss of hope started to siphon the minds of two desperate officers. However, outside of town a sliver of hope glittered when McDill knocked on one more door. It was a small farmhouse with bright blue curtains. A wrinkled hand appeared with the squeak of the front door. Then a warm voice joined the hand and invited Dennis to enter a tidy, comfortable living room. "Colonel, please come in. It's freezing outside. My wife started a fire a while ago." He took the officer's coat. "Sit and warm your hands. My name's Ralph Amesworth. We are always glad to see servicemen. Colonel, I was in the army during the war." McDill ignored being called "Colonel."

Dennis' long fingers and palms reflected the fire's glow. "I appreciate your fireplace, Mr. Amesworth," he said. "My fingers were getting numb."

Ralph admired his fireplace. "I had this built special, larger than most. We old folks get colder by the year." Amesworth was shorter than most, so he lifted his chin to see the officer's face. "But enough about us. I figure you came here for a reason. Can we help you?"

"Yes, I'm looking for room and board for my crew of seven. We're here to repair those rotting ships tied down at the pier."

Amesworth raked the gray stubble on his chin, pondering. "It's still not too dark," he noticed. "Look out this window. See that barn in the back?"

McDill squinted. "Yes, I can barely see it."

"We don't use that space any more since I retired. My wife and I can spruce up the place so your people'll be comfortable."

McDill was tempted to jump up and clap, but restrained his eagerness. "Sir, we'd be eternally grateful." Dennis looked out the other window. "Oh, I forgot. My name and rank is Lt. Commander Dennis McDill, U.S. Navy. My lieutenant is out there in the cold searching the other side of town for rooms."

At footsteps, Amesworth turned. "My wife's name is Sally. See, she's coming out of the kitchen now."

Sally heard part of the conversation and gave the officer a maternal smile. "Our children're grown and gone. We live alone in this little house. You could use it, but it won't hold seven sailors. I heard you talk while I was cooking. You and your lieutenant can be our guests."

"Thank you, no. We will live with our men." Dennis moved back to the fire for warmth.

Ralph extended his hand. "Our barn is yours, Commander McDill."

"Mr. Amesworth, this is the best news we've heard since we arrived!" Dennis shook Amesworth's hand violently. "We brought a boxcar loaded with food, tools, and other provisions. Is there any way we can prepare our own food?"

"We've got an old stove and a few old pots, bowls and pans you can have." Sally offered.

"Great! This is better than I expected. Frankly, I almost lost hope. You have given us a great relief," he sighed. "Now I'll get Lieutenant DuBois. You and Mrs. Amesworth can show us what you have. Is that agreeable?"

"Of course, but call us Sally and Ralph." Mr. Amesworth gently put his arm around his wife.

"In private, call me Dennis."

"Then let's shake on that, Dennis." Instant friendship melded a commander and the old farm couple. To Dennis, Sally looked very much like his mother even though she was not as aristocratic as his. "She'll be a mother to my men," he thought.

Later, McDill found DuBois and scurried to the Amesworth farm. After introductions, they both engaged in a friendly conversation with the Amesworths. Then two happy men galloped down to the dock to order every sailor to clean up and march in file over to the Amesworth farm nestling on the edge of town.

During the war Sally Amesworth served food to large numbers of army personnel, so she prepared her favorite chicken and dumplings for eight men and one woman. When the meal was over, the entire group converged on the old barn behind the little white house. They constructed makeshift bunks and stored their food in unoccupied horse stalls. The old barn's leaky roof steadily dripped water into the loft. Wet straw hung down in limp strands. McDill inspected the defect then declared, "We can fix that in the morning. Most of the space in the barn is dry enough."

Two of the crew moved their clothes near the drier wall while the others worked in the dark to bring down just enough provisions for one night. Ralph uncovered an old stove in the rear of the barn, opened the lids to start a fire and bring warmth and light for the men to work in a degree of comfort. From a distance one could see a small yellow glow coming from a red barn behind the Amesworth house. Neighbors could hear sailors dancing jigs and singing their favorite song, "Fifteen Men On A Dead Man's Chest. Yo, Ho, Hum and a Bottle of Rum." Ralph and Sally joined them in the jigs. For an elderly couple they were surprisingly spry. Commander McDill and Lt. DuBois grinned for hours. Every crew member shook Ralph's hand and bowed to Sally several times.

Serenity covered them like a calm zephyr—at least for a while. Finally, six sailors settled on their make-shift bunks for a peaceful night's sleep. Before he fell asleep, their commanding officer wondered if this was too good to be true. His sixth sense predicted more strife lay in ambush for his people. After a while he fell asleep, and dreamed of ghost ships floating overhead. McDill knew his crew could not repair the seven pitiful ships expiring at the harbor dock. These miserable craft haunted him all night. Even with a small degree of physical comfort, his soul was caught in a web of torment that forced him to stay awake all night.

⚓

Next morning, Commander McDill and his men drifted down to see again the deplorable sight of seven ships heaving and groaning at their moorings. "Men, we may have to abort this mission. These hulks are beyond repair. We could spend our time doing something better." McDill removed his cap to scratch his head.

"Sir, I can answer for the rest. Your crew and I are trained shipwrights. We all agree with you." Rogers nodded to each crew member. "For me, I don't want to spend the rest of my career trying to salvage junk."

"So be it. I'll get Comer to send a telegram requesting us to discontinue and tell our superiors why. Lieutenant, you and the men rest. No need to waste your energy." McDill bolted over the tracks to the telegraph office.

Comer pushed his chair back and stood when he saw Dennis coming. "Commander, you're in a bit of a hurry. Must be something important?"

"Very important. I want you to send a message for me. Give me a pen."

Urgency was plain to Comer. He ripped a piece of paper off his tablet, grabbed a pen and pushed over a bottle of ink. "Here, Commander. You write and I'll tap it to whatever destination you desire." McDill began to scribble and talk at the same time.

"This is a message for Headquarters."

Confused, Comer read the request and gawked. "You really want me to send this, Dennis? I thought you would be able to repair."

"Send it. I need an answer soon."

Comer surrendered. "All right, then." Comer's nimble fingers wiggled over the keys.

TO: HEADQUARTERS FROM: LT. COMMANDER DENNIS MCDILL: RESPECTFULLY REQUEST PERMISSION TO DISCONTINUE REPAIRING SEVEN NAVAL SHIPS AT DOCK IN CITY POINT, VIRGINIA. THE GUNBOATS ARE BEYOND REPAIR. THIS IS A REQUEST TO SEND THEM AWAY AND JUNK THEM COMPLETELY. ALSO, RESPECTFULLY REQUEST REASSIGNMENT OF THE CREW FROM CITY POINT TO ANOTHER LOCATION.

Comer spun around. "It's sent. Anything else?"

"I'll wait here for an answer." Dennis paced over to the rocking chair.

"That might be a long time. Stay here if you will, however if you get hungry, I'll bring you some dinner."

Recently, Captain Mort was transferred to Headquarters at his own request. As he was arranging his new office, a yeoman sprinted down the corridor so fast he bumped into three people who glowered at him and tossed him several disdainful comments. The young yeoman held a piece of paper and waved at the man behind the desk. "Captain, here's a telegram transferred to this office. It's important, Sir."

"Thank you. Just lay it on the front of my desk."

"Sir, with all due respect, you may want to read it soon and give a reply. I'll wait."

The squinting officer gritted his teeth. "Oh, give me the darn thing." The Captain read the message twice. Twice his face reddened deeper and deeper until it was dark crimson. "Hand me that pen."

He scribbled. "Give me a minute and send this back as soon as you can." Politely, the yeoman waited. Captain Mort's terse words were to the point.

FROM: CAPTAIN NORMAN MORT TO: LIEUTENANT COMMANDER DENNIS McDill. PERMISSION TO ABORT MISSION IS DENIED. YOU HAVE A DIRECT ORDER TO CONTINUE YOUR MISSION. REPEAT. REQUEST DENIED.

"Send this immediately. Understand?"
"Understood, Sir."

Dennis read the Captain Mort's answer and clamped his jaws until his teeth made clicking noises. "It's going to be impossible to repair those dead boats in the harbor. Besides, they may be seven ugly ogres to everybody in this community."

DuBois entered without knocking and asked, "Skipper, the crew's curious. Did you get an answer?"

"Yes, but not the one I wanted."

"It was denied, wasn't it, Sir?"

"Yes, but I want to try something." McDill pulled out several dollars from his tunic. "Lieutenant, I want you to do something."

"Yes, anything, Sir."

"Here, take this." Dennis jammed dollars in Phillipe's' hand.

Surprised, DuBois ogled the little fortune. "What's this for, Skipper?"

McDill twisted his neck and glared at the seven sick ships as though he was going to vomit. "Take this money, find a photographer and pay him to take two tintypes of those pathetic things tied at that old rundown pier. We'll mail one of the pictures to Captain Mort and see if he'll change his mind."

"Commander, I'll do my best but I don't think there's a photographer in town."

McDill brushed off the epaulets on DuBois' shoulders. "You're an officer of the U.S. Navy. You are resourceful. Go to Petersburg or Richmond and find a cameraman. I don't care how or where, but get one."

"I will, Sir. You can depend on me."

"While you are on that assignment, I'll do some thinking. Let the crew take off a day while I decide what to do."

"I'll tell them. They'll be sad to know we can't abort, but glad to have a day off."

Dennis McDill secured the dinghy and paddled upriver. Cormorants followed him as if he had some delicious fish for them. One of the birds almost jumped into his boat. McDill wanted to be alone, even alone from the shiny black divers. Sun rays slanted in the water and mild wind made waves waggle under his craft. He stopped paddling. Drifted. His mind seemed to float with the currents. Dennis had to clear his head. Soon the moon took charge of the sky and looked at him as if it were about to speak. Fresh water flowers threw their perfumes at him as though preparing him for something important—to dress him for a parade or a funeral. A night-hunting kingfisher plunged the water in front of his bow, and proudly brought up his prey as if to offer it to Dennis as a sacrifice. Trees danced with the breeze inviting him to join them. Then he realized he wasn't really alone. Nature was attempting to demonstrate its drama. The dilemma marched on stage. Should he obey or not? The specter of obedience-disobedience split his mind two ways. Dennis McDill had never disobeyed an order from a superior. He could feel the frigid fingers of solitude. He sensed another feeling, a yearning for his wife Helen to be with him in such a crisis. She helped him think clearly. He wanted to be away from people, but suddenly he was lonely. Thinking about Helen pried another thought from his mind—his crew, who had families, ached for them. To Commander McDill, their families were important. The ominous pendulum of the dilemma began to swing. Sometimes it would level, resting at ease. Sometimes it would swing skyward, sometimes earthward. Thrusting itself skyward, it halted in midair. Suddenly he felt his oar pushing him faster and faster heading for the dock.

Rogers sat on the boat landing peering in the moonlight for his commander. The dinghy glided into view, heading ashore until it bumped against the edge of the pier. The chief pulled Dennis' dinghy to the dock.

"Glad to see you, Sir. Lieutenant DuBois told me you wanted to be alone to think. Have you decided what we are going to do?" Rogers asked eagerly.

"Yes, Chief, I have."

Chief Rogers knew his Skipper by now and hesitated to ask any more questions. Dennis dropped into a daze. Rogers concluded his boss would inform him when he was ready. Dennis tied up his dinghy and motioned his Chief Petty Officer to walk with him. They circled around the Point twice without a word. At the last turn, McDill let go a high-pitched voice. "You know what? Let's build some houses."

37

"What's that, Sir?" Taken aback, Rogers stumbled slightly.

"Build houses for the men who have families, and find a permanent place for you and the Lieutenant."

"But, Sir, the order...."

"Belay that order. Our people are far more important than seven half-sunken boats. We'll salvage the good wood from those wrecks, cut some timber, and build some homes. What do you think of that?"

"Won't we get in trouble for this, Skipper?" Staring at the sky, Rogers scratched the back of his neck. "Sir, you and I know our Navy thinks bucking orders is very serious."

"Perhaps. I'll take full responsibility for this decision." His hand patted his chest as though he were taking a heartfelt oath. "It's a matter of priority."

"Sir, won't you be in trouble?"

"Maybe. I'll take that chance. It's worth it." Secretly, Dennis realized the harsh consequences of such an action.

"Shall I tell the men, Sir?"

"No, wait until morning and have them form in rank on dock. I'll tell them what I want. Now I'm tired. The weather is getting warmer. It's a great night to sleep under the moon. You sleep in the barn and I'll find a nice soft place here."

Three late winter nights had warmed the earth. Dennis fell asleep on a grassy knoll above the river. At dawn, a cricket hopped on his nose and roused him suddenly. Dennis brushed the tiny insect from his nose and squinted at a blazing sunrise. Hunger gnawed at his stomach so hard he could even smell Mrs. Ellis' fine cooking. In minutes his fist hit the panel of the front door of Dr. Richard Ellis. Mrs. Ellis opened the door. Her neck stretched in surprise. "My, Commander, you're up early. Have you eaten?"

"No, Ma'am. I'm starving. May I purchase a breakfast?"

"For you, Commander, you will get one more free meal. Dr. Ellis is across town helping a young mother birth her first child. He'll be a while, Commander. The first one comes slow, you know."

Dennis wanted to tell the Ellis couple when they were together what he decided, but he couldn't force himself to keep a secret. Actually, he wanted to tell the whole town after he met his crew. Soon as the hasty meal was finished, he had to tell her. "Mrs. Ellis, we're going to build homes for our sailors and their families. We are done with those boats dying in the harbor. Headquarters could have made the decision. Just tear them apart, use what is good, and burn the rest."

"They made that decision?" she asked, confused.

"Ma'am, Headquarters didn't make the decision. I did."

Her apron dropped from her hand. Her arms fell limp to her side. "You did?" She seemed to be viewing a man in a coffin. "But if the United States Navy wanted you to continue, it wouldn't be a choice. It would be a command, wouldn't it?"

"Yes. I'm taking full responsibility. I'm going to tell the crew as soon as I leave here. By the way, this is one of the best breakfasts I've eaten since my mother fed me."

"Commander, we like you and we don't want you to get in trouble. Are you sure that's what you're going to do?"

"Yes, I'm sure." Dennis nodded with a "thank you" and left.

The noncommissioned shipwrights received his decision with a mixture of gratitude and dreaded apprehension. They wanted their families, but the fear of being court-martialed bore deep into the psyches of every sailor. "Commander, may I speak?" Rogers requested.

"Affirmative, Chief. What's on your mind?"

"Skipper, I'm happy for the men and their families, but I've always been a law-abiding person."

"I know that, Chief. However, you and I know that job the Navy gave us is impossible."

"Sir, I will abide by your decision, but I'll admit I'm uneasy."

"Chief, I'll take total responsibility."

At that, Rogers smiled. "Yes, Sir. Tell us what to do. I, for one, will enjoy working on something else. And I think I can speak for the men."

"First, we will pry the good wood out of those hulks, then we will search for some good timber to construct homes we'll be proud of."

Rogers' fear vanished. The crew broke rank and shouted.

"But, men, before you celebrate, we'll have to find some good land for those homes." McDill cautioned.

Some of the men did not hear the last sentence. They had already started to rip out several solid boards of the ships.

During the din of labor, a large buggy had pulled up beside the workers. "Wait, we want to get a picture of those wrecks before you wreck them more," DuBois called out. "Someone help the photographer get his equipment set up."

Two volunteers scrambled into the buggy while a wiry, steel-gray haired man guided them. He inspected the terrain and found a spot high above the river's edge. "Put the tripod on that hill. I'll mount my camera and load the flash." Photography was complicated in the 1800s. It took eons to place everything in its right place.

Soon, amid pops and flashes, two pictures were taken. Acrid smoke curled across the harbor. "I'll have these ready shortly," the cameraman said. "You can have the proof you need. What could better than a picture?" he bragged. The wagon was big enough to provide instant processing, otherwise the tintypes would be ruined.

When finished, Dennis mailed one image to Captain Mort immediately.

⚓

Over a week passed. Comer delivered a telegram to Lt. Commander Dennis McDill.

> TO: LIEUTENANT COMMANDER McDILL. RECEIVED YOUR PHOTOGRAPH. YOU HAVE YOUR ASSIGNMENT. YOU ARE HEREBY COMMANDED TO COMPLETE YOUR MISSION.

Dennis' face was livid, but it sparked his determination. "By all that's Holy, I'm going to defy those confound orders. If Captain Mort is not convinced by pictures, we'll take our chances." McDill read the message to Lt. DuBois and Chief Rogers. "All right, men. Get the crew to finish making skeletons out of those corpses. Get all the good material and pile it up in neat rows."

In two days, the entire job was finished. A large pile of wood grew at the edge of the river. McDill confirmed it was not enough, but it was a start.

At dusk, DuBois dove into the river to clean off the dirt he collected from the day's labor skinning ships. A shadow looped over his head. "Lieutenant, when you're dressed, come with me."

"Aye, Sir."

Both officers inspected their work until dark. DuBois couldn't wait any longer. "Commander, where can we find enough land to build houses around here?"

"Amesworth."

"Amesworth?"

"Comer recommended that I see him. He has a lot of land." Dennis braced for the next question.

"Do we have money to buy enough lots, Sir?"

"Probably not enough, but we can bargain."

When they arrived, the old couple were rocking in their favorite chairs. Ralph was shuffling the newspaper. Sally was knitting a sweater. Both stood as the men approached. "Come, sit with us," Sally offered. After they settled down from extending their cordialities, McDill asked. "Would you by any chance sell some of your land for us to build new homes for our sailors and their families?"

Ralph and Sally's eyes met trying to read their thoughts. They paused, then he asked. "How much land?"

"Four or five acres, I'd guess." McDill answered.

Sally and Ralph intercepted each other's signals. Ralph cleared his throat. "Well, I'll answer for both of us. You can have all the land you need free."

"Did I hear you say FREE?" McDill crowed.

"You can have it free, Dennis. That's the least Sally and I can do. We both want this town to grow and prosper. New homes will improve things."

Chief Rogers joined the crew in the barn and gave them orders from the C.O. A premature celebration erupted, but Rogers broke it up. "I want you gobs in shape ready to work tomorrow." Obediently, every sailor dropped in his bunk.

Just before dawn, Armstead drove his horse and wagon to the barn to pick up the crew. It was daylight when they reached the farm. With men using measuring tapes, Armstead carefully divided the land into five parcels. The largest was set aside for O'Malley's family of five children. Their house needed at least three bedrooms and a large living room. O'Malley repeated his favorite quip: "We started having children and couldn't quit."

With the land allotments finished, the next task was to gather and load the recovered lumber from the ships. One load was enough, since good lumber was scarce. Chief Rogers almost bit off his pipestem. "I knew it. This ain't enough."

At the pier, DuBois, left alone, stood on the boat landing and lamented the dismal fate of seven ships. His head turned at Rogers' approach. The Chief came to report the problem to DuBois. "Chief, are you sure there won't be enough saved lumber to build even one house?"

"I'm sure, Sir. We gotta' tell the Commander."

DuBois and Rogers found Skipper McDill outside the barn talking to Comer. "Sir, we hate to tell you, but there isn't enough lumber to build even one house," DuBois reported.

Dennis grimaced at the Lieutenant and then the Chief. "You're sure that won't be enough to build one house? I could have sworn we could salvage more."

"Sir, we measured good. It's correct, or my name ain't Rogers."

"Well, we've got to find enough to build five homes somehow." McDill thought as he pushed dirt aside with his boot. In a helpless moment, he stared up at a cloudy sky.

⚓

Some mornings Horace Comer would straddle his little mare and trot through the town and country. This morning he neared the Armstead farm. In the distance he saw a wagon with several men standing around. He questioned himself. "*What's this all about?*" He reined his horse to get a better look. It was Amesworth talking to several men. "Betsy, let's talk to those folks up ahead," he said to his steed who was anxious to run again. The aging horse leaped at his command as quickly as though she were a yearling. Within twenty feet of the wagon, Comer pulled back on the reins. "Whoa, Betsy." Dennis met them, grabbed her bridle, looked up at her rider, and smiled.

"Just the man I want to see. Your timing is perfect." Dennis released the bridle and walked Comer over to the group standing beside the wagon. In minutes, Dennis explained his predicament to Comer.

Comer was astonished that so much lumber was needed, responded immediately. "If you don't have enough money, maybe a little rum will do. I know where you can get more timber. And you can cut it to sizes." This caught Dennis' attention quickly.

Rogers reluctantly reported. "Skipper, we didn't drink all the rum at the last party."

"Comer, who do you have in mind that will sell or give us timber?" McDill asked.

"Cousin Elmer."

"Who?" McDill asked.

"We call him 'Cousin Elmer.' He has a farm farther out. It's well-timbered."

Dennis' attention intensified. "Yes, go on."

"We might get some trees from Cousin Elmer who lives in the country not far from here. He'll bargain with you for rum. But beware, he's smarter than he looks."

"What are we waiting for? Let's go see Cousin Elmer." McDill started for the woods.

Rogers, McDill, and Comer pushed aside a dozen thickets of forest. It was like struggling in the jungle. Ticks and bugs did their best to impede the little caravan. One narrow road, an Indian trail, guided them until they saw a thin shaft of light leading to an opening with a dim outline of a spooky shack. Beside it was a barn that leaned into a cattle pasture. Both house and barn, crowned by tin roofs, curled at their ends as though some tornado had attempted to pull them heavenward. Side planks of the barn were separated so much that one could see through them without getting close. Pungent odors rolled out to meet the arrivals. Barnyard goo collected on each boot as they approached the property of Cousin Elmer. Soon they heard the whacks of a butcher knife plunging into a calf hide impaled by long nails on the side of the barn. One small figure sat on a granite rock in front of the hide. The figure scraped and swore with every stroke. It stopped when he heard the squish of boots mashing into the barnyard mix of muddy manure. "Cousin Elmer, this is Commander McDill and Chief Petty Officer Rogers from the Navy."

Elmer extended a bloody, grease-covered hand that made McDill hesitate for a moment. "Welcome, Gents."

"Likewise, You raise cattle here, I see." McDill observed and wiped his hand on his leg.

"Yeah, ye can see me cattle over there. I sell their meat and skin 'em for a livin'. Elmer looked at Comer. What brings ye out here?"

McDill answered. "Trees. We need lumber." McDill didn't want to palaver with the little man long. "We want to get enough to build five homes. Do you sell trees?"

"Sometimes." Elmer waited for more information.

"We figure it'll take six or seven large ones." Rogers shaded his eyes sizing a grove of white oaks outside the pasture fence.

"Over there, you seen 'em. They'd make good lumber, me thinks."

Dennis cranked his neck to see. "Let's take a closer look."

"Yeah, Gents, follow me. The path's over there. Ye can look all ye want."

Walking toward the trees, McDill couldn't avoid noticing the dwarfish man walking in front of him. Elmer looked like an elf. When he stood, his legs bowed. His back was bent as though he had sustained some great injury.

McDill was two feet taller than Elmer. The elf-man looked like an ogre in one of Dennis' nightmares, however Elmer's oaks were straight and tall, a shipbuilder's most pleasant dreams. In spite of his appearance, Elmer was hospitable, especially since he rarely had human visitors.

All the sailors inspected the trees by sighting up to see how straight they were.

"These four look good to me," Rogers observed.

"Can you let the men have them, Cousin Elmer?" Comer asked. "I think they'll bargain."

"For me price," Elmer said and held out his hand toward Dennis. "You have an offer?"

Dennis rammed his hand in his pocket. "The Navy didn't give us much money." He pulled out several dollars.

"Can you offer me anythin' else?" To Elmer, Dennis looked as tall as one of his trees.

"We can offer you rum," Dennis said.

The elf-man stood as tall as he could, smiling through stained teeth. "Rum, ye say?"

"We have a little." McDill pretended he knew nothing about what Comer told him.

"I like me rum as much as any seafarin' mariner."

"We have about six bottles left." Rogers winced, like saying goodbye to his best friends.

"Four bottles and fifty dollars'll do." Elmer liked money as well as alcohol.

Dennis searched his pockets again. "I have thirty dollars."

"I like rum and Yankee money. All right, since ye're Navy, I'll take it. But ye'll have to cut and haul it out."

"We plan to," McDill agreed. "Chief, go back. Get our men. Hook up the horse and wagon." Dennis faced Elmer. "Do you have an extra ax or two?"

"Commander, me got three sharpuns, and ye can borrow me big crosscut."

"Okay, Elmer. Here's your money. Oh, Chief when you come back with the wagon, bring Elmer the rum he wants."

"Aye, gladly, Skipper." Rogers was anything but glad to part with any rum.

Somehow the meticulous Naval officer found it difficult to picture himself dealing with a little rum head like Cousin Elmer. He could even smell Elmer's greasy handshake. It made him shudder inside. McDill was a shipwright himself and didn't mind the grease of a ship, but this was the deadly smell of animal's blood coagulated with grease.

Since most ships of this day were wood internally, some shipwrights were often assigned to cut trees and plane the wood into planks to be used for hulls, decks and the insides of their ships. After the wooden pieces were in place, metal covered the iron clads. Most of McDill's crew could manage both building phases.

At the end of two weeks, the trees were cut down, trimmed and planed. Their lumber was placed in front of the parcels of land selected by Amesworth. Members of the crew, however, were forced to cut a wider path for the wagon from town to Elmer's farm. Cousin Elmer lay beside his shack in a delightful rum stupor.

Official spring arrived after one more week of warming weather. Each week furnished more good working days. By late March, hammers pounded nails straight into the hardwood boards. Structural skeletons grew as fast as watermelons in a fertile patch. Whitewashed homes were designed for all families to move in as soon as possible. By June 1, lookouts were posted on the dock every day. By June 5, sails and smoke of a full-fledged frigate ascended under a sun showering light over the entire Point. Small boats shoved out to meet the ship. Little boats and canoes were filled with women, children and their belongings. Happy men rowed their precious cargoes ashore as fast as they could. Knots of men, women and children were hugging and greeting each other. Histories of the past separation were exchanged frequently. Their last leaves were granted two Christmases ago, and the married men were overjoyed to be reunited with their loved ones. Although letters had described the houses, the women were overwhelmed to see such masterful construction. Sailors had to give credit to many of the townspeople and were proud to introduce their families to everyone at the dock. Because the crew had become so popular, many citizens in the town had helped erect every home. Every friend waited for this day.

By the end of the second day, all women and children were settled in their new quarters. Women cooked their husbands' favorite foods, and children played in spacious yards and became acquainted with their neighbors. Soon, Doctor and Mrs. Ellis started plans for a new school. The old school was crowded, but teachers and parents made accommodations for the pupils anyway. Settling into a new home pleased Dennis, but his unsettled conscience continued to plague him. Uneasy visions of a military tribunal and the ghoulish disposal of a convict's remains tumbled in his head every night. Some nights he felt he was chained to the bed producing a nervous sweat and groans which would wake his wife Helen at times. Dennis could truthfully pass it off as a bad dream and urge her to go back to sleep. He hoped his thoughts weren't ominous predictions of his future. Trying to escape his tormenting dreams, he pressured himself to keep busy with whatever tasks Helen wanted done.

Chapter III

Gaith Johnson matured to a broad-shouldered, hairy athlete, not the fine young lawyer his rich father wanted. Colonel Johnson carried Gaith to several doctors to cure his habit of stealing. Gaith often thieved what he didn't need. Stealing grew into a recurring compulsion. When he joined the Navy, he and his father decided to conceal his problem from his recruiters. By the time he reached twenty, he was sentenced to the Navy Prison for grand larceny. One weekend he and some other sailors stole a Navy training boat for a wild ride in the bay. To make it worse they went AWOL for an extra day. All three were tried in military court, and locked in prison for two years. While in prison, Gaith lost his love for the Navy although he still loved boats and ships, and he never lost his love for trains. The walls of Gaiths's cell became canvases covered by penciled and painted portraits of trains and ships he cherished. He would stand back, hold a small brush in his teeth, and admire his artistic achievements. The young creator celebrated each with one final, sweeping stroke.

Gaith's escape from the prison house was successful. Under the camouflage of a pitch black night, he immobilized a train engineer and he learned quickly how to drive one of his most coveted prizes, a shiny new locomotive. Shoveling coal into the boiler was a joy. Like a professional, he blew the whistle twice at every crossing.

Late afternoon brought the amateur engineer in sight of the village of City Point. Gaith stopped the train and slithered out of the engine's cabin. Quietly he hid behind a large red oak. With deep owlish green eyes, he spanned the whole area with his head leaning out from behind his cover. Below him lay a harbor holding seven ships moored to a broken down dock. Gaith's gleaming eyes savored the sight. Seeing seven water crafts made his mouth salivate in large drops. All of his senses seemed to soar at finding such prizes.

The seven old vessels tempted him, even beckoned him, like beautiful sirens ashore once beckoned lonely seafarers. But this had to wait. Gaith needed food and, above all, he needed to stay out of sight. He mumbled to himself, "I'll wait till dark and search for food. I'm sure there's some around here." Gaith settled behind the old oak and fell asleep.

At dawn, O'Connell wanted to make one last try to repair the Leland. His hammer banging against metal woke Gaith abruptly. The escapee sprang up straight as a lightening rod and poked his face around his protective tree. His body dropped into the tall grass and snaked its way toward the noise of O'Connell's hammering. Names of the ships were barely visible. "Leland" was the nearest and easiest to read. A faint sputtering surged out from the vessel's inboard. "*What a beauty!*" He could even admire the rusty, battered Leland straining at its tether. To him, anything that floated would be beautiful. He could almost kiss the "Little Queen of the Appomattox."

"*I've gotta have this little one!*"

Gaith's stomach growled, reminding him of his hunger. At another sound, he rotated in the opposite direction to view three men struggling out of a boxcar, staggering with something heavy on their shoulders. Bags of flour. Careening under their loads, men climbed up the road to a barn sitting just beyond the town limits. The convict could see no one in the barn when they left. A leg of some animal swung by a rope inside the barn, invited him. It was cooked and ready to serve. In minutes Gaith squatted in the tall grass behind the barn gnawing on a large deer leg. Satisfied but thirsty, he remembered a small stream he crossed as he following the men to the barn. Prone on his belly, he lapped up enough fresh water to end his thirst.

Gaith's mind flicked back to his joyful discovery. "*I'll wait till tomorrow after that gob leaves.*" Gaith stepped through the woods behind the train station where he found a huge magnolia to conceal his mammoth frame. Even at twenty, his body was tired. He slept soundly, until dawn. He heard voices. Carefully he peeked from behind the big tree. Near the train he could see a carriage. Two men lifted a body while two others brought over an old worn out stretcher that somebody had sequestered for decades. The body was laid reverently on the stretcher. Dr. Ellis bent over to listen to its heart, feel its pulse, and raise an eyelid. Ellis shook his head slowly.

"He's dead, ain't he, Doc?" O'Connell had seen enough dead men to know.

"Yes, he's gone, I'm afraid…."

Suddenly, Dr. Ellis' attention split.

"Hey, Doc. Over here! There's blood on this piece of iron railing the train inspectors brought with the body." Right away the lawman held up an object, pointing at it with his forefinger. "Some guy must've picked this up and slammed it on his skull." Deputy Sheriff Seeley held the weapon high enough for all the witnesses to see.

"There's a deep depression on the back of the skull. I'll have to take a closer look and check his body thoroughly." Dr. Ellis lightly placed his hand on the chest of the dead man.

"Looks like murder, don't it?" Sullivan questioned the deputy.

"Yes, maybe murder," Seeley answered.

Hearing loud talk outside, Comer emerged from his office to find out what was causing the noise. Seeing the body he halted, numb and speechless. For a moment he couldn't breathe. Then in a loud voice he cried out, "Mother of God, it's Clyde! What happened?"

"Looks like someone split his head open," Deputy Seely replied looking at the gruesome gash plunged deep inside the back of the dead man's head.

His lips trembled. "With what?" Comer blurted.

"This here piece of metal." The deputy pointed to the blood-stained article.

"We've got to know if it's Clyde's blood or not. I learned how to match blood. I have equipment in my office to help me find out." Ellis rose up and ordered. "Move his head over a little to the right, so I can get a spot of blood." The physician drew out his handkerchief and lightly dabbed up a tiny speck of the victim's blood. Next, he dabbed blood from the weapon.

When O'Connell turned Clyde's head, some bystanders cringed and delivered a sharp concert of gasps when their eyes caught the corpse's open wound revealing a mass of wrinkled grayish matter. "Somebody beat his brains out!" An elderly lady in the crowd sobbed.

A young mother with a little girl quickly covered her child's eyes from seeing the hideous scene. One teenaged girl vomited when she saw the dried blood caked around the brain tissue of the victim.

News traveled like a windstorm fire. People converged from all directions. Five sailors and a deputy locked hands and formed a circle to keep the curious away. Anxious spectators crowded so close the human chain almost broke under their collective pushing. They kept shoving hard against the barrier to get a glimpse of what had happened.

"Please move. Let the doctor and the deceased through," the deputy dictated in his loudest official voice. "The doctor wants to examine the body."

Before he could leave, Ellis looked around, signaling for help. "Will someone go to Petersburg and get the sheriff?"

"I'll go," Deputy Seeley volunteered. "That's my job."

"All right, but hurry," Dr. Ellis pleaded. Then he covered Clyde's body with a white sheet.

Seeley looked at the victim again and shook his head. "As unpleasant as it is, I'll notify his wife Lizzy that Clyde's dead and it looks like murder."

"Doc, where do you want us to carry the body?" O'Connell asked sadly.

"Keep him covered and take him to my office. I'll give him a thorough examination. Then I'll report my conclusions to the sheriff. Lizzy can tell us what to do afterward." Dr. Ellis bowed his head devoutly and followed the corpse.

O'Connell and Sullivan gently lifted the body onto the stretcher and inched their way through a bevy of onlookers. Because everybody wanted to gape at the victim, it took them an eternity to get to Dr. Ellis' office. With difficulty, they carried the corpse into the doctor's house. Then the crowd dispersed as fast as it appeared.

Hours later, Sheriff Elkinson drove his carriage to the front of the doctor's house. Elkinson was a slightly built, square-bearded man with a county star on his chest. A sobbing, worried, middle-aged lady rode shotgun beside him. The shade of her bonnet hid her tears. She leaped out and rushed into the house. Lizzy pulled the makeshift pall from the man's head. "Oh, my God! Oh dear Jesus!" She wailed loud enough for every citizen to hear her lament. "He's the only man I ever loved. Who'd want to kill my Clyde? He was a good man who never hurt anybody in his life." Her impassioned grief brought tears to the tough lawman and three leathery sailors.

"What did you find, Doctor?" Elkinson asked.

"Dried blood on Clyde's wound and on the piece of iron are an exact match. He was killed by this blunt weapon, I'm sure. I can't say, but it looks like murder."

"It's not suicide, for sure," Elkinson noted. The law officer gently put his hand on Lizzy's arm. "By all that's holy, Lizzy, I'll find who killed Clyde," Elkinson vowed.

"If you didn't bring a casket, I have one in the shed," Ellis offered.

"Thanks, Doc. I'm a coroner too, you know. I always have one in my wagon. I prefer to use my…."

Harsh coughing of an engine rifled the air over the harbor. Even seriously crippled, Little Leland was chugging away from the dock. It was heading for

50

the center of the river. O'Connell had repaired the boiler enough for it to run.

A heavy form bent over the boiler. Gaith's muscles rippled. Sweat ran from his shoulders to his fingernails. The big kleptomaniac shot rapid glances back to the shore to see if he was being followed. The further away from shore, the greater confidence he gained. His sarcastic smiles of triumph goaded the people who rushed to the dock to see his attempt to escape.

McDill was the first to leap in a dugout canoe. DuBois followed behind in another boat, grabbed an oar and paddled as fast as he could. Gaith pulled away ten feet further from the canoe. Little Leland was sailing faster and faster. DuBois strained until veins bulged on his forehead and neck. Commander McDill's bare knuckles gripped his paddle, but Gaith still drew away. McDill cuffed his hands and shouted at the figure on the Leland. "Avast! Bring that ship around. You'll never make it."

Gaith's face mocked the officer's command. His facial expression returned the command with the derision of a man who deeply resented every officer in the Navy. His avid scorn showed utter contempt. He shoveled in more coal. His face glowed red with torrid hate. Gaith's compulsion and contempt coiled like a two-headed cobra inside his head. "Eat more coal, you poor excuse for a boiler."

It happened. A spine-splitting blast ripped branches from nearby trees on the opposite shore. Gaith was thrown ten feet in the air and landed belly flop in the water. Injured slightly, he flailed his limbs violently to regain balance. Quickly he got control, ready to challenge anyone. As DuBois reached the thieving convict, DuBois and McDill felt their boats rock, then capsize pouring both officers into the water with Gaith. DuBois caught the force of a thousand pound uppercut causing his body to float in the water semiconscious and helpless.

Gaith roared and charged at McDill like a raging water buffalo. Suddenly, McDill was being held by two adamantine hands while a hammerhead butted his forehead three times. Blinded by a bleeding cut on his forehead, Dennis couldn't see the fist coming. It landed with the velocity of a comet. McDill's mouth was bleeding in two places. He turned his head to look for his lieutenant and caught another blow—this time it crashed into his midriff, bending him double to swallow a pint of the green river water. Coming up for air, he coughed and spat out some of the muddy fluid. Summoning his last milligram of strength, Skipper Dennis took hold of his enemy by the waist. Dennis' wrestling muscles tightened around the criminal with the strength of an anaconda. Gaith struggled to loosen the commander's grip. Dennis did not let go until Gaith fainted from the lack of oxygen and collapsed. By then, Phillipe recovered and clenched his hands against Gaith's arms to hold him upright.

"Thanks, Lieutenant. I thought you'd never get here." McDill coughed out more river water. McDill turned the canoe right side up, pulled his assailant by his wrists and heaved him in the boat. Both men paddled ashore with legs straddling their captive like two cowboys on a saddle. Rogers and O'Malley commandeered another canoe and towed what was left of the Leland, while the officers propelled ashore with their bounty. Gaith was tossed on the top of the boat, landing like a big fish. He wobbled unsteadily, stood up and faced the lawman.

Sheriff Elkinson cuffed the thug and frisked him several times. Elkinson stood close to Gaith. So close that Gaith could see the sheriff's shiny .45 resting in its holster. "Trying to steal Navy's property, weren't you?" Elkinson continued his inquisition by asking the felon's name. "Who are you?"

Gaith spat at him and didn't answer.

"Who are you?" Elkinson drew back his fist to hit the con, but held his temper.

No answer.

"You hear me? Who are you?" Elkinson shook his fist in Gaith's face.

Gaith stepped backwards to keep from being hit. "Gaith," he yelled.

"Gaith, who?"

"Just Gaith."

The lawman's steaming anger turned his face dark red. Boiling agitation burst forth from under his ten-gallon hat.

"All right, Gaith or whoever you are, why were you trying to get away in that boat?"

"I just like boats," he answered sarcastically and glowered at the sheriff's handlebar moustache.

"You just like boats, eh? I ask you again, why'd you steal that ship?"

Gaith refused to budge. Elkinson kicked the back of the con's knees making the criminal fall. Elkinson pushed to be sure Gaith fell head-first.

The sheriff got a better look and observed the captive's shoes. "Man, I can smell it. You're running away from something."

Gaith looked out toward the river and back at the sheriff, saying nothing.

"You're wearing prison shoes. Where'd you get 'em?"

"From a friend."

Elkinson inspected both shoes again. "Your size, huh? You escaped from prison, didn't you? Those are prison shoes."

No reply.

"I want an answer."

"What's it to you, cowboy?" Gaith sizzled.

Gaith's handcuffs weren't securely locked, allowing him to twist and pull his wrists free. He jumped up, lunged at the sheriff and snatched the .45. "Back off!" he squalled. Slowly and carefully everyone backed away from Gaith and the sheriff. "I'm getting out of here, and no one can stop me. Yeah, I killed a man. One more won't make any difference. Now back off! Move!"

A weak smile hinted that Gaith was enjoying his role. He slowly cocked the pistol and aimed it just between his victim's eyes. Never had he enjoyed being the center of attention so much. His zest soared as he looked at terror crisscrossing the lawman's face. "After I kill this 'un, I'm gone. If anyone follows, they'll be buzzard food."

Elkinson shut both eyes, stiffened his body and braced for certain death. He knew Gaith was close enough for a sure shot. Everyone flinched when the trigger hammer snapped into position. DuBois, O'Malley, Rogers, and the rest of the crew stood rigid, helpless to save the sheriff. Everyone froze except McDill. Comer was immovable. Time stopped! No one breathed! No one moved! No one talked! Dennis could see the sun flash off of a shotgun barrel leveling at the criminal. In the tenth of a second Dennis knew what was happening. He sprang for the gun. It was too late. The blast tore their eardrums. Bodies hit the ground. Then silence. Time stopped again. McDill stood and faced the felon lying still on the ground. Two humans stood erect with Dennis—Sheriff Elkinson and Lizzy. Lizzy nervously held a smoking, double barreled shotgun. "You killed my husband! I hope your soul fries in hell for what you did to my man." She was talking to a prone, motionless body. Gaith could not answer.

Elkinson turned to Lizzy. "Thank God, Lizzy. You saved my life. I knew I was a goner when that thug got my gun."

Slowly, Dennis took the shotgun from Lizzy and gave it to the sheriff. "Lizzy, you won't need this anymore. All of us are your witnesses. We'll help you all we can."

"Thanks. I was hurting so much. Then I saw the sheriff was in danger."

Comer felt the man's pulse. "I think he's dead, Lizzy."

Elkinson placed his hand gently on Lizzy's arm. "It'll be all right." Elkinson comforted. "No judge or jury in the country could find you guilty of homicide. When we get to my office, I'll get it all in my report."

"Hold on, Sheriff," Comer protested. "Why write anything about this?

Let's all swear to keep this a secret. We'll bury this rat's body in the swamp and keep mum."

"Is that wise?" Dennis challenged. "I'm sure that any fair-minded judge would declare this justified. What do you think, Elkinson?"

"It could be second degree." Elkinson stroked his handlebar and looked at Gaith's bleeding corpse.

"And she could serve time for it." Comer added. "I say, let's bury this creep and keep quiet. What'd you say, folks?"

A pack of wolves would envy the group of men barking and standing around dead meat. One woman stood alone crying a waterfall of tears. Her future swayed back and forth. When the barking ceased, a majority of the men agreed to bury the body and keep it secret. Let's all swear, okay?" O'Connell appealed.

Elkinson, DuBois, and McDill were out voted. O'Malley and McEaton wrapped the body in an old blanket and tossed the body in a canoe. Two sailors rowed down river toward the swamp. In his mind, Elkinson thought he need not report everything, but he had to make the gesture of justice. That was enough. However, McDill was adamant. With him, it was like the Code of Honor. He would have his way, but he realized he had no civil jurisdiction. Momentarily Dennis lost command of his men. It rendered him more helpless than he had ever been in his life. It was a most pathetic feeling. At that moment, Dennis craved to be alone.

Lizzy wanted to be cleared forever, but she could say nothing.

Elkinson asked Comer and two men to put Lizzy's husband in the sheriff's carriage, now serving as a hearse. Lizzy mounted and sat beside Sheriff Elkinson. Her hand rested on her husband's chest.

One by one the crewmen returned to the dock. McDill met O'Connell climbing out of the little ship onto the dock. "Commander, the Leland's broke. It won't run no more."

"Is it the engine?" he asked. "O'Connell, you're sure?"

"Yes, Sir. That no good murderer killed her engine. Her boiler's busted. In her shape, it won't be practical to get another engine."

Dejected, Dennis curled his fingers through his hair. "By the Almighty," he prayed. "Another setback. What else can possibly go wrong?"

Chapter IV

A heavy knock rattled McDill's front door. Dennis saw a gold sleeve and saluted. "Are you Lieutenant Commander Dennis McDill?" the Captain asked looking aloof.

"Yes, Sir. I'm Dennis McDill."

"I'm Captain Fritzgerald from the Inspector General's Office."

"Come in, Captain. I was just getting dressed."

"Commander, I want to ask you some questions." Without asking, Fritzgerald barged passed Dennis and sat in Helen's favorite chair.

Dennis remained silent waiting for the question.

"Did you take government funds and government material to build your crew's houses?"

"Sir?" Dennis pretended he did not hear the question.

"Did you take the funds and materials to build your own house?"

"Sir, I...."

"All right, Commander. You're not talking. Finish dressing and come with me now."

Dennis wanted to argue but he hesitated.

"Get dressed and come with me. On the double. Right now!"

Dennis flew into the bedroom, dressed, and stamped to the door, hoping to wake Helen. In the meantime, Fritzgerald sat in Helen's easy chair twiddling his thumbs.

Seeing the Commander, the I.G. jumped to the door. "Follow me."

Both men walked down to the shore where Fritzgerald's little sloop was anchored. Helen slid downhill. She could see two men had boarded a boat, leaving the dock in a hurry. The little vessel was out in the center current before Helen reached the shore. She dove in the river's cold water and swam as hard as she could. It was no use; the boat was too fast and she was exhausted.

Dennis tried to go overboard, but the I.G. blocked him. He stopped, for he couldn't hit a superior officer.

As they sailed out of sight, McDill's wife stood weeping bitterly on the dock.

⚓

Choirs of fog horns sang deep bass notes across the river. Washington's single river harbor was not a large as City Point's. Ships and boats of all nations and descriptions jockeyed for position in and out of the Capital's crowded docks. Not only was it the nation's capital, the town bristled with increasing commerce.

Little conversation occurred during the voyage. Ashore, McDill and Fritzgerald walked in silence together like twins, dodging horses, carriages and carts. "Where are we going, Captain?" Commander McDill dreaded the answer.

"I want to ask you some more questions. The Inspector General's office secured a separate room in the barracks. It's two more blocks away. We turn right at the intersection of the next street." Pedestrian and vehicular traffic decreased, leaving a few servicemen going home from work. Dennis recognized the uniforms of Marines and Navy shore patrols. Three men in civilian clothes mingled with the home going crowd. A knot of sailors with weapons marched in formation in front of an old building erected years before the Civil War. A white washed anchor officially declared the ancient structure to be Navy property.

At the top of the steps, two armed Marine guards met the I.G. and Dennis. Fritzgerald flashed his identification. "Enter, Sir. We'll escort you to quarters on the second floor. You'll find what you need there. We'll be outside if you need anything else." Dennis was ushered into a room with two single beds, one single table with one side directly under a glaring gas lamp. On the other side there was a basin of water with a bowl and two cups. Four sandwiches and bags of tea lay beside a dingy white basin. Behind a small door a privy closet, barely big enough for a single person, was almost invisible. Two straight chairs were parked on each side of the table. Bare barracks wasn't Dennis' idea of a comfortable living.

Sitting in the gloomy room, McDill knew the order he disobeyed would be an unforgivable sin for a U.S. sailor. *"Should I confess everything, and get it over with? Plead for mercy? Should I duck the questions and give little or no information? Should I request a lawyer?"* His own questions rolled like tidal waves in his mind.

"Now, Commander, a few questions." The I.G.'s long nose pointed like a finger.

Dennis sat erect as a flagpole at the small table in front of the Inspector. He was deliberately forced to sit in front of a blinding light that could shine directly in his face.

Fritzgerald shoved a piece of paper in front of Dennis. "Read it and sign it, Commander."

In spite of the heat from the gas lamp, Dennis could sense the chill of a freezing reality. He pretended not to recognize the document.

"It's your confession. Sign it. We might go easy on you then." His narrow smile almost hid his sunken eyes and his walrus beard.

"Sir, I can't sign this. I'd automatically be convicted. I don't want a dishonorable discharge or something worse without a chance to explain," McDill pled.

"You deny that you disobeyed an order?"

Dennis sat still and turned his head to avoid the dazzling lamp.

"Commander, I'll ask you again. Did you or did you not disobey a direct order?" Fritzgerald's fist crashed the top of the table until the room shook.

McDill looked back at his captor and quietly folded his arms.

"Answer me!" Fritzgerald roared.

"I have nothing to say." Dennis gave his broad shoulders a roll backwards.

Fritzgerald jumped up, jerked his chair from the table and pranced to the door. "Guards, take this man to the brig."

"Am I arrested, Sir?"

"You'd better think of a good lawyer. Our Interrogation Panel will question you tomorrow."

Dennis thought the word "question" should be "arraign."

Two marines shouldered their rifles and escorted Dennis across the street to a squat, spotty gray-colored building with bars punctuating each window. Each bar seemed to be holding the weight of a heavy roof. The two sea police took the officer inside a dungeon that Headquarters called a brig. The musty smell of something rotting insulted his nostrils. His escorts dubbed his cell their "holding tank" for Headquarters. Dennis thought Headquarter judges could afford a better jail than this dank black hole inside a concrete jungle.

McDill was placed in an eight-by-eight cell with a six foot bunk, too short for his frame. He grumbled to himself at the sight. *"If they want to make me miserable, this is the perfect place."* Walls sweated and leaked from rain the previous day. Ancient cell doors down the corridor squeaked and rattled as though they were begging to get out of hell. His feet hung over the end of the bunk, causing him to jockey several times for a comfortable position. He stared at the cracked ceiling and tried to imagine what kind of fate lurked ahead—a fate that pursued him constantly. He envisioned a slinking jaguar pouncing on an unsuspecting victim. In the middle of the night, Dennis realized he had not eaten. He was so miserable he doused the thought and tried to sleep again.

McDill was already awake when a few sun rays squeezed through the bars of his slim window. Tin cups banging against steel issued a loud commotion. Hungry shouts added to the clamor. A server slipped a tray under his cell door. The breakfast consisted of mush and a cup of water. *"Lord, I hope I don't have to come back here again,"* Dennis beseeched his Maker.

After breakfast, two jail guards ambled past his cell and turned around. "Here he is. We're supposed to turn him back over to the Marines."

"What's he in for?" The shorter guard looked up to the taller one.

"I don't know. Somebody must think he did something real bad, cause we don't get many high ranks around here. Ain't it nice to see someone like him getting his due? One time a high rank kicked me in the shins. I didn't deserve it. If that one's guilty, I hope he goes to prison for life. Here's the key. You unlock while I watch to keep him from escaping."

Dennis had no time to shave. Two marines stood at the end of the hall with bayonets clamped to the muzzles of their rifles. They escorted Dennis and the I.G. to a carriage which took them to Headquarters. They passed by two giant anchors crisscrossing to identify the United States Headquarters. Inside, the I.G. required Dennis to sit in the chair directly opposite a long table in front of a podium. The expansive conference room contained leather chairs placed behind a sturdy maple table, splashed by a pool of sunlight. Cynically amused, McDill smiled to himself. *"Headquarters did the 'cry poor' routine. Why should they be concerned about a small amount of money paid for a little room for some houses?"* McDill gazed at the room's opulent furnishings. "Marble floors, Captain?"

"Maybe. Imports from Italy or someplace. All this stuff we acquired during the war. Congress would give us anything we asked for then." Fritzgerald squeezed his broad hips in a chair beside Dennis.

"I see," Dennis uttered an envious twang.

"McDill, I want you to sit directly in front of the Panel's President. He'll be in the center. I warn you, they'll look straight into your face when you answer their questions."

"I've looked into the jaws of hell. Why should that bother me?"

"Well, you may be looking at them again. Now's not the time to brag, Commander. This is serious business. They could decide to put you in the brig forever. Civilians might call misusing government property a petty crime, but Navy thinks it serious." He pulled his chair away from Dennis in order for the Panel to get a singular view of the accused. "And, remember, we're not civilians. I...."

Creaks of a nine-foot iron door echoed across the room. Quick steps paced toward the huge maple table.

The I.G. nudged his arm. "Stand up, Commander, and salute."

Five men in white with wide gold braid marched in like a parade, pulled out chairs and the officer in the center returned McDill's salute. Dennis was suddenly stunned to see a familiar face. He was staring at his old boss, Captain Norman Mort! The Captain's cropped gray hair stood up like a porcupine in heat. Mort never looked at Dennis. Before McDill could say anything to the I.G. about Mort, Admiral Hicks pounded his favorite gavel. "Be seated, gentlemen. We are in session. Inspector, what is the name of your suspect?"

"Lt. Commander Dennis McDill, Sir."

All ten eyes nailed McDill's until he squirmed slightly.

"Is that your name, Commander?" Admiral Hick's face, leathered from many missions, contrasted the commander's lighter complexion.

"Yes, Sir."

"Inspector, what is the charge?"

"Misuse of government money, misappropriation of government property, disobeying orders and dereliction of duty," Fritzgerald expressed with a flair.

"How do you plead?" The leathered face of the admiral was crowned with a shock of white hair and a neatly trimmed beard.

"Not guilty, Sir."

Fritzgerald could not believe why McDill pled "Not Guilty." He looked at Dennis and glanced over to see the Panel leader.

"Details, Inspector," Admiral Hicks ordered.

"Admiral, this officer willingly disobeyed a specific written order from Headquarters. He was appropriated government funds to repair seven ships. He asked for permission to abort the mission. It was denied. The mission was aborted by his orders and he used government funds to buy building materials for homes for his men and their families instead of ship repairs."

Admiral Hicks asked. "Then permission was not granted?" Dennis looked at Captain Mort who bore his eyes into the lobes of his brain. It felt like bullets ripping his chest apart.

"Correct, Sir. Commander McDill received an order to continue with his mission, but he proceeded otherwise." Fritzgerald had launched the offense.

"He aborted the mission and you believe it was dereliction of duty. Is that correct?" Hicks summarized and asked.

The I.G. continued to gather confidence. "As I see it, that is correct, Sir."

All five chairs pulled closer to detect the defendant's expression. It looked as though their eyes were harpooning him with the sign saying "Guilty." Dennis' eyes dropped under the vicious optical stabs of his antagonists. He spiraled around seeming to hunt for exits. All the doors were securely guarded. Each marine held a rifle and a bayonet firmly mounted in place. *Prison guards?* he wondered.

Dennis had heard that military court panels grew into Court-Martial Tribunals. Also rumored, a sailor was automatically guilty as soon as he stepped in front of a panel of officers. A hand carved gavel pointed to the victim. Panel President Admiral Hicks asked bluntly, "Is this true, Commander?"

"With all due respects, Sir, that answer will incriminate me." Dennis could feel the gavel pounding his head.

Admiral Hicks pushed back his chair. "Then, Commander what do you have to say for yourself?"

Dennis stood at attention, eyeing his superior. "Admiral, our families were sent down to our station in Virginia. We were grateful. However, we didn't have enough permanent facilities for our families to live in. I have always obeyed orders, but our families seemed to have priority over some old ships that are beyond repair."

"You asked permission from Headquarters to build homes. Is that correct?"

McDill glanced at Mort. "No, Sir."

"You were ordered to continue with your mission, were you not?" Hicks' face wrinkled with annoyance.

McDill felt the noose tighten around his neck. "Yes, I received that order."

"Would you not consider that disobeying a direct order?" Hicks glowered at the Lt. Commander.

The imaginary noose began to choke the accused trying to swallow hard and remain silent.

Hicks paused for an answer. Hearing none, he confronted Dennis. "You are aware that is a serious breach?"

Dennis swallowed again and remained silent.

"You risked court-martial. Didn't you?"

"Yes. I did, Sir." Dennis answered relying on the word, "risked."

"How many women and children did you provide housing?" Hicks continued. The old man seemed to provide some relief by changing the subject.

"Five wives, three sisters of the wives, and fifteen children."

"How many houses did your crew build, Commander McDill?" The Vice President leaned over and asked with a brassy voice.

"Five were planned," McDill answered, trying not to admit the fact they were already built.

Eyebrows lifted up to every man's scalp seated in front of the accused. "Did you say FIVE?" The brassy voice blew like a trumpet.

"Yes, Sir. Five." McDill cowered and sat in his chair as low as he could get.

"Where did you get enough lumber for that?" The brash commander asked.

"From a man in the country named Elmer," Dennis replied.

"Did he know you used government money without permission?" The commander pressed the inquisition further.

"No, Sir. He knew nothing about that. He's just a solitary farmer living in the country, who had very fine oaks for lumber."

"Fine enough to repair those ships?" the starched inquisitor prodded.

"Sir, those ships were virtually impossible to repair. Our government could have used the money more wisely to build new and better vessels, rather than repairing those worn-out ones at the dock." Dennis knew the man was getting agitated, and quickly said politely, "With all due respect to the Panel, Sir."

Hicks checked his watch. "Any more questions?"

No one spoke.

"Then, Inspector, ask your men to find the Commander a nice bunk in our brig."

"Aye, Sir." Fritzgeral saluted.

McDill saluted, turned about-face, and marched toward the guarded door. Both marines escorted McDill out of the room.

"Stay Inspector. We want you in on this," Hicks commanded.

Approaching the door, McDill felt like a criminal being carted off to prison.

One marine closed the iron door with a slam that iced McDill's spine.

Inside, Hicks asked for discussion and looked up and down the table. "May I, Admiral?" Captain Mort's hand shot up. "It's no question. Lt. Commander McDill is guilty. There's plenty of evidence, and we could see it in his face. I move we convene tomorrow for court-martial."

"A little irregular, Captain. We haven't discussed all elements of this yet." Captain Ore pipped.

"Admiral, I've learned enough to find him guilty." Mort's granite statement shocked some of the panel members.

"Whoa, Mort." Captain Ore moved to the other end of the table. "You're moving too fast. I'd like to consider all of the circumstances."

"Ore, I know you've worked on more of these panels than I have, but can't you see this officer is guilty, guilty of disobeying an order? That's enough to court-martial any sailor. A senior officer like him should know the consequences."

Hicks intervened. "I'm sure he realizes the consequences. He knows he took a risk. Now before we argue more, let's ask the Inspector some questions."

I.G.'s face reddened. "Sir, I'll tell you all I know."

"Did you take a good look at those ships?" Hicks questioned.

"Sir. I glanced at them when I went ashore and when we left City Point."

"Go on."

"Pretty bad, Sir. None of them were able to sail. They were skeletonized."

"We realize you're no shipwright. Do you remember how long they've been working on those ships?" Captain Ore got to his feet and confronted Fritzgerald.

"From what the Commander told me, not very long," the I.G. answered.

"Then, you'd say they had shirked their assignment?" Hicks asked.

"Yes Admiral, I would think that, Sir."

"Gentlemen, I'm going to adjourn until tomorrow. Inspector, find out who gave the order for McDill to continue his mission. Give me the answer tomorrow morning. We'll need all the answers. Oh, Inspector. Check with our telegrapher and see if he has a copy of that written order."

In the brig, McDill's eight-by-eight cell looked exactly like the one he had the night before. This night was no better. It was worsened by several dogs braying outside his window. He was so restless he got a shorter nap this time. However, this morning he had enough time to bathe and shave.

Promptly at 10:00 a.m. the marines marched Dennis McDill inside the metal door of the "interrogation room."

Behind the big table sat the Panel dressed in their whites. Before each was a writing tablet as though they were going to take copious notes. Their eyes pierced McDill's pupils.

He saluted, with surprise. Instead of Mort, a strange officer sat in Mort's chair.

"Sit, Commander," Admiral Hicks commanded.

"*Here it comes*," Dennis choked to himself.

Hicks spoke. "You know, Commander, you can be tried, convicted and sentenced to prison for several years."

McDill's throat was dry as a tumble weed. He mumbled, "Yes, Sir. I know."

"You took a great risk, you know." Hicks moved closer to the table to emphasize his point.

"Yes, Sir. I know."

Hicks held up something in front of Dennis. "You recognize this piece of paper?"

Dennis looked up, paused, and sucked in his breath. He scanned it briefly.

"Your orders to continue the mission, Commander?" the admiral asked.

"Yes, I believe so." McDill could feel the sharp fingernails of doom.

"We see there that Captain Mort signed it."

"Yes." Dennis held his tongue, hoping that Hicks had recognized a conflict of interest since Mort was assigned to the Interrogation Panel the first time they convened. However, Hicks was preoccupied with another document.

"I see here on your record, you've never been cited for disobeying an order." Admiral Hicks looked over his bifocals.

"No, Sir, never." Dennis affirmed, praying that information would sway the group.

"Well, the Navy sent your dependents down to stay with you without further provisions for them. Is that correct, Commander?" Hicks rested his wrinkled hands on the arms of his chair.

"Yes, they had only their clothes and personal items." Dennis prayed that no one would mention houses again.

Hicks continued. "It's our considered judgement that our Navy shouldn't have sent them down in the first place. We'll look into this. Commander, we realize you were concerned about the welfare of your men and their families. You were well-intended. However, there is enough evidence to have you tried in a court of law. The date will be four weeks from today to allow you to have a defense counselor. You will be remanded to the brig until that time. We are now adjourned."

Dennis remained at attention, but his mind slumped to the floor. "*A court-martial? Won't they at least sympathize a little?*" His brain churned and his heart stopped for a few seconds. He felt as though someone had poured hot lead over his whole body to use it as a mold. While the marines cuffed him, he realized the sickness of his miserable condition. Once again, they released him to the brig jailers who promptly pushed him into a cell that he'd seen before. "Oh, God. What can I do?" he beseeched aloud to his Supreme Being.

For days, McDill managed to move around in cramped quarters and eat jailhouse food. Brig jailers were not interested in his plight. They only kept close watch to see that he didn't escape. Things were so bad he wasn't able to communicate with anyone. He waited for some kind person to send him a lawyer.

$\downarrow$

Fritzgerald put ashore at the boat landing at City Point two days after McDill's arrest. O'Malley was the only sailor in sight when the I.G.'s little single masted sloop tied up. After returning a brisk salute, Fritzgerald told O'Malley he represented the government's Inspector General's office. Without inhaling he told O'Malley that Commander McDill had been arrested and would face a military tribunal in less than four weeks. O'Malley flinched as though a giant mosquito had speared him. "What, Sir? Arrested?"

"Yes, arrested for misappropriating government funds and property. He is cited for disobeying a direct written order and dereliction of duty." Fritzgerald smirked with pleasure to be the one to bring the bad news.

Temptation urged O'Malley to defend his boss immediately, but something halted him, so he stood quietly in front of the Captain. Fritzgerald looked up into the eyes of the towering sailor and took one step toward him.

O'Malley wanted to take a step backwards, but thought better. "Seaman, who and where is your second in command?"

"It's Lieutenant Senior Grade Phillipe DuBois, Sir."

"Take me to him. Now, sailor. On the double."

"Yes, Sir. Please follow me." O'Malley marched with a huge lead ball in his stomach.

Phillipe was sitting near the barn door cleaning his shoes. O'Malley and Fritzgerald's shadows floated over Phillipe's head. Dodging the sun, the lieutenant leaned into the shadows and recognized a sleeve full of gold. In one motion he came to attention and saluted. "Lieutenant, this is Captain Fritzgerald from the Inspector General's office." O'Malley introduced the I.G. and fled.

"Sir, I heard that Commander McDill went with you…to Headquarters…I see…he didn't come back with you?"

"No, he's been arrested for violations of the Code: Disobeying an order, absconding Naval material, misusing government funds, and dereliction of duty. We have him confined to the brig at the moment."

"This is most serious, Sir." DuBois swallowed.

"Indeed it is, Lieutenant."

"Can he get bail?" Phillipe asked.

"Not unless an attorney can convince the Admiral."

"Then he must have a lawyer, Sir." DuBois concluded quickly.

"Yes, but he will need one as soon as possible. It's less than four weeks before the trial."

"Offhand, I know no lawyers, but I'll try to get one for our C.O. Is that all, Sir?"

Fritzgerald stepped closer. "No, Lieutenant, one of the main reasons for my visit is to leave you in command."

"Sir, I really don't know…."

"No excuses. You're in command. You are to cease all action. Take charge of your men and see that they don't do anything they'll regret."

Lieutenant DuBois was dazed, worried, and puzzled. Captain Fritzgerald returned his salute, spun around and headed for his vessel. In five minutes, Fritzgerald shoved off heading upriver. DuBois rubbed his hands until his fingers turned red. Immediate action was the order of the day. An idea descended like fresh summer rain. "I'll see Miss Josephine Ellis at the Manor. I bet she knows some important lawyers." With that thought he dashed uphill with the speed of a frightened gazelle. He managed to stumble up the steps and knock frantically on the front door. Alarmed, Roberts opened the door.

"What is it, Lieutenant? You look like you have seen a horrible apparition."

"I think I have. Is Miss Ellis at home?" DuBois looked around Roberts to peer inside.

"Out in the back room. I'll tell her you're here." Robert clicked his heels like a Cossack.

"Please. And hurry," DuBois beseeched the butler.

Overhearing, she sensed the urgency. Josephine Ellis glided in as fast as her long dress permitted. "Lieutenant, is there something wrong?"

"Yes, Ma'am. Commander McDill has been arrested in Washington and will face a trial. I believe he has no lawyer."

"My good man. Arrested for what?"

Between rapid heaves for air, DuBois explained charges to the hostess. When she heard it, she sat down lady-like on her couch, exhibiting her thinking frown. A long pause made the room feel like a tomb filled with several silent coffins. Finally she rose, drew a long sigh, and said, "My cousin once knew an outstanding lawyer who lived—or still lives—in Fredricksburg, I hope."

"Ma'am, he'll need a very good lawyer to get out of this awful mess."

"Lieutenant, I'll write down this name and his last known address. Go to Comer's and have him telegraph this message for me. In the meantime, I'll tell Helen McDill what's happening to her husband. She's frantic to find out something."

When Phillipe reached the door of the telegraph office, it was locked, no one inside. For a second, panic struck like a bomb. He circled the building twice hoping to find anyone in charge. Wheels of his mind rolled like a runaway cart. *"Time's precious. Where can Comer be? Home?"* His mind twisted like a tornado. Uphill, he hustled as fast as his legs could carry his six-foot frame. DuBois knocked on Comer's front door until the hinges rattled. No one answered. He knocked again. *"He's fishing, but where?"* Lieutenant DuBois slid downhill, as if he had on snow skis. His eyes scanned several sweeps. Only a barge could be seen by the naked eye. The dinghy. That's it. One was tied to the dock. No time to ask. Its oars seemed to jump from the dinghy's floor into his hands. The light craft was pushed into the center of the river where it was aided by the strong southward current. Down river he could see only two unfamiliar water crafts. DuBois decided to fight the current and paddle upstream. Searching river and shore, the mariner found nothing upstream. He calculated, *"I'll have to go back to his office and wait until...."*

Suddenly a shot jerked his head toward the west shore. A white object flashed. A shirt. A slim figure bent down at the edge of the river. "Hello, you over there. Are you who I think you are?" DuBois bellowed.

"Leave my dog alone so he can get my duck."

"I can't see you too well. Are you Comer?" DuBois squinted at the form ashore.

"Yeah, what'd you want?" he shouted back, irritated.

"An emergency. I need to send a most important message." DuBois stood up in his boat enough to make it wobble.

Comer ignored Phllipe. "I got my duck. Good boy."

"Comer, did you hear me?" he screamed, cuffing his hands on either side of his mouth.

"Something about an urgent message?" Comer replied, still a little irritated.

"Yeah, let's go. I'll explain." The lieutenant's voice lowered.

"I'll meet you at my office, okay?" Comer yelled back.

"Yes, but hurry." Phillipe pleaded. His oar turned the dinghy into the down current, and he paddled as fast as he could.

DuBois was waiting at the telegraph office when Comer mounted the hill.

Still out of breath, DuBois explained the devilish predicament that his boss was facing and shoved Miss Ellis' message into Comer's hand.

"This is for a good lawyer Miss Ellis knows. Maybe he can help."

"Here goes. Hope we can get a response." Comer's skilled fingers tapped rapidly as he read the note.

"Can I wait here until we get a response?"

"Yeah, Lieutenant, if you want. We have a small office in Fredericksburg, and I think it's probably closed. It's opened part time."

"No matter. I'll wait." DuBois settled down on Comer's couch.

Comer was right. The Fredericksburg office was empty. Unheard clicks of telegraph keys continued into the night. "Boy, I wish there was some way their office machine could write down my message and send me an answer, but it's gotta have pen, paper and a human being." Comer's face wrinkled in frustration.

"Please keep trying if it takes all night. This is imperative and extremely urgent," Phillipe begged.

At dawn, familiar clicks woke two men who had slumped in their chairs.

"Comer. Is that our answer?" Phillipe stood, walking off his cramped legs.
"Be quiet! Let me get this down."

DuBois locked his hands until his finger joints popped.

"You'll like this." The telegrapher pushed a small piece of paper into the sailor's hand. It read:

ALBERT MONROE, ESQUIRE, WILL ARRIVE NAVAL
HEADQUARTERS IN WASHINGTON TOMORROW AT 11
A.M. HE WILL BE HONORED TO DEFEND LT.
COMMANDER MCDILL, IF THE COMMANDER WISHES.

"By the hands of Mother Mary!" DuBois leaped out the door to tell Miss Ellis and Mrs. McDill. He knew he must tell Helen McDill the good news.

News of Dennis' court-martial spread like a plague. Because of his misfortune some people sympathized with Dennis McDill and wanted to help, but how?

Lt. DuBois quickly gathered his men for a powwow. "Sailors, you know the problem. Let's figure out what we can do."

"We can get to Washington by train in a day. One leaves at 9:00 each morning," MacEaton offered.

"Okay, we go by train, then what'll we do?" O'Connell asked, a bit doubtful.

"At least cram our bodies into the courtroom to show our support," the Chief responded. "You know we're all a part of this. It wouldn't surprise me if all of us ain't court-martialed, too."

"Lieutenant, you think that lawyer's any good?" O'Malley questioned. "Military court is tough. Defense has gotta' be good."

"My Lord, I certainly hope so. We're partly responsible for this mess." Phillipe looked at each man as though he were inspecting him. "Yes, I know what you're thinking—we were just following orders. But if the Skipper's found guilty, the trial counsel may pounce on us next."

"Say, I have an idea," Rogers spoke. "Let's organize a rally and get a train full of townspeople to go with us to Washington and support our C.O."

"Great idea, Chief. We'll get the railroaders to agree to pull three or four carloads up to D.C." DuBois slapped the old salt on his back so hard he almost stumbled. "Comer will know who to ask."

"Maybe they can give a good ticket price if we got a lot of passengers." Sullivan, who had been quiet, finally spoke. McEaton agreed in a shout. He was small, but he had a loud voice.

"All right. Chief, you and O'Connell go to Comer, tell him our plan, and if he approves, start negotiating with the railroad bosses. Got it?"

"Aye, Sir. We got it." Rogers answered. "We're off, Sir."

DuBois ordered, "O'Malley, the rest of you and I will divide the town into areas, knock on every door and solicit help to go to Headquarters. We'll rally right in front of Headquarters—with signs high enough for everybody to understand our cause. Military courts often forbid spectators in the courtroom, but we'll insist until they let us in. If not, we'll parade around Headquarters and let the whole world know we want a fair trial."

Rapier thin clouds fanned out from some hidden epicenter near the horizon. They looked like streaks of white fire. A sea of bouncing signs engulfed a new locomotive and its six passenger cars. Inside there was just enough room for all of McDill's sympathizers and their signs. No one really minded being packed in, for they firmly believed they were traveling for a good purpose. Naval personnel mixed themselves throughout the crowd encouraging every soul to give them their utmost support for an unfortunate skipper. The long ride didn't deter any of the enthusiasm that mounted by the hour. Headquarters was about two miles away from the train station. More than a hundred friends marched vigorously holding signs reading: "A FAIR TRIAL FOR MCDILL." McDill's crew shrewdly informed the crowd that in the service a man is often believed guilty before his trial begins. Determined, Helen McDill led the entire caravan like a modern Joan of Arc. She held up a sign nearly as large as her body. Only the light brown crown of her head could be seen when she jabbed it in the air. Helen McDill was the most enthusiastic marcher in the entire procession.

When Helen stopped at Headquarters, everyone else stopped. Albert Monroe stood in front of the two large anchors in front of Naval Headquarters. Right away the crowd hushed when they saw him. Albert shouted to be heard. "Ladies and gentlemen, I am very glad to see such a large turnout. I have studied the charges and have some information. It is my belief that this trial is a farce. It is not justified under the mitigating circumstances that your man has faced. I shall stake my reputation to see that this will be a fair trial. Your friend and my client will be free."

Applause was loud enough to be heard across the Potomac. It roused all the occupants of Naval Headquarters. Four marines, stationed at the front door, were stampeded when the crowd shoved past them into the huge courtroom. One admiral, three Navy captains and a Marine general sat with starched backs behind the large maple table fastened onto an elevated platform, each one sported his official medals. Admiral Hicks took charge. Seeing the huge audience fill the room, Hicks figured it would take an entire fleet to force them outside. Dennis McDill and his lawyer settled behind a table on the main floor directly in front of the senior officer of the court. To McDill's left was the trial counselor who served as the Navy's prosecuting attorney. Dennis was relieved that Captain Mort was not on the Court's Panel.

Admiral Hicks lifted his gavel. "Order in the Court." He looked to his left and to his right. "I see everyone is present. We shall begin. Trial Counsel, you may proceed."

"Sir, if it please the court, this officer is accused of misappropriating and misusing government property and funds. Also, he is accused of disobeying a direct written order which I will submit later as Exhibit 1. Specifically, he has taken funds to buy lumber to build houses rather than repair naval ships as he was ordered. In fact, the ships were to be his top priority. Albeit, he requested permission to change his mission. This request was denied. He changed his mission on his own, thereby aborting the mission. This man is accused of one of the most despised crimes in the Navy—disobeying a direct order. Herewith, I have a certified copy of the written order he did, in fact, disobey. I now call from the Inspector General's office, Captain Fritzgerald." Fritzgerald wobbled and sat down behind the stand to the right of the court.

"Do you swear to tell the truth and the whole truth, so help you God?" the court clerk asked.

"I do."

Admiral Hicks started. "Captain, did you have an occasion to visit the place where ships were to be repaired?"

"I did."

"Did you see any ships being repaired?" Hicks probed.

"No, but I saw something else. The ships were stripped down to their keels. Most of the metal and some of the wood were removed. Also, I saw one being loaded on a barge to go some place, perhaps to be completely destroyed."

70

"What else did you see?" the prosecutor inquired.

"Some new houses on newly prepared lots. They were occupied."

"Occupied by whom?" Trial Counselor Bailey asked.

"The crew and their families." Fritzgerald answered confidently.

"You say they were new homes?" Hicks interrogated.

"Yes, Sir. They occupied the new houses."

"Go on." Hicks rolled his gavel in his hand when he looked at the crowd sitting quietly, hearing every word.

"While I was there, I discovered those new houses were built by McDill's crew and some others. I also found out that McDill himself was living in one of the houses."

"What else did you find out?" Commander Bailey inquired, already knowing the answer.

"After checking around, I learned that he had money, and bought trees to saw into lumber for the houses."

"Do you know where he got enough money to buy lumber?"

"Probably from Navy's allowance."

Monroe pushed his chair back so hard it scraped the floor. "Object. This is speculation, your Honors."

"Trial Counselor, do you have an exhibit for this?" Hicks glowered.

"No, but I heard some talk." Fritzgerald cleared his throat.

"Please, your Honors, this is unidentified hearsay," Albert objected.

"Since it may be germane to the case, I will allow this testimony to stand. However, clerk, make it so that all objections are in the record," Hicks ordered.

"How would you describe the progress of repairing the ships at that time?" Commander Bailey continued.

"It appeared that the mission was aborted."

"Then the mission was changed by that man sitting as the accused in front of you," Bailey declared.

For more than two hours the I.G. testified against Dennis McDill. Court members leaned on every word of the I.G.

Trial Counselor Bailey seemed to be gaining ground with every answer.

"Mr. Monroe, this is beginning to look pretty bad," McDill whispered. "How am I going to get out of this mess?"

"We'll have our turn later," Monroe whispered back. "I want to stall the Court so I can do some research, and I want to talk with you again in private."

Each time Monroe objected, it was overruled.

Finally, Monroe had his chance. "Your Honor, I respectfully request a recess until Monday, so I can check some facts and talk with my client," Monroe asked.

The Marine general raised his hand. "Let's continue with the case, Admiral."

Hicks looked over the audience, paused, and lifted his gavel. "The Court is recessed until 10:00 a.m. Monday morning. Guards, allow the defense counsel into the cell to talk with his client."

As McDill and the guards were turning to leave, Helen shoved people aside as she pushed her way to her husband to grab his sleeve. "Don't worry, Dennis, we're all here and we will wait a week if we must." A guard forced Helen to release her grip and led Dennis off to his dreaded cell. It was another cell. Slightly bigger and cleaner than the one he endured earlier. At least the bed was long enough to support his entire body. He lay thinking and numbering the cracks in the ceiling when he heard a creaking sound. It came from the outside brig door. Dennis, surprised, sprang up like a frightened deer. One stocky guard with short cropped hair and a thin off yellow beard, escorted Monroe directly to the cell, unlocked its door, and pointed to McDill.

"How long can I stay?" Monroe asked.

"You have an hour." Dennis' cell door was locked immediately.

"Sit on the bed, Dennis. I'll sit on this excuse for a chair. I want to ask you some questions. I needed the court to grant me the weekend to verify a hunch."

"A hunch?" McDill sat slowly onto his bunk.

"Yes. Let me start at the beginning, or at least I think it's the beginning."

"Fire away, Mr. Monroe. I'll tell you all I know." Dennis sat back in the bed with his feet dangling over the edge.

"You can call me Albert. No need to be formal from now on."

"All right, I'm Dennis, if you wish."

Albert placed his briefcase on the table and pulled out a writing tablet. "First, why were you given such a stinking low level job to repair some old junk the Navy should have discarded years ago?"

"Jealously, I think."

"Explain." Albert pulled out a pencil.

"Well, I learned not only to build and maintain ships, I learned to design ships. Even if I do say so, I became good at it."

"Were your designs accepted?" Monroe asked anxiously.

"That's the point. They weren't. My superiors became so jealous they refused to submit my designs. I think they planned to take the credit themselves. So, they plotted to cart me off to some trumped-up assignment. Then I wouldn't be in their way of claiming they invented the new ship."

"Anyone in particular?"

"Yes, Captain Mort."

"Did you later see any ships that looked like your design?"

"No, few government craft traveled the waters off City Point, where I was stationed. Mostly we saw barges, fishing boats, a dinghy, lots of canoes, and, of course those run down gunboats we were suppose to repair. There was one exception. Headquarters sent our families down in an old frigate which carried midshipmen for training."

"Well, Commander, there was no way you could patent your inventions. Right?"

"Right. Everything I designed would belong to the Navy, and they often sent out bids to civilian companies to construct new craft."

"Somebody at the Navy's Maintenance Terminal might be able to give us a lead," Monroe pondered, chewing on his pencil.

"What do you mean?" McDill asked.

"Maybe those jealous men got your plans. After you left, they may have attempted to sell them to someone who'd take the risk of buying them secretly. Dennis, that would be illegal." He turned a page in his pad. "So, if they snatched your schematics and actually sold them undercover, they'd be in a barrel of trouble," Albert speculated, still chewing his pencil. His narrow, black moustache bobbed up and down with each word.

"Sure, they would, I hope." Dennis replied.

"It may be a slim lead, but I want to go to the terminal this weekend and talk with anyone I can."

"If he is still working at the terminal, Chief Sam Giles would be helpful enough to tell you the truth, if he knows. We've trusted each other for years."

"I'll look him up, if I can get a pass. In the honor of justice and a fair trial, as your people are demanding, someone might see that I get a pass."

"Do you know where to find him at the Naval Repair Terminal?"

"Don't worry, Dennis. I'll find Giles even if he's under water trying to catch barracudas."

Dennis McDill smiled for the first time in weeks.

Slamming cell doors unleashed doom's frigid fingers to cascade down his back every time Albert Monroe visited a client in jail. Leaving the dreary brig was a warming relief to him. Sympathy for every incarcerated soul flowed through his heart when a slammer banged behind him when he entered or left. Just before he left the cell compound, Albert stopped a passing shore patrol. "Can you tell me where I can find the officer in charge of the Judicial Section?"

"Yes. Next building to your right, first floor. Tell the guard who you are, what you want, and who you want to see."

For some reason, Monroe wanted to thank the informant. He shook his hand.

When he stepped outside, two pearly stone buildings almost blinded him. The larger one stood 90 degrees to his right. He counted fifteen steps as he climbed to the front door. Inside, a sentinel behind the desk stood up. "May I help you, Sir?"

"Yes, I'm a defense counsel and I have a client in your brig. I would like to talk with your officer in charge."

"If you'll wait a few minutes, I'll have my assistant check for you."

Large murals in the hall impressed the lawyer as he waited. Sea storms seemed to roar from their canvasses. Battleships blazed their guns directly at him as he gazed up at their pictures. The guard had to interrupt Monroe's uncontrolled gawking. "Sir. SIR! The Rear Admiral will see you, but for only a few minutes."

"That's all I'll need."

A tall wide door greeted them as they marched down the hall. Inside, a stoop shouldered figure sat bending over a desk. His eyes seemed to reject any interference. "I haven't much time. What do you want?"

"Permission to visit the Repair Terminal."

"A most unusual request. Why?"

"I am defending a client who's being tried in court, and I need to interview a possible witness on his behalf."

"I'm inclined to deny your request, young man. This seems out of order," the admiral smirked.

Albert had to play his trump card. "Admiral, there may have been a prejudiced individual on the Inquisition Panel."

"What do you mean, Mr. Attorney?"

"Lt. Commander Dennis McDill is being tried. Captain Norman Mort was once McDill's immediate superior. He seemed to manage to be assigned to my client's Inquiry Panel. I think Captain Mort is an enemy to my client. He'll do all he can to get the commander in prison for a long time. Captain Mort did not excuse himself. He must have some nefarious reason to be on the Panel. In defense of the Panel, they probably didn't know Mort was my client's superior officer. I believe it's Captain Mort's way to send my client to prison."

"What a disappointment! Mort was highly recommended by our adjutant. We don't check personnel an officer commands, just his own superiors and his record. I personally checked his record. It's clean." Still unbelieving, the rear admiral stared at Albert.

"Admiral, I know you'll be relieved to know that Mort was not permitted to serve on the Tribunal."

"Yes. You can rest assured if there is more evidence concerning Mort and your client, we'll find it"

Albert, believing his point was made, asked directly. "Will you honor my request, Sir?"

The admiral paused for several seconds, then started to write on a short piece of paper. "Here is a note you can take to the terminal. I'm sure this will get you in."

Before he left, Albert felt the need to talk to Admiral Hicks in person. Since Hicks' orderly had already seen the lawyer, Monroe had a easy time seeing the admiral. He entered and gave a brief description of his immediate past actions. Hicks drummed his suntanned fingers on the edge of his desk. "Mr. Monroe, we'll have to have the prosecuting attorney present. I will have him in this office this afternoon. Meet us here. Make your request. For the record, I'll have a steno ready. Commander Bailey will need to know the reason. In the meantime, I'll have my staff glean from McDill's record to discover his superior officers." Hicks appeared cooperative. This relayed some hope for Albert.

Albert informed the admiral. "Sir, I believe you will find that Captain Mort's was my client's superior. If not, I can produce a witness."

"It won't be necessary." Hicks hailed his orderly. "Ask Trial Counselor Bailey to come here tomorrow."

"Thank you, Admiral. I will be here as you ordered." Albert Monroe left feeling good that he may have won one battle for McDill, but he reminded himself that the war wasn't over. Right away, he sped over to the brig to let Dennis know what had been accomplished. A blink of hope broke through.

Dennis grinned. "Thank you, Albert. I knew Miss Ellis would know the best lawyer on this side of the country."

Dennis slept soundly with both feet inside the end of his bed.

Later, the sun beamed into his eerie castle like a harbinger of good news. He could see Albert Monroe standing in front of the cell.

"Ready, Dennis? We have a date with an admiral."

"I'll be ready in a minute."

Commander McDill's steps sprang happily under his feet, being led to the "courthouse."

Armed men, posted outside, joined the two as they walked down the street to a horse-drawn paddy wagon. The defendant and his lawyer rode while a shore patrol, armed with a .45, sat on top of the wagon urging their horse to move. Washington streets were busy with commerce. Many people cluttered all the walkways.

For the first time, Dennis McDill did not dread going back into Headquarters. Inside, Headquarters seemed brighter. In fact, the whole world lifted his soul. Marines escorted the lawyer and his client to the front of Admiral Hicks' desk. Beside Hicks' desk stood a bewildered counselor still wondering why he was ordered to such a meeting.

"Mr. Monroe is here to make a motion, Commander Bailey. I want you to hear the motion and be given the opportunity to respond."

"Isn't this most unusual, Sir?" Bailey pleaded.

"Yes, but this is an unusual circumstance." Hicks responded as his chair swivelled toward Albert. "Proceed, Mr. Monroe."

"Thank you, Sir. I move that my client, Dennis McDill of the United States Navy be released on bail and that the trial be delayed two months."

"Commander Bailey, do you object?"

Baily, aghast, choked. "Sir, I can't imagine why we need to delay. This man is guilty. In fact, why not speed up the trial so everything will be settled sooner?"

"Defense, it's your turn." Hicks nodded for his stenographer to continue.

"We are aware that one of the panelists was once the defendant's superior officer. He is namely, Captain Mort." Albert said firmly.

Bailey's face went from red to purple. "Your Honor, I didn't know…."

Hicks' pivoted to face the prosecutor. "I certainly hope you didn't know." He swivelled his chair over to face Monroe. "Before I make a decision, I want to ask who will take the responsibility to see that this accused returns to trial on time?"

Without hesitating, Monroe answered, "I will, Sir. He will be in my charge at all times."

"Will you swear to that?"

"I will swear to it, your Honor."

"Very well, I leave this man in your hands and the hands of the local law enforcer. He is confined to stay within five miles of his home. The bail will be $5,000. Under these rare circumstances, if you need more time, I will consider it if it's defensible. I will inform the Panel of my decision." Admiral Hicks looked for his gavel. It was not on his desk, so he rapped his fist on the top of his desk. "Court is extended for sixty days. This meeting is adjourned."

The moment Albert and Dennis left, they could see Bailey running to catch a carriage. "I bet I can guess where he's going, "Dennis observed. "Straight to see Captain Mort."

"You'll win that one." Albert laughed and hailed a carriage.

"Where're we going?" Dennis asked.

Monroe stopped and turned his client to face him. "To get you on a train home. You look a wreck. I want you to get some rest." He continued. "But first, when he arrives, I want you to report to the lawman in charge. Also, I took the opportunity to tell Helen and her friends to go home. I'll send the sheriff a telegram."

Dennis let fresh air fill his lungs. "Helen and the gang should be home by now. Boy, it'll be nice to see them again."

Old Iron Lady that DuBois loved so much was waiting for her cargo. "All aboard," the conductor shouted as the tired mariner stepped into the passenger car. He flopped into his seat and waved at Albert through the window. The rocking train car lulled him to sleep soon. He traveled about thirty minutes when he began to stir in his sleep. Nightmares controlled his mind. He dreamed that Bailey, Fritzgerald and Mort were comparing swords to see which one was the sharpest. They engaged in a contest to find out which sword could cut a clean face into a Halloween pumpkin. *"Pretend this is McDill's head." Mort said. "Whoever can cut out this jack o' lantern the fastest will have the honor of decapitating Dennis McDill."*

Enormous clanging noises caromed over the sides and ceilings of the large building where the U.S. Navy had given care to numberless flotillas over the last decades. It was a weekend. Albert expected a quiet place. Unknown to him, the repair shop needed overtime to complete their largest ship repair job on time. He approached the first sailor he saw. "Tell me. Where can I find Chief Warrant Officer, Sam Giles?"

"To the rear, up the ramp, the right side room with the big window." He pointed. "Look, you should be able to see it from here."

"Is he on board today?"

"Yeah, we're all working. We gotta' meet our deadline." He looked up at the great gash in the starboard side of the ship hanging in dry dock. "You see what we have to do?"

"Yes, I guess that would require a great deal of work," Albert observed.

"Yeah, a heap of work." The sailor shrugged his shoulders

Albert searched for the window. "Thank you. I'll be on my way."

"Wait, Sir. You'll need permission to go any further."

"Oh, I forgot. Here's my letter from the JAG Admiral."

The sailor scanned the note. "Yeah. I know him. Served under him during the last war. That was before he became a lawyer."

"All right. Where do I start?"

"See those guards at the entrance just beneath the window?"

Torch flares blinded Albert, causing him to shield his eyes and squint in the right direction. "Can't see much. I'll wait until they snuff out their torches. It won't take long," he hoped.

Soon, Albert could see a rugged man with bushy eyebrows and arms covered with coarse black hair. His goggles reflected Albert's face when he walked down the steps to see his visitor. "Are you the man in charge?" Albert wanted assurances since he was almost blind.

"Yeah, one of 'em."

"Are you Sam Giles?"

"Yeah. That's me."

"My name is Albert Monroe. I'm a lawyer and I need a little information. Do you remember an officer named Lt. Commander Dennis McDill?"

He removed his goggles and looked down at Albert. "Lawyer, are you for him or against him?"

"I'm his counselor. He's facing a tribunal over at Naval Headquarters. There may be some information you know that will help his case."

Giles grinned. "Okay, what do you want to know?"

"Do you remember him when he worked here?"

"Yeah, I hated to see him go. He's one of the best friends I know. What's he being tried for?"

"Misappropriating government funds, stealing government property aborting his mission and disobeying a direct order."

"Oh, my God! That's BIG trouble." The burly giant dropped his goggles and pushed the hair out of his eyes.

"Yes. BIG trouble, as you put it."

"But, how can I help the Commander?" He fixed his gaze at some unknown object. Albert looked down at the platform.

"Can we take a seat over there at the edge of that platform so we can talk in private?"

Giles and Monroe dangled their feet while the barrister dug into his briefcase for a pencil and pad. Giles glanced at him. "You're going to write everything down, aren't you?"

"Yes, I might want you to testify, and I will want to know what you'll say."

"I'm ready. What do you want to know?"

"Was McDill a good draftsman?"

"One of the best. One time he drew the plans for a future steamer that could travel over thirty-five-knots-an-hour. That's faster than any bigguns' we have now." Giles stretched out his arms for emphasis.

"Most impressive. Was that ship ever built?"

"Don't know. The Navy may have contracted it out. They do that often."

"Commander McDill tells me that he was transferred because some senior officers were jealous and conspired to steal his plans." Monroe reported.

"Well, I might not be able to tell you very much. When Captain Mort ran this section, I could sense he was getting kinda funny about the praises Commander McDill was getting. At first, I couldn't figure if it was jealously or if that Dennis was doing something out of place."

"Did you know that Captain Mort had served on his Inquisition Panel?"

"My God, Counselor. He's responsible for shoving Dennis into that terrible job trying to restore some old dying rigs down in Virginia. He recommended that the Admiral have him transferred."

"Then, at least there was one enemy on the Panel who would surely find him guilty and throw the book at him." Albert calculated.

"Counselor, if there is anything I can do, just let me know."

"There is. Can we certify that Captain Mort was against McDill?"

"Let me think. I remember one day a congressman came to inspect the terminal. Mort was showing him around, and while they were walking through the drafting room, they stopped to look at some drawings. I recognized they were looking at Dennis' work. The congressman was impressed. They didn't see me passing by. I overheard Captain Mort say, 'Thank you. I drew that one myself.'"

"So! It appears HE took credit for the plans?" Albert laid his pad down and stood in front of Giles.

"Yeah. I told Dennis about it, and Dennis told me he wasn't surprised."

"Then why wasn't he surprised?"

"He told me that Mort was jealous of his work. I advised Dennis to report it, but Dennis didn't think anyone would believe him and if they did, what could he do about it?"

Albert's pencil scratched rapidly on the surface of the paper as fast as he could write. "Mr. Giles, do you know what happened to those drawings?"

"No Sir. I remember our clerk reported them missing one day. He searched everywhere but found nothing."

"We have a start anyway. Are you willing to testify?"

"You can count on me to help an old friend."

"On the stand, I want you to tell the Court exactly what you told me, today. Can you do that?"

"You bet I can. Let me know when you need me."

"It's a deal. Will you tell your man to let me out?"

Torches had been doused out of consideration for the visitor. Sam and Albert walked in stride toward the entrance. They shook hands. Albert felt like hugging "Goliath," but figured that he'd be crushed to death if Goliath hugged him back. He followed the guard to the front entrance and left to hustle to his train waiting to pull off to D..C and Naval Headquarters. There was just enough light for Albert to write on his pad. He knew how difficult this trial would be. He thought, *"I've got to have more time to find those drawings. They could be in any number of places in the country, and God forbid, perhaps in another country."*

He pondered for an hour and fell asleep. Two loud whistles woke him. His train was pulling into the station. Albert stepped out into a waterfall of rain. It slanted sideways, hard enough to pound on his cheeks. He pushed his pad under his shirt and struggled to find a taxi. "Where to?" the driver shouted above the torrents.

"Naval Headquarters."

Chapter V

Helen McDill heard the thud of boots dropping on the porch. Not surprising. Helen already knew that her husband would return. Smiling, she opened the door. "Dennis, before I got word, I thought something awful had happened to you. I was afraid I'd have to visit you in the brig often."

"Helen, I'm out on bail."

"Thank God you're here under any circumstance. Take off your coat, sit down and tell me what happened. We were worried to death."

"Guess I'm on a strange leave of absence."

"What happened?"

"Albert Monroe persuaded the Panel's President to allow me to have bail and extended the trial date. Albert got permission to go to the ship terminal and interview a possible witness. You know, my friend Sam Giles."

"He's one of your best friends, Dennis."

"Precisely, I wanted Sam to tell him, first hand, how Captain Mort treated me when I was given this lousy assignment. Admiral Hicks probably was livid because Mort somehow weaseled himself on the Inquiry Panel. He quickly recovered by saying his department would look into it. I'm sure he'd find out that Mort should have excused himself before the court-martial was ever convened. And I'm sure a good fleet officer like Admiral Hicks will take care of the matter."

"Careful, Dennis, Mort is dangerous. He may do something worse."

"Well, I'm here at least for a while. I'm starving, Helen." Dennis rubbed his stomach and licked his lips twice.

"You can have your favorite. I bought a tenderloin steak in case I'd ever see you home again. It's in the spring down the street. It's from a good-looking farmer," she teased.

"Oh, you don't say?" He pretended to be jealous. Helen draped her arms around his shoulders and kissed both cheeks.

"No one's better looking than you. Commander McDill."

"It's been eons since I had any kind of steak. I'm famished."

She held him at length and inspected. "Dennis you look tired. Take the easy chair while I prepare your specialty."

"Honestly, I haven't unwound until I got home. When the I.G. came here, it meant trouble."

She agreed with a gentle sob. "That man was cruel to whisk you off so fast."

"I even spent long nights in the brig before I got bail."

"We were so busy campaigning for a fair trial, I couldn't visit you in jail. Dennis, every day you were in jail, it seemed like a year."

"I was under arrest the moment I stepped on Captain Fritzgerald's vessel."

"I know you love the Navy almost as you love me, but this...."

"Let's forget all of this and have one good night at home. I've missed you, especially when I was in that dreaded dungeon." Dennis returned her kisses and leaned back in his easy chair.

Helen stared out the window for a moment. "Dennis, I hate to bring it up now, but something's been bothering me."

"What is that?"

"On second thought, let's wait. It's not that important right now."

"Are you sure it's not that important? I'm starved and a bit exhausted." He sank deeper in his seat.

"Yes, supper will be ready soon. Sit and read your paper."

His nostrils quivered and his mouth watered when the incense of steak enveloped the living room. It hypnotized him. Dennis settled, realizing he was doubly glad he had his house built, even though part of it was taken from the Navy's ships.

After breakfast, Dennis couldn't wait. "What's been bothering you while I was gone?"

"I went to church with Mrs. Ellis. We sloshed in a driving rain to the brick church two blocks away from her house. It was thoughtful of her to invite me. But Dennis, it wasn't the same, no Mass, no confessional as we have. The people were nice to me, but Dennis, it wasn't the same."

"Well, we'd have to spend an entire Sunday if we went to Mass somewhere else. We can go to the church down the street. It's almost the same."

"But, I still say, it's not really the same."

"Oh, come on, Helen. We'll be just as happy." He leaned over the table and took her hand.

"Dennis, you don't understand. I like the people here, but I feel out of place in their churches."

"Aw, aren't you being a bit unreasonable?" Dennis put his hands on his hips.

"Not when it's about our beliefs. Yours and mine." She pointed a finger at Dennis and then to her. Her bright hazel eyes dropped tears on her blouse.

Helen and Dennis argued most of the morning. Unresolved, he left piqued without any answer that would satisfy him and his wife. Helen took her anger out on some onions she had dreaded to peel for dinner. In doing so, she sliced her finger with a small cut. When he left, he stamped hard enough to knock a plate off the table. It clattered and bounced on the kitchen floor shattering into a dozen pieces.

Confused, Dennis skirted down to the dock to express his compassion at Leland's rusty turret, one of her few recognizable features. "Little one, what must I do? We can't make a church out of you. Your companions are too far gone." Small waves whispered to the sailor in front of the little craft. Their ripples stroked her like a lady rubbing her cat. Soft sibilant sounds repeated a word—*Bishop, Bishop, Bishop.*

Just then boots vibrated against the deck of the pier. The soft whisperings ceased. Vibrations were advancing directly behind his back. Dennis could feel them as he turned to see a shining badge that almost made him sightless. A gritty voice seem to come out of the badge. "Are you Dennis McDill?"

"I am Dennis McDill. You are?"

"U.S. Marshal Jonathan Moore." The gritty voice came from under a broad brimmed hat that stamped the insignia "U.S." just above the brim. Marshal Moore was slightly shorter than Dennis, but his eye level was almost the same. His steely eyes were sharp as daggers.

"Can I help you?" Dennis pretended to be nonchalant

Moore's stone face looked as though it was carved into the side of a granite mountain. "You know a man named Gaith Johnson?"

Dennis' pause sucked in his breath.

The marshal sneered at the lack of immediate response. "Understand my question? Do you know a man called Gaith Johnson?"

Dennis stalled again. "Why do you ask?"

"I think you know he's an escaped convict from federal prison."

Dennis could see impatience leaping from the marshal's question.

"We traced him to this location. We thought you or somebody might have seen him or heard of him."

"What did he do?" Dennis asked pretending not to understand.

"He and some buddies stole a boat belonging to the U.S. Navy. He was serving a two-year term for grand larceny, but he decided to leave a bit early."

His brain was begging Dennis to stall longer. "Can you describe him, Marshal?"

Moore's chin twitched with ire causing his voice to reach a higher pitch. "Muscular, scar on left cheek, tattoos on his right arm, about six feet. We believe he might be dangerous if he doesn't get what he wants. Seems to have a compulsion to steal almost anything."

"A kleptomaniac?" Dennis kept stalling, but realized that the truth might have to be told.

"Yeah, you might call it that." The marshal was about to say, *"Tell me or I'll choke it out of you."*

"He'd do anything to steal something, you think, Marshal?"

Moore stood straight as a board, with eyes flaming, they looked directly into the face of the officer. "Commander; from your tone and your questions, you know something, don't you?"

To add to Dennis' problem of being confronted by a U.S. Marshal, a sharp scalpel stabbed his mind. He was burdened by another dreadful dilemma. If he told the marshal what happened to Gaith, he and his crew might be in trouble. He chose full silence about the soggy burial. On the other hand, it was honorable to tell the truth. *"And how about Lizzy? My God, what'll they do to Lizzy?"* Dennis tightened his belt another notch. *"All right. Here goes."* Dennis squared his shoulders. "Marshal, a thief launched one of the ships, or what's left of her." Dennis nodded to the Leland. "See, her skeleton's still hooked to the landing now."

"Did he match the description I gave you?"

"Pretty well, I'd say."

"Did he bring the ship back?"

"No. He tried to escape with it, but fed the boiler too much too fast. It blew up and died on the water." Dennis held back information about the final disposition of Gaith Johnson. The commander pulled his arms behind his back and crossed his fingers.

"Can you tell me anything else?" the marshal asked.

"Tell the man everything." Doctor Ellis, bringing down some fish bait, overheard the questioning. "Dennis, you and I were against the decision. We were outvoted, remember?"

"Our people will be in trouble, Doc." Dennis rebutted.

"We'll give you witness protection," the marshal offered.

"I'm afraid that won't help, but thanks anyway." Dennis calculated that would not be enough for him. He certainly did not want the marshal to know he was out on bail.

"Can't you see, Dennis? Secrets often imprison us," Ellis pleaded.

Frustrated, the marshal relented. "At least tell me where he is."

"Marshal, he's in the swamp down river." Ellis looked up at the marshal and pointed in the direction of the swamp.

Surprised, he asked, "Living in the swamp?"

Dennis hesitated and looked at the doctor. Two sets of eyes locked in combat, each one parrying for position.

"Dennis, we've got to tell the truth, even if it gets us in serious trouble." Dr. Ellis pleaded.

Dennis hesitated again, then confided calmly. "No, buried in the swamp."

"Did you say BURIED?" Moore nearly stepped off the boat landing.

"Yes, buried."

"How did he die?"

"He was shot," Commander McDill replied modestly.

"By you?"

Dennis pondered, hoping to dodge the question. "No, someone else shot him."

"Who?"

Ellis and McDill faces froze, petrified like two fallen trees. Finally, a nod from the doctor gave Dennis the signal.

"A woman," Dennis answered reluctantly.

"I need a name. Who?"

Ellis and McDill faced each other again. Four eyes locked in a battle again. Lips searched for moisture. Lungs raced for small intakes of oxygen. McDill answered in a raspy voice. "It was Lizzy. She heard Johnson confess that he killed her husband. She saw Johnson snatch the sheriff's .45 and threatened to kill him with it. Johnson bragged about killing the engineer, Lizzy's husband. At that point she realized who murdered her husband. She saw the sheriff was in the clutches of immediate danger. Lizzy seized a shotgun from the sheriff's carriage and shot Johnson before Johnson could pull the trigger."

"Where can I find this Lizzy woman?"

Dr. Ellis frisked his pockets. "Here's her address."

Marshal Moore tucked two fingers in his lips. His shrill whistle could be heard for blocks. "Come on, Old Boy. We've got some riding ahead of us." With one jerk of the reins the marshal rode west.

"You think we're in trouble, Dennis?"

"Doc, I hope not, you and I were witnesses. However, we really did nothing to stop it."

"You think we're involved in hiding the evidence or permitting the evidence to be buried?"

"Could be." Dennis shrugged. "We can't stand here and worry. Why don't you go home?" Soon Dr. Ellis disappeared over the hill.

McDill, alone again, kept hearing "*Bishop, Bishop.*" Was he going insane, or was something or someone trying to tell him something? "*Bishop, Bishop*" followed him into his living room.

Helen was busy knitting a sweater. "Dennis, I didn't hear you come in. You're quieter than usual."

His eyes tightened in a trance.

"Dennis, you hear me?" She shrilled.

In a second he stood up straight as a telephone pole. "Helen, I've got it!"

"What?"

"Bishop."

"Are you all right? Sit down and let me get a wet cloth." She couldn't tell whether he was seeing and hearing things or having a fever.

"I've got the answer. I'll see the Bishop. Comer told me that he's in a large church in Richmond."

She stopped in the middle of the room. "You think it'll do any good?"

"He may have an answer. Bishops can buy property, you know."

Confused, Helen puzzled. "Yes, but what do you have in mind?"

"Well, if he could buy some land around here, we can build a church right here in town."

"Dennis, that's the best news I've heard since we moved here!" She embraced him so tightly he had to move her arms so he could breathe.

He looked down at his little woman and held her cheeks. "Helen, I'm off right now to see if Comer's in his office."

"Let me know what you can do. Come back soon. I don't want to be disappointed."

In military style, Commander McDill marched out of his house, double-timed until he spied the telegraph office. Comer's back was turned with his hand on the lock to close up for the night. "Wait, Comer. I need your help."

Comer turned his neck to face Dennis. "You scared me."

"Can you send a telegram this late?"

"Yeah, I can send it anytime, but I don't know if anyone can get it on the other end at this time of day. Tell me what you want to send where."

"I want to send a message to the Diocese's Bishop. Since you're Catholic, you might know his name."

"Yeah, I know him. Bishop King."

"Please address this message to Bishop King, will you, Comer?"

"This late, I'd better send it in care of the police department. They're willing to deliver for me."

"Okay, send a short message to Bishop King that we want to see him about some land to build a chapel here at the Point."

"Dennis, he'll probably see you but he may not want to build another church."

"We'll ask him anyway."

"Did you say WE?" Comer's eyes opened in mild alarm.

"Yes, I'm hoping you can go with me if the Bishop can see us."

"I'll send the message and hope to get an answer. But wouldn't it be better if we had a piece of land in mind and how much it costs before we go?"

"That was on my mind as I came over. Miss Josephine Ellis has a great deal of land around here. She might be willing to sell some for a reasonable price since it's a good cause."

"Man, you're good. You've thought of everything."

"Not everything, but I try. When we get a firm date to see the Bishop, we'll go see Miss Ellis at the Manor."

"You said WE again."

"Comer, would you be willing? This is a friendly/official request," Dennis beseeched.

Comer considered as he picked his teeth. "I've trained a man to take my place while I'm off." Comer's finger was already tapping the Morse Code on the little machine in the corner of his office. Jerky telegraph taps always fascinated Dennis. *Someday I'll learn the Code,* he promised himself.

Comer kept tapping until the last syllable. He slowly wheeled around. "You may need the Code. I'll give you lessons." Comer's sixth sense told him that Dennis had a keen interest brewing.

"It's a deal. You read my mind." Dennis peered outside at a blazing sunset. "Tomorrow we'll have a date to see Miss Ellis. She's usually home early in the morning. Can we meet at her house at 8:15? She's a very organized woman, you know...." McDill's trailing sentence drifted as he stepped outside.

"I'll be there," Comer agreed. "I'll make the visit You meet me there early."

At home Helen sat anxiously rocking back and forth, waiting. Her husband slammed open the door as she ran to meet him. "Tell me. What happened?"

"Let's go inside and I'll tell you."

"Don't wait, tell me right here, Dennis McDill." Her demanding arms arched in a wide akimbo fashion. To Dennis that constituted an order.

"Comer and I are going to see Miss Ellis tomorrow and find out if she'll sell us some land to build a church. Comer sent a telegram requesting an audience with Bishop King. If Miss Ellis will sell and the Bishop will buy, we can build. How's that, Helen?"

"What a grand idea!" Her arms encircled his neck.

Next morning, stiff breezes caused several trees to sing in unison as two men rang the doorbell of the Manor. Roberts immediately answered the ring. "Oh, come in, gentlemen."

Comer bowed slightly. "May we see Miss Ellis?"

"Please stay here, gentleman. I will see."

McDill could not resist looking at the triple-dental molding on the ceiling. "What an admirable place. Roberts has done a splendid job keeping it in shape."

"Miss Ellis hires the best," he boasted. A rustling sound announced her presence. "Oh, here she comes."

"How nice to see you two gentlemen." Her white glove extended toward the sofa. "Have a seat. Shall I order you some coffee?"

"No, thank you, Ma'am." Comer answered.

"Miss Ellis, if you will allow me, I will explain why we're here. It's on business."

"Gentlemen, I'm always interested in business. May I be of help?"

"We are trying to build a church and wondered if you could sell some of your land," McDill explained.

For a moment her eyes focused on the ornate ceiling. "Land to build a church," she mused quietly. "Another church might be good for our community."

"It would be Catholic, Ma'am." Dennis reported in a quiet tone.

"You and your crew's families are of that faith, I believe," she said factually.

"Yes, Miss Ellis. We are all Catholic."

"You're going to build the chapel yourselves?"

"Yes we can, with the help of a few like Comer, here." He nodded to Comer.

"Before you came, there were only two Catholic families in town," Miss Ellis acknowledged as a matter of fact.

"We're twelve miles away from our church now. That takes up most of a Sunday traveling," Comer added.

"Gentleman, I have a small lot near Dr. Ellis' home. It's really no bigger than his. Do you think it will be large enough for a church?"

"I know something about Dr. Ellis' lot. It's small, but we can make it fit. What do you think, Comer?" Dennis asked.

"Yes, for a small chapel," he answered and turned to his hostess. "Miss Ellis, there'd be only about twenty-five in all to attend."

"Well, I'll be willing to take $150 for the lot. Do you have the money?"

"We need to ask Bishop King if he will buy the land. Bishops hold title to all church property, as you know."

"Yes, I've heard. Go and ask your Bishop. If he can pay $150, I will sell it to him."

Miss Josephine Ellis lifted the silver pot on the nearby table. "Won't you have some tea or coffee?"

"No, we must be off to Richmond—I hope not later than tomorrow. We thank you for your gracious hospitality and your willingness to sell the land." McDill shook her hand in gratitude.

Knowing he might not hear from the Bishop until the next day, McDill wrestled his covers all night. After midnight he stumbled into the kitchen, drank a glass of milk, and tried again. No results.

The sun rose on a calm, warm day. Dennis hurried to the telegraph office and waited for Comer.

"What are you doing here so early?" Comer rattled his numerous keys to find the right one. "I doubt we'll hear this soon."

"I couldn't sleep, so I thought I come over and wait if I have to."

"All right, Commander, I have a question. Even if you get the land, where do you think you'll find enough lumber to build a church or a little chapel?"

"I'll use the rest of the lumber the I.G. thinks I stole."

"Think again. Will that be enough?"

"I don't know. We've never built a church." McDill admitted gesturing with his hands.

Click, click. Comer's clicking keys clamored for attention. "I hear a message. Dennis, quiet, please." The clicking stopped and Comer finished scribbling.

"Oh, boy. Bishop King will see us tomorrow at noon," Comer quaked.

"We can get there on time by train. Do you know where he lives, Comer?"

"It's a big church near the center of town. I was there a long time ago. I believe I can find it."

Dennis rushed home and brushed off his finest dress uniform. Comer got out his new tweed. By 9:00 a.m. they were seated on the train heading north.

Commerce in the big city rapidly increased by the late 1800s. Buggies, carts, horseback riders, and carriages clogged every major thoroughfare. Scores of people bustled past the two men. "There are almost as many people here than I've seen since Washington," Dennis observed.

"Yeah, this town's getting crowded, all right."

"Comer, we can't waste time. Let's ask a policeman where we can find the Bishop."

A traffic cop, with a crimson face and a huge whistle was directing traffic. He glanced at the two men crossing to meet him. "Laddies, you're in the wrong lane. Move over."

"Sir, we'd like to ask you something," Comer shouted.

"Step over here if you want to risk it."

Two brown horses, pulling a wagon, nicked Comer's leg.

"You hurt, Laddie?"

"No, just a bruise I think." Comer rubbed his leg and hobbled over to the policeman.

"Waja want?"

"We're looking for Bishop King," Dennis inquired while helping Comer regain his balance.

"Over there, turn right, and go three blocks. The church is on the right. Now move over before somebody really hurts you."

They dodged three carriages, a trotting horse, and a wagon. Finally they got on the right street and found the church. "That cop wasn't very nice, but we found the church didn't we, Dennis?"

"Yes. Ring that bell above your head."

A narrow slit in the door revealed a hooded frame with two eyes staring between the opening. "May I help you?"

90

"We want to see Bishop King."

"Is he expecting you?"

Not wanting to waste time, McDill raised the bishop's telegram aloft. "This will explain it. It's on this paper."

The monk cracked the door wider and looked at the message.

"Yes, Bishop King is in the parlor to your right." He bowed.

Dennis straightened with surprise. He expected to see an old man looking like St. Nicholas. The bishop was very slender. His gray-streaked hair displayed a man of middle age. A long-fingered hand stretched out to shake hands with his two guests. "Welcome to our humble place."

Dennis could not believe it. The church was almost as large as a cathedral, but very plain inside except for some exceptionally beautiful windows. Stained glassed saints lived in every one. He stood still in reverential awe for several seconds.

"You received my answer," King acknowledged.

Dennis searched for the voice. "Yes, we did and we are most grateful you can see us."

"Gentlemen, our chairs are hard, but please sit and join me over here." Bishop King pointed to some plain ladder-backed chairs in front of a dark brown desk.

The cleric pulled back his robes and sat behind his desk in front of Dennis and Comer. "Gentlemen, what is your mission?"

"As we mentioned in our message, we want to build a church at City Point." Dennis sat so erect his spine did not touch the back of his chair. He leaned a little toward the Bishop. "Yes, Sir. We have about twenty-five Roman Catholics at City Point, and we'd like to have a chapel there. It's a day's round trip journey to the nearest church of our faith if we attend a full service."

"Who would build such a structure?" The bishop often speculated with a question.

"Sir, my men and I could, with the help of some citizens."

King's eyebrows arched slightly. "Most commendable, but most unusual. Are you certain you could build a small church?"

"Yes, our crew members are shipwrights. If we can build ships, we can build a church."

Bishop King did not answer until he cleared his throat twice. "Commander, you look like an honest and able man. I know you need money. How much?"

"We met with Miss Josephine Ellis of the Ellis Plantation. She's willing to sell a small lot for $150. We are not allowed to use federal money to build a chapel, Sir."

King pondered thoughtfully. "If I buy the lot, where can you get the materials to build it?"

"Sir, we already have the lumber, or almost all the lumber. It was secured to help us repair seven old ships at the dock in City Point. Those ships are too dilapidated to repair, and our superiors know it."

"Commander, you won't have any trouble with your superiors, will you?"

"I pray not, Sir. But the land will be yours to sell, if we don't succeed. We won't fail, Sir."

"If you are that dedicated and determined, I will take the chance."

"Thank you, Sir, we'd be most grateful." Dennis affirmed.

"Please give me a moment. I believe there should be just enough money from the last collection."

A little door near the corner of the room opened with a squeak that seemed to recognize its master. The prelate disappeared and returned quickly. "There is $150 in assorted bills. You can carry them more easily in this envelope. I will come down in a few months to check your progress. Go with my blessing." Comer kissed the bishop's ring. "Bless you my son, but that gesture is for the Pope. Go in peace."

Dennis tucked the money inside his uniform jacket. He and Comer bowed and left.

Streets were just as busy as when they entered the church. Traffic policemen worked hard to untie the blockage. "How far to the train station, Comer?"

"The way we came, it was about half an hour."

"If we have no trouble, we should catch the next train south."

Comer pulled his watch chain to check his time. "We'll have to hurry."

Both men sprang into a trot. Comer almost knocked an old man into a moving wagon. He apologized and continued. Half way down the second street they heard the clomping of speeding feet. Feet not loud enough for horses. Feet of men behind them running. "We're being followed. Faster!" Dennis shouted.

Dennis McDill always kept in good physical shape, but Comer didn't. Dennis had to slow down for Comer. Dennis looked back. Three figures were gaining. Dennis tugged at Comer's shirt dragging him as fast as he could. Too late. Hands clutched their clothes. One assailant had a long stick and rammed it into Comer's stomach. Three thieves were pulling at Dennis' coat.

"They're looking for the money!" Comer shouted, recovering from the blow to his stomach. Instinctively, McDill swung his elbow hard into a set of ribs. One mugger's body was banged severely. Dust flew everywhere when he landed in the sidewalk dirt. Dennis threw his left fist to catch an extended chin. Comer wrestled another attacker to the ground. Finding all three villains grounded, Dennis grabbed Comer's shirt again. "Let's run!"

They made it a second before the Iron Horse pulled away from the station. Dennis and Comer mounted the steps of the passenger car as it started to move. "Phew! That was close. I could see our little chapel vanishing. Let's relax. We're safe now." Dennis smiled at his brave companion, gulping for breath.

The rhythm of the train, as it bounced down the track, rocked them into a drowsy state. Comer leaned forward. "By the way, if we don't have enough lumber, what'll we do?"

"Go to sleep. We'll find a way."

Later, Helen and four wives waited at the platform. "Did you see the Bishop? Miss Ellis told us she would sell her lot for $150. Did you get the money?"

"Hold on ladies! One thing at a time. We got the money. Miss Ellis set the price. When she gets the money, I'm sure she will deed the land to Bishop King in the name of the church. And, Helen, I think the chapel can be completed soon."

"Congratulations, fellows! Success! Come have dessert on us." Helen and the wives were thrilled.

"Before you honor us with sweets, we are on our way to pay Miss Ellis." The men left in a hurry.

After Dennis gave the money to Josephine Ellis, she had the deed made ready and handed it to McDill to take to the bishop.

Miss Ellis threw a great party. Most of the town congregated in the Big House. It was the biggest party since the war ended. Several toasts were offered to Miss Josephine Ellis and honor was bestowed upon all her ancestors.

Dennis was compelled to interrupt. "Crew, listen! When the party's over, get a good night's sleep. Report to me at the pier. We'll go to Miss Ellis' lot...er...former lot. She'll show us the exact dimensions from her plat. See you in the morning. Good-night, men."

Miss Ellis met the crew at the lot near Dr. Ellis' house. She unfolded the drawing which delineated all the lines precisely. Before this, she had Roberts place tiny poles at each corner of the lot.

"Miss Ellis, you were kind to think of everything." Rogers congratulated her several times.

O'Connell took a look at her and nudged O'Leary. "You think the Chief has a crush on her?"

"Who knows? Maybe." O'Leary smiled.

For a day, men moved tools and lumber on the lot. They carefully measured each piece of lumber. Chief Rogers brought a sketch of a ship's schematic. "What are you doing, Chief?" Lieutenant DuBois turned his head sideways to look at it.

"It's the plan of a boat."

"Are you going insane, Rogers?"

"No. Just look at this picture upside down. Tell me what you see."

"I see an upside down scheme of an iron-clad like the ones we tried to fix. I still don't see it, Chief."

"Sir, please let me call the Skipper down here to see it. I'll spread it on the ground so we can all get a good look."

O'Connell alerted his C.O. Holding back his curiosity, McDill walked over as requested.

"What is all this, Chief?" McDill accidentally stepped on the edge of the drawing.

"Look hard. Tell me what you see, Commander."

"Did you drag me over to see the plans of some old ship? I've seen enough of them already."

"Look, Sir. The keel is a broad 'V' and the deck is flat."

"So?" Dennis began to suspect the Chief was drinking too much.

"Sir, the chapel could be an upside down iron clad about the length of the Leland."

McDill walked around the plat three times. Three times he rubbed his chin. He slowly paced over to Rogers. "Chief, I believe you're right. Our chapel could be an upturned ship." He looked away and called out, "O'Connell, get Sullivan and MacEaton to cut to scale the entire portions of this drawing. That will be our floor. Of course, at the same time, get O'Leary to design and build four cornerstones to hold up the floor. He's a good mason. Maybe Smithy can let him use his shop."

"Commander, just one thing. We don't have enough lumber." DuBois hated to tell his boss, but he had taken several more measurements. "Commander, we have less than two-thirds of what we need. To have adequate sloping for the 'A' roof, it will take more lumber."

"We don't have enough money to buy it from Cousin Elmer." McDill calculated again.

"Commander, let Rogers and me go down each street and ask for money to help. Would you approve?" O'Leary asked.

"Some people may throw rocks at you. We've begged enough." He stopped to rub his neck. "Are you willing?"

"Yes, Sir. The Chief and I have already agreed to do it if we had to."

"All right, go. Let me have what you collect, then we'll see. In the meantime I want all of you to clear off enough trees and shrubs to give room for the building and a walk from the road to the church."

Digging up shrubs and cutting down unwanted trees was drudgery for any set of sailors. Bodies were scratched to bleeding, backs ached with every muscle movement, and sweat rolled down into every mariner's eyes. Women helped by bringing fresh cool water to drink and gauze to bind wounds. "This job is almost as rough as the war," the old salt injected and rubbed his back. "I'm not built for this kind of job," Rogers moaned. "I'm as tired as those old ships down there."

"Cheer up, we'll have this job finished in two weeks," Dennis urged.

In two weeks the job could be finished, but the lieutenant and the chief could collect only half the money they needed to buy enough lumber.

"Boy, another problem," O'Connell muttered. "Well, men, at least we have enough to lay the foundation and two walls. Sullivan, MacEaton do you have enough clay for foundation bricks?"

"Aye. We have." Sullivan pointed to a large pile of clay lying near the road's edge.

"Get Smithy to fire up his furnace and bake enough for our cornerstones," Dennis ordered.

"We'll load the wagon and be on our way, Sir."

When the wagon rolled into Smithy's shoe parlor, he was ready to bake clay. "*I've never baked bricks, but it'll be fun to learn.*" He grinned to himself and humped his shoulders while laughing at two gobs covered with red clay.

Meanwhile, at the lot, four men skinned a poplar log. They rolled the heavy log a hundred times to level the foundation as much as possible. They began their second hundred when they heard a chilling scream. It was MacEaton's voice, echoing blocks away. Fire coals had popped out on his

95

legs. His clothes blazed, blistering his skin in three places. Horrified, he ran in circles. From nowhere McDill yelled, "HALT!" Being a sailor, MacEaton obeyed. McDill threw him on the ground, and rolled the screaming sailor over several times in a clump of green grass. Finally the fire went out.

"MacEaton's hurt real bad, Sir." Sullivan lifted the burned victim.

"O'Leary, O'Connell, grab a horse blanket and wrap this man. Take him to Dr. Ellis. On the double! You don't have a minute to lose."

DuBois glanced over at McDill. "Look, Sir. Your hands."

"What?"

"They're burned!"

"Oh Holy Mother of God! Wrap 'em immediately! I'll see the doctor, too, but MacEaton goes first. His burns are worse than mine."

On the examination table McEaton wrenched in pain.

"Nurse, move the light so I can see better." Mrs. Ellis carefully cut off MacEaton's clothes to expose his wounds. "These are almost as bad as our worst battle. Get me some ointment and some gauze."

MacEaton twisted and yelled until he passed out. "Poor boy, he won't feel the pain when he's unconscious. Let's do our work while he's out." Dr. Ellis directed every move.

Gaping wounds covered both legs. When Ellis finished with MacEaton, he examined McDill. "You saved this man's life. The fire could have spread to his organs. Then he'd be gone. You won't be able to use your hands for several days. I want to change the bandages every day for the first week."

"I won't be able to work, Doc? Helen will have to feed and dress me?"

"You won't be helpless. You can still give orders. You're good at that. I'll keep MacEaton here a while and check him everyday. You can't count on him to work for some time."

"Can you estimate the time?"

"With good luck, two months."

Under handicaps, the work continued. Every day, Dennis came to the site to supervise. They did finish the foundation even without the muscles of MacEaton or the commander's brawn.

"Do you like it?" DuBois frequently asked townspeople passing by to inspect unofficially. Usually he got an affirmative nod. Sometimes a jealous skeptic would shake his head and give suggestions that he knew DuBois would reject. A few citizens didn't like northern intruders. Building a church in their midst was an intrusion. Vice Mayor Brewer strenuously objected. He resented their presence, the sale of the land by Josephine Ellis, and the Catholic religion as a whole. Brewer was disappointed when the town council announced their support for the church.

Brewer stumped, "We've got enough churches in town. We don't want another one." Brewer held several outdoor meetings to rail against the construction. Many people believed his statements cloaked Brewer's profound prejudice. However, Brewer was powerful and had gained avid supporters. Secretly he would think to himself. *"I've got to find a way to stop 'em."*

Another week passed. The crew had collected and used all the lumber they had. Rogers and DuBois collected a small amount of money to buy more lumber, but not enough. They knew Headquarters would not allocate any more money. Construction slowed to a stop which made Brewer happy. At last MacEaton was able to work some and McDill's hands healed. But their misfortune clung like wall plaster. "We're defeated," O'Leary cried. "We can't do any more."

"We can pray," DuBois suggested. "Tomorrow's Sunday. Let's gather at the foundation of our church and pray that help will come to us. After all, it is God's work."

Sunday supplied a heavy rain. In spite of the weather; every crew member, every Navy family, and all of their friends congregated in a rectangle around the entire foundation. Their favorite hymn was sung twice—"The Church Is One Foundation." Commander McDill had never delivered a sermon, but he talked and prayed for almost an hour. They went home drenched, but serene.

With several weeks without progress, morale sunk to its lowest, and some braved the trip to Petersburg to worship.

At home Helen and Dennis prayed, but Helen frequently asked, "Dennis, what are we going to do?"

"Prayer is the only hope we have. I...."

"WHOA! Ye mangy animal "

Dennis rushed to the sound of the bad-tempered command. "Well, I'll be a...It's Cousin Elmer! What are you doing here?"

"I hear ye need more lumber, or ye won't finish the job. I'm not a religious man ye know, but I can help a fella who's down 'n out."

"Praises, you are the most welcome sight we've seen in a long time."

Elmer had enough body odor to offend the nostrils of a goat and stubby hair all over his face and neck, but Dennis didn't mind. He hugged the little dwarf anyway. "Come in. I want you to meet my wife." Helen was a little startled. McDill had tried to describe Elmer to her earlier, but this was astonishing. She noticed a wagon full of prime logs and forgot how Elmer smelled. She shook his hand vigorously.

"Very pleased to meet you." Unnoticed, Helen wiped both her hands on her apron.

Dennis climbed on the wagon and inspected every log. "These are the finest I've seen. They'll make perfect lumber."

"May the good Lord bless you, Elmer," Helen invoked God for the little nonbeliever.

"Ye appreciate me logs. That's enough for me and my old mule here. By the by, ye got any hay for my old nag?"

"Yes, and I will prepare the best meal I can for you and your old mule. That's the least I can do." Helen walked into the kitchen to check her firewood. Helen was a good cook and a quick learner. She spent much time obtaining ideas from other townsfolk women.

"Elmer, you came when we were about to give up." Dennis couldn't stop shaking the little man's hand.

"I heard ye had trouble personified. So's it's the least I can do."

In addition to feeding Elmer, the McDills invited the entire crew, Comer, and half the town to a feast. The meal was so big Helen had to summon several neighbor ladies to help her. Helen was a great organizer, and could have made a good Naval officer.

Elmer, even sloppy and odorous, was accepted. Everybody poured thanks on the little elf-like person for his timely rescue. In honor of Elmer, festive singing launched their appreciation. He was toasted until midnight—of course with his favorite rum.

Around 1:00 a.m. the guests left. Elmer was bunked in the bedroom farthest from Helen and Dennis. Only the sound of an owl cracked the black silence. The night sky was clear, but the moon had disappeared over the horizon. The men slept soundly. Their sense of smell and hearing was asleep. Suddenly, something jerked Helen awake. She sniffed. She shook her husband and snatched off his cover. "I smell smoke!" she hollered loud enough for the next door neighbors to hear.

"It's after midnight. What'd you want?"

"Smoke."

"Smoke. Where?" He sat up straight and threw off the rest of his cover.

"Outside near our window!" She jerked the window open.

McDill hopped across the room frantically pulling on his pants. He elevated his nose for directions, and hobbled over to the window. "Holy Creator! The logs are on fire! Ring the bell, Helen."

Blazes flew fifteen feet high. Burning hulks of wood exploded like fireworks. The alarm bell brought a fire brigade of fourteen men with buckets. One dipped into the well and passed full buckets down the line to the fiery wagon. Elmer's knees buckled as he shouted until his lungs burst. "Me wagon, me wagon! What'll I do without me wagon?"

The bucket line was too late. The entire shipment of logs and Elmer's wagon shrunk to a pile of ashes. "Who would do something like this?" Helen moaned.

"This fire didn't ignite on its own, Helen." Dennis peered into the darkness. "There's an arsonist out there. Smell the kerosene?"

"Yes, but who would want to do a thing like this?" Helen wailed.

"Someone who doesn't want us to build the chapel. They must object very much."

Neighbors consoled Elmer when they saw him burst into tears. Fortunately his mule was in back tied to a pole. "Look, Elmer, your animal's safe," Comer joined the consolation. "We'll all chip in and get you another wagon. You've helped us so much already."

"I can get more logs, but those bad 'uns will burn 'em again."

O'Malley's huge hand patted Elmer on his shoulder. "Don't worry little guy, we'll get 'em and we'll guard you. If we did, would you be afraid to bring us another load?"

"Not with ye at my side." Elmer hugged the huge man's waist.

"You can count on me, too, little man." Sullivan placed his hand on Elmer's shoulder.

McDill ordered without hesitation. "O'Malley, Sullivan, you two guard Elmer night and day. Also, help him with the logs. I want him protected at all times, the logs cut, and the logs delivered even if someone has to stand watch and work all day and night."

"Aye, Sir. You can count on us. We'll take care of everything."

"Comer, will you report all of this to the sheriff? I want him ready to arrest those hoodlums," Dennis requested.

"On my way. I'll tell him everything."

"Oh! Check with Lizzy and ask her if the U.S. Marshal made contact and ask if there's anything we can do."

"I will, Sir."

"Lieutenant, you and Rogers have a special assignment. I want you collect all the donations from our neighbors you can and get a new wagon for Elmer. We'll chip in. I'm sure everybody knows what happened by now. Besides, a merchant might give him a reduced price. If you have any extra money, give it to Elmer."

"Commander can I go with 'em?" Elmer brushed black more ashes from his coat. His tired eyes waited for an answer.

"Sure, if you have the energy. I'll be satisfied if you would bring us more logs. That will be most appreciated."

With the little man at his side, DuBois politely knocked on each door and explained what happened. Miss Josephine donated half enough money for a good wagon.

On their way for donations, they saw a dim light flicking in Vice Mayor Brewer's dining room window. He was eating a gigantic ham hock with both hands. Brewer's chubby fingers curled around muscle and bone while his bloated belly scraped against the table Tufts of hair sprang from both ears. Greasy hands sported six rings that reflected light from several precious stones. DuBois' knock stirred him from his concentration of sucking fat from bone. He grunted and squeezed his blubber out of the chair. Instantly he recognized them. "Yeah, I heard what happened. Here's some money." This surprised them. They thanked him and left, really wondering why.

After the collection was finished, the men found they had collected enough money for a wagon and two loads of logs from Elmer's farm.

Inside, Brewer could see his wife standing in the doorway between the dining room and the kitchen. Her thin lips widened into two straight lines. They trembled with anger. "What on this earth did you do? Give money to those Catholics who want to build their church in our town?"

"Hey, wait a minute. If I refused, they might get suspicious. Everyone knows how I feel about another church in our neighborhood. People ain't stupid. They'll put two and two together and point the finger at me."

"So what? You're only guilty of setting a little fire. Nobody got hurt, did they? Lots of folks will side with you."

"You are my wife and I say to you, I didn't leave any evidence."

"I certainly hope not." She crossed her arms and stood as though she were daring him to move her.

"They may think some bum came to town to have a little fun," he rationalized.

"Brewer, you know nobody'll believe that."

"My friends will thank me for it," he boasted.

"Wouldn't it be better if you didn't tell anybody, even your closest friends?" Mrs. Brewer often hesitated to offer her husband advice.

"Right, but I can't help being proud that I pulled it off while their eyes were closed."

"They'll get the sheriff, I bet. Elkinson's a brainy one, you know."

"What if the sheriff suspects it's me? Nobody saw me and there's no one to rat on me."

Her eyelids left a slit for her green eyes. "I know you took the kerosene up to their house."

"You wouldn't?"

"If nobody asks me anything."

"Woman. Look at me. Are you going to be a backsliding traitor?" he threatened, and glowered.

"I won't be if you promise me you won't break the law to keep 'em from building that church."

"You know I can't promise that."

"Then I'll tell 'em what you did, if they corner me."

"Oh, no you won't!" Brewer rose up like an elephant seal and roared. "Confound you, woman, you won't tell anybody anything!"

"Just wait and see."

Brewer's blood boiled like a kettle over a blue flame. His rage came in torrents. His hands searched for anything in sight. They gripped his heaviest chair and brought the weapon high over his head. Before she could duck the chair, it collided with her head. She looked at him with eyes flaring in disbelief. Her body collapsed. A small stream of blood dripped from her head wound. Mrs. Brewer lay soundless on the floor while the room lapsed into an eerie hush. Vice Mayor Brewer stood staring at an immobile figure lying helpless in a spread out position. He had to decide. He rolled the body in a blanket. With a spurt of his greatest power, he pulled it out of the house and heaved it into his wagon. Quickly he hitched his horse and drove down to the river. The dinghy waited to be included in the drama. Brewer rolled the body in the small craft and paddled out to mid-river. His wife's body made a belly flop into the river channel. "She can't talk now," he grinned.

Dark clouds obscured most of the dawn when the sheriff's body cart bounced to a halt in front of the telegraph office. "Comer, you know anybody wanting to keep the chapel from being built?"

"A handful, maybe five or ten who don't like northern Catholics."

"Names, Comer. I'm interested in hardened criminals now."

With O'Malley's help, they gave Sheriff Elkinson five names who might have the nerve to do such a thing. They told him that one citizen had once been accused of arson.

That same morning Elmer rode his mule to Richmond and bought a new, stronger wagon…but not too heavy for his trusted animal. When he hooked up his cart, the mule's pride flushed with the idea of having a new wagon to pull. What a sight—a lowly equine prancing down the road for miles. The animal moved so fast it took only two hours to reach the farm, a record for a mule-drawn vehicle.

Before Elmer reached home, he could hear saws whirring and axes chopping in rhythm. Sound waves rippled from its epicenter to the edge of the woods. Seven oak trees fell, destined to become planks for the walls and seven pines were cut to be slats for the floor. All trees were trimmed and cut to fit the wagon for transportation. Oaks were converted into sturdy planks, four-by-fours and boards. The iron smith forged buckets of square heads to hammer into each piece of wood. A perfect square of bricks was shaped to fit the cornerstones and base. Upright boards, side to side, created firm walls to support the angular "A" framed roof. During his younger years, Smithy had learned to be a tinsmith. With the "A" frame finished, smooth sheets of coated tin hooded the entire roof. It was time to order church furniture.

Sunday afternoon, Comer paddled down river to catch fish. Shallow edges and tree branches provided sanctuaries for catfish and other river denizens. Even the main current slowed to a lazy crawl. Warm sunlight and placid water forced Comer to yawn and stretch. He almost fell asleep. When he lowered his head from a sky reaching stretch, a white buoy appeared. "*No buoys out here.*" His partly closed eyes shielded the glaring sun. Seized with curiosity and a wish to stay awake, Comer slowly rowed toward the buoy. It undulated slightly, pushed by tiny ripples. *"My God! It's a woman!"*

A body, mistaken for a buoy, morphed into a corpse floating face down with stiff arms extended. Gingerly his paddle turned the body over in the sun-drenched water. *"It's Mrs. Brewer! Floating dead for days!"* he screamed silently and stiffened as rigid as the body beside his boat. For an instant he was mortified. Finally, his senses recovered. *"Gotta get her to shore."* He searched the boat and spotted a rope about twenty feet long. He looped it over the cadaver until it reached the nearest wrist. He tugged the line and wrapped the one end around the stern of the boat. For more than an hour, Comer rowed until his palms looked like crimson burlap.

Two figures stood on the dock. They saw Comer was out of breath, almost exhausted. Mrs. Brewer weighed slightly under two hundred pounds, and sometimes the river currents opposed Comer's destination. "Help me, will you, men?"

Rogers tossed a rope. "You must've caught a whale," he yelled.

"No. It's a CORPSE!"

"A corpse? By St. Sebastian." DuBois genuflected three times.

"Who is it?" Rogers bellowed. He bent to help Comer pull the boat around and pull the body up to the deck.

"Mrs. Brewer."

"The Vice Mayor's wife?" DuBois asked.

"Yeah. It's her. I found her body about a mile down river. It was caught in the bushes."

Rogers sprinted to summon the doctor. He spied Ellis swaying peacefully in his rocker, enjoying a quiet Sunday afternoon's rest. The doctor's eyes sprang open at the sudden sound of Rogers' footsteps.

"Doc, come down to the pier. Quick. There's something you've gotta see."

"It's Sunday afternoon. Can it keep?" Ellis yawned and looked helplessly at Rogers.

"Afraid not. Comer found a dead body in the river."

"Wait, I'm coming." He hopped out so fast, the rocker keep its steady motion.

Ellis and Comer raced against others to view the gruesome specimen lying prone on the boat landing.

Dr. Ellis learned forensics the hard way—experience. "Cracked skulls seem to be my specialty these days," he remarked and examined the rest of the deceased's body. "Indentures indicate some blunt weapon crushed her head, maybe a large club or board. That's definitely the cause of death."

"Somebody killed her?" Several people mumbled while they bent down to look at the remains.

"Another murder. Get the sheriff," someone from the gathering audience cried.

"He's interrogating the arson case," O'Malley pointed toward the eastern part of town. "I'll get him. I know he'll want to check on this one first."

"Anyone gone to tell Mr. Brewer?"

"Doc, I just got back from the Brewers'. Nobody's home." O'Connell puffed hard and squatted to catch his breath. "His horse and buggy are gone, too."

Knowing he could do nothing for the deceased Mrs. Brewer, McDill decided to search the Brewer house himself. O'Connell was ordered to come to witness. "We'll scan everything, but leave every part exactly in place." McDill dictated. "Sheriff Elkinson can do his job better."

O'Connell and McDill found the back door ajar, swinging slowly, propelled by a mild western breeze. "You left the back door open?" McDill asked.

"No Sir. It was that way when I saw it a few minutes ago."

Both men searched all rooms in the home thoroughly. Suddenly O'Connell stopped. A shape in the corner of the dining room floor lay on its side. It had landed in the darkest space in the room. "I think I found the weapon."

"Where are you?" Dennis circled around the room he was inspecting.

"I'm in the dining room, Sir." His grim expression emphasized the horror of something that was not accidental.

McDill quit searching. "Where?"

O'Connell's finger trembled. "There in the corner. It's so dark, I almost missed it."

"Did you touch it?"

"I wouldn't want to." O'Connell cringed.

"The blood's dry. I'll bet it's been on that chair for at least a day or more." McDill speculated. "O'Connell, we'll leave everything in place. While I wait for Elkinson, you go and tell the mayor what happened, or what we think happened."

"Sir, remember? He's gone to visit his mother in England."

"Yes. He won't return for another two weeks. We'll leave this in the hands of Elkinson anyway and give him a hundred percent of our help. I have my own suspicions, but the law must handle…."

Elkinson's boots pounded the floor. "You men touch anything?" Sheriff Elkinson questioned as soon as he opened the front door. "If you did, you may have screwed up the evidence."

"Sheriff, we touched nothing, just searched. Look over there, in the corner." Dennis pointed.

Elkinson gyrated in a blur. Quickly he left, snatched his lantern from his buggy and promptly lit it with his cigar. After a time, lantern light swept the lower edge of the chair. "It's blood, all right. The perpetrator must have used this chair as a weapon. From what the doctor said about the deceased's wound and what I saw, it sure looks like this big piece of furniture did it." Elkinson walked over to McDill. "Where's Brewer?"

"O'Connell got here first. He found no one. He also found the horse and buggy are gone."

"Men, we'll shut up the house. You guard the entire premises while I go back and get some help," the sheriff decreed, serious and stone-faced.

McDill ordered his crew to stand watch until Elkinson rounded up several citizens to form a posse. One man brought two bloodhounds to sniff the house and the stable for the scent of a human or a horse. Bloodhounds ran three circles around inside the stable and finally caught a scent. They vaulted and nearly dislocated their master's arm that held their leashes. Braying bloodhounds could be heard upstream and downstream. Two canines strained to the choking point. They barked, tugged and pulled the posse along with them. Dogs yelped and darted up the west road. At the next intersecting trail, men and dogs turned north. Trees bowed low to discourage trackers to plod down their dark lane covered with thick weeds and thickets. Through the darkness, a thin streak of light directed them to a clearing just ahead.

"Halt! Muzzle your dogs." Elkinson pulled out his six-chambered pistol. Quick, cautious steps got him closer to a shack in the middle of the clearing. The two dogs settled down and rested quietly. The posse whispered while the sheriff searched. In spite of tacit motions for him to stay back, McDill crept behind the lawman. "Get back," the sheriff whispered. "I can handle this."

"You might need some help," McDill whispered barely audible.

"All right. You go left. I'll go right." Elkinson motioned with his gun. "Be careful. Don't forget you're unarmed. A dead hero is no help."

McDill remembered a familiar military strategy—the pincer movement. Converging, McDill dropped to his knees and crawled to the nearest door. His hand touched something cold. His eyes rested on a tarnished metal doorknob that clicked with a hard turn. Inside, an obese figure reared up at the sound of the click. Dark shadows obscured his vision. The vice mayor remembered he had placed his shotgun in the corner of the room. Brewer shoved the table aside and stumbled toward his shotgun. In one quick motion, the fat man grabbed his weapon, pointed its muzzles toward the door, and pulled the trigger. Wood and glass scattered over the floor and outside the door. One pellet creased McDill's skull, leaving him dazed in pain. Brewer moved toward McDill's disabled body. He found Dennis alive and pointed his gun at his target's chest.

"Hold it!" Elkinson shouted. Brewer turned around and pulled his trigger again. The sheriff was thrown back five feet by the pellets' impact. Blood splashed great blotches on the door and side of the house. Elkinson relaxed, motionless.

Brewer twisted his huge frame around and charged inside to scramble for more shells. Pictures were strewn sideways and fell crashing onto the floor. His shaking fingers clutched the shell box. Two shells. That was enough to finish off an officer from the north, and a sheriff for certain, he grinned. Two shells popped into their chambers. Brewer slowly crept toward Elkinson. He said, barely audible, through his teeth, "I never liked this guy. This one always got in my way. I'll blow his face off for sure." Brewer aimed his muzzles at the constable's forehead, and slowly squeezed the trigger.

Dennis, conscious but groggy, could hardly see Brewer standing four feet away holding his shotgun directly at Sheriff Elkinson's head. With all his strength the seaman griped the assailant's leg. A shot rang out through the wooded thickets. Unmuzzled, the dogs barked and ran toward the noise. Another shot was fired. Both Brewer and Elkinson lay stretched out and bleeding.

Dennis could barely hear the posse arrive. O'Connell helped his C.O. get to a tree for support. "You all right, Commander?"

Dennis felt his head. His hair was matted with half-dried red fluid. "Yeah, I nearly got scalped. How are Elkinson and Brewer?"

"I think Brewer's dead, Sir."

"And the sheriff?"

"My Lord! Skipper, the sheriff looks dead, too!"

Dennis stood on wobbly legs and hobbled toward the lawman's body. He bent down and listened for a heartbeat, then felt for a pulse. He looked up at O'Connell and several who stood beside him. "I feel a very weak pulse. He's barely alive. O'Connell, get the posse and take this man to the doctor, pronto.

Every second counts. Find somebody's horse and get going in a hurry. On the double, sailor."

⚓

Cousin Elmer not only gave lumber for the chapel, he helped with the painting. Giles secretly shipped down some whitewash and brushes. Astonished citizens often complimented Elmer's skill and he nodded politely to his admirers, "Ye know, me painting was learned when I was sixteen." Elmer gave two strokes for each admirer and continued. In three days the little chapel glistened, even on cloudy days. Some neighbors plowed around the church and sowed grass. One brick mason donated bricks and labor for a solid walk in front. Smithy learned to make sturdy pews. Commander McDill designed and supervised the building of the entire church and ordered Sullivan to take charge of roofing. Sullivan's body could carry a heavy beam and scurry up the incline as fast as a squirrel. O'Malley's hammer could hit square heads until sparks flew everywhere. MacEaton and O'Leary could skin bark and plane boards as fast as they could be nailed in place. Lieutenant DuBois not only was a shipwright, he had studied and practiced horticulture. He planted beds of flowers. Chief Rogers helped DuBois design the entire landscape to fit and enhance the church property.

For a while, McDill forgot he was still out on bail. So did nearly one else in City Point. Helen was the happiest because the little church grew from an idea to a worship center. For once, she contributed the best of her skill creating wall designs.

As promised, Bishop King sailed down to inspect the newest Diocesan investment. His praises were frequent and sincere. One day, he and McDill looked at the plans and noted that the vision was taking shape. McDill deliberately held the plat upside down. "What do you see, Bishop?"

"Why, I see a ship."

"Look closely, Sir."

"It is an upside down ship. The chapel?"

"Yes, the chapel."

⚓

October brought its full pallet of vivid colors. Yellows of the poplars, and hickory trees, reds of dogwoods and red oaks, oranges of several small plants and the shiny greens of the holly trees and magnolias. After a long recovery Sheriff Elkinson regained his health and returned to duty.

Also, October brought out scores of hunters, including DuBois. He had earned the U.S. Navy Marksman Medal two months after he joined the service.

On the first day of hunting season, Phillipe found his boots behind the closet door and water-proofed each with oil, fully knowing they would attract mud like magnets. He fetched a carton of bullets precisely made for a bolt-action Springfield. DuBois relished the challenge of the hunt more than any sailor in Virginia. His feet were ready to carry man and his rifle into the forest.

DuBois bounced down to the harbor where a small dugout lay on its side in the rocks and sand. He turned the small craft over on its slender keel, took hold of the oar, and pushed off. With care, he had placed the gun inside the hull while his pockets jingled with ammunition. Man and paddle pushed the boat upstream for about a mile. He discovered a clump of bushes held firmly by a maze of planted roots. After floating through some underbrush, he secured the craft's line firmly to a sycamore branch. Water sloshed around his boots while he waded into the dense woods.

Fresh smells elicited a feeling of energy, causing the hunter to walk faster until he reached a path almost completely obscured by prickly holly bushes. The perfume of the rosin almost intoxicated him. Dry leaves barked quietly back at his feet as he stepped closer to the watering hole where deer and other game often lapped heartily to satisfy their thirst. The patient marksman squatted and waited to hear a twig crack or the gobble of a male turkey looking for a mate. Except for a distant mocking bird, the trees and plants were silent. Not breeze blew to warn the animals that a killer was waiting upwind to take aim at them while they cautiously crept toward the watering hole.

DuBois crouched near a willow when a twig broke and send tiny ripples of noise that made him stand up slowly and lean against the disguising tree. Another twig broke. He pointed the Springfield directly at the sound. Something came closer and closer. It approached head-on directly in front of him. *"Oh, no, not a bear! He'll get me if I don't shoot."* Phillipe drew back the bolt, ready to fire immediately. Instead, Phillipe was looking at the sinister end of the twin muzzles of a double barreled weapon. "Who are you?" Both yelled simultaneously. Still aiming at each other, they moved slowly toward each other.

"Hey! You're a woman!" DuBois gasped. "Don't shoot. I'm harmless," he yelled.

She inched closer to her prey, still pointing the double barrels at DuBois' chest. "You are trespassing on our hunting ground."

"Your hunting ground? I thought one of our farmers from the village owns this land."

"Maybe, but we own the hunt. You don't hunt here. We hunt here."

"Little lady, I have as much right here as you do."

"White man, this shotgun says were have more rights."

DuBois had never killed a woman before. He lowered his rifle and looked at the angry person in front of him. Her jet black hair was pag-tailed with shiny eyes flashing when she focused hard on his. Her irises were as dark as a baby sea lion's skin. The young woman's tannish red face had to look up to see the face of Phillipe DuBois. "You leave or I'll shoot."

"Woman, I said I mean you no harm."

"I'm not worried about that. I can defend myself, but this land cannot defend itself. You go away or you'll be fertilizer for the trees or food for the buzzards."

As he backed away, he got a good look at the determined young native at the other end of a 12-gaged shotgun. He was absolutely astonished by her beauty. Her skin was smooth as a baby and she had perfect teeth which were clenched to show her wrath. The young woman's dark eyes supported long curved eyelashes and her black pigtails brushed her waist. For a few seconds, Phillipe could not speak, only gaze at the pretty young person in front of him.

She broke his spell when she shook the gun barrels in front of his nose. "Go, I say! Go before I feed you to the hawks."

Phillipe slowly backed away holding his rifle beside his leg, seeing that she meant business. Very cautiously he turned and quickly slunk back to his canoe.

On the way home he dreamed about the most beautiful woman he had ever seen. He easily overruled her determined hostility and concentrated on the wonderful things they could do together. But, how could he ever court a person who considered him to be interloping on her hunting grounds? He decided to go ashore and ask those who know about women, what to do.

McDill was on the dock catching fish. Rogers was approaching from a nearby boat.

"Ahoy, Lieutenant. Come join us." McDill held up his catch. "Where have you been so long?"

"Well, Sir, I met a girl."

"Go on, Lieutenant," the skipper ordered.

"When I was hunting for deer in the forest upriver, a young woman jumped into my sight. I mistook the sound for a bear, but it was a woman—a beautiful young woman. She's the prettiest one I've ever seen, but I have a problem."

"A good looker like you, Lieutenant, should have no problem with young lassies," Rogers observed and took out his pipe.

"This one might have shot me."

Both Rogers and McDill yanked their necks in amazement and gawked at the junior officer. They were struck dumb for a moment. McDill cleared his throat first. "Did you say she might have shot you?"

"Yes, Sir. She could have killed me. In fact she aimed to kill me if I didn't get off her hunting ground."

"What happened?"

"Lowered my rifle, backed away, and left in a hurry." Dubois, brave as he was, had to yield to a woman.

"Do you really think she would kill you?" McDill asked.

"By the determined look in those flaming eyes of hers, I believe she would have shot me if I hadn't retreated."

"Let me guess, Phillipe, you fell in love with a dangerous woman." McDill placed his hand on DuBois' shoulder. Rogers gave a fatherly look.

"I want to see her again. You men know about marriage. What should I do?"

"Mrs. McDill and I did not have that kind of problem. We met at a graduation ball, fell in love, and married in a year. We are evenly matched. Both had strong wills."

"My Missy, bless her soul, met me at a picnic on the Jersey shore. We both like the same food. She was such a good cook, I asked her to marry me. What she saw in me, God only knows."

DuBois listened politely, but his attention was elsewhere. "But what can I do, gentlemen?"

"Lieutenant, exactly where did you meet this lovely lady?" McDill pressed.

"At a watering hole to hunt for game, not far from the rock jetty."

"What makes her think you were on her hunting grounds? I think an old farmer owns most of the land immediately upriver. You can identify it by an outcrop of large rocks."

"Yes, Sir. I passed them."

"The townsfolk call it the 'Point of Rocks.' There's a branch running on one side of the rocks." McDill identified it instantly.

"Yes, Sir. I saw the stream."

"Then, Lieutenant, we can prove that land is owned by a white man who has the title to prove it."

"Sir, I don't believe this woman cares about titles. She's a native."

"A redun'?" the Chief asked.

"She is a reddish-tan beauty from a tribe, I think."

Apprehension made McDill's face wrinkle. Dennis put down his rod and pushed over his tackle box. "Sit down, Lieutenant. Let me give you some advice. First, that woman is of another race. If you marry her, it may cause some serious problems. Second, she's hostile toward you for encroaching on her territory. And third, she might shoot you if you go down there again. What do you think, Chief?"

"Yes, Sir. I agree. I hate to see my good friend killed over some hunting property."

"I've got to see her again. I loved her when I saw her, even when she pointed her gun at my chest."

"Lieutenant, I will not order you on personal matters, but as a friend, I advise you to stay away from that woman, no matter who she is." McDill chopped the air to emphasize each word.

"Thanks for the advice, gentlemen." Lieutenant DuBois saluted and left.

After he left, Rogers and McDill lingered, comparing notes.

"You think he'll take our advice, Chief?" McDill's eyes followed DuBois until the lieutenant strutted out of sight.

"No, Sir. I don't. A guy in love will take chances, even the most dangerous chances. Remember a lover named Romeo?"

"That makes me worry, Chief. But when he's off duty he can do anything he wants—even get his head blown off, I guess."

"Yes, Sir. That could happen to our young man."

"Well, it's getting dark and we need to get some rest. I want to get back to the church construction. It will please me if we could finish it before I have to go back to Washington for the trial."

"Count me in, Commander. I'll see you in the morning."

A peaceful silence descended like a zephyr-driven cloud over the pier. McDill could see the sunset as he gathered his gear. The evening sun had used the sky for a painter's canvas. Swirls of red, gold, and blue moved, mixed into the sky bowl. Streaks of white sky rocketed through in the dark blue foresail of the heavens. They painted the sun to resemble a golden half moon at rest half under the earth and half over the edge of the earth. Dusk declared its conquest as the river ceased to reflect light back to the boat landing. It was one of the most beautiful displays of nature Dennis McDill had ever seen. He gazed, stood still and relaxed to enjoy the present God gave him that evening. His reverie over, he picked up his tackle and sauntered home to his wife.

Helen was knitting in their front room when Dennis arrived with his catch of the day. He flopped his bounty on the floor of the porch, and crowed, "We can have enough for two or three meals."

"All right, Dennis McDill. You clean them and I'll cook them. You know I hate cleaning fish."

"Yes, I'll do it just to get a taste of some fresh fish."

"Dennis, since the weather's improved, aren't you going to work some more on the church tomorrow? I hope you can get it done before the trial."

After dinner, Helen and Dennis talked a long time. Most of their conversation included the building of the church and the trial. They slept with their arms around each other until a sun ray slipped in between their bedroom curtains. With a full breakfast, Commander McDill walked briskly to the church site nestled among several hardwoods and cedars.

Elmer and O'Connell were retouching paint on the inside of the chapel. Windows were shipped in from New England at the request of Josephine Ellis of the Manor. She was so particular that she personally supervised the unloading of the crated packages from the transport ship to the chapel site. Painting window trims was not Elmer's best talent, so he asked for O'Connell's help. Often the little elf-man's hands would shake after a night of alcoholic bliss. McDill inspected the work and suggested that Elmer stain the floor instead. Actually, Elmer appreciated the change. "Ye want me to stain anything else?" Elmer dipped his brush deep in his pail of stain and sloshed it on the floor in large pools.

Dennis looked at the level floor and rubbed behind his neck. He considered Elmer's question and decided he was right. "No, Elmer just paint the deck...er...I mean the floor. Don't forget, spread the stain evenly. We want a pretty church that we can admire."

O'Malley and Sullivan secured flattened layers of tin that Smithy had pounded into thin sheets in his shop. Their job was tedious, climbing on an unsure ladder and lugging long sheets of metal up over the eaves of the roof. It became teamwork. The smaller and more agile Sullivan climbed to the top of the ladder while O'Malley lifted ray-reflecting sheets up to him. Once in place, the heavy pounding began. Hammers would bang square heads on the sides of each sheet. It was so deafening Elmer and O'Connell couldn't talk without shouting.

Miss Ellis donated eight ancient gas lamps, which her father brought from England, surplus from the construction of the Manor. She was happy to find a nice place for the beautiful unused pieces from her home. O'Leary and McEaton were entrusted to erect the lamps carefully at precise points near the windows. When finished, Miss Ellis filled each lamp bowl with oil, and tested each with a flame from a burning candle. To her satisfaction, all lamps worked perfectly.

Rogers and Smithy busied themselves with the pews. McDill figured the chapel needed eight pews, eight feet long, to be placed in the middle leaving narrow aisles just wide enough for two people on each side. He calculated the church should accommodate about twenty-five men, women and children who had room to sit, stand and kneel.

Phillipe and Dennis designed the altar and the podium where the priest could stand and kneel according to the rituals. A two-foot high altar was designed to provide just enough room for the priest to administer communion to ten parish worshipers at a time. Rogers and Sullivan stained the podium and altar exactly as planned.

By the time the chapel was almost finished, it was time for the trial to begin. Monroe was hurrying to find enough evidence to defend his client. He got permission to visit the ship terminal again and talk with other people who might know something about Mort and the missing drawing. One day he questioned an old shipwright who mentioned that he saw Captain Mort walk out of the office with a roll of paper under his arm. The shipwright was getting off work when he saw Mort meet another man at the main gate. "Can you describe the other man?" Albert questioned

"Yeah. He was about five foot nine, walked with a slight limp, had a ruddy face with a short black beard. I'd guess he was in his late forties."

"Did you see where they went?"

"I sure did. They went into the pub where I go after work. They sat in the corner while I finished three drinks."

"Do you know where they went after that?"

"No, I left before they did."

"Where's the pub?"

"Out the main gate, turn right, go two blocks. The pub is in the third building. It's down in a basement."

Monroe thanked the helpful ship builder and rushed outside. He increased his steps to the basement of an ancient brick antebellum building. Down the steps a darkened room opened. Strong beer fumes met the lawyer as he waited for his pupils to become adjusted to the dark. Four men sat on stools and leaned over a long bar making it invisible for Albert to see the other end. Small gas lamps struggled in vain to brighten the midget room that seemed to squeeze everything into its narrow tunnel. One big grizzly bartender wiped a glass, inspected it, and wiped it again. "What'll it be?" He sat the glass down and wiped his apron.

"A glass of your ale, if you have any." Monroe thought if he bought something, the barkeep would be more cooperative.

"Yeah, we have plenty. A tall one?"

"Pour it in the glass you just cleaned. That'll be enough."

"Here you are, Mac. That'll be a half dollar." The bartender held out his hand as usual.

Albert drew a five-dollar bill from his pocket and positioned his rear comfortably on the bar stool. "I need some information."

Money for information was not new to the bartender. In fact, he even accepted bribes if the price was right. "What kind of information?" he asked.

"I'm looking for a man."

The barman nodded meaninglessly, continuing to wipe another glass

Albert pushed the bill closer to the big mixologist and described a man exactly as the shipwright had described. The barkeep pushed a full glass of ale over to Albert. "That sounds like Hal Thompson."

"Do you know where I can find him?"

"In the graveyard." The bartender frowned and polished another glass.

"Oh no, not dead?" Monroe could not hide his surprised expression.

"Yeah, dead."

"When did he die?"

"About a month ago, I'd say."

"Bartender, you'll earn another five, if you can tell me where he lived and who lives there now, if you know."

The barkeep gazed at the other crisp five resting about a foot from his belly. He grabbed it and shoved it in his apron pocket. "No one has bought or rented his apartment to my knowledge. It's on the second floor of the white building across the street. Customers tell me it's unoccupied."

Albert took one large gulp and looked at his watch. "Not bad for domestic stuff. I've got to be going."

Late afternoon sun was almost touching the horizon. The barrister knew he had little time, so he crossed the street and knocked on the front door of the white building. No one answered. He knocked again. No answer. He knocked the third time so hard it hurt his knuckles. "I guess no one's in the entire building," he thought out loud.

Monroe scanned the side of the building. A narrow alley between the structures preceded a small open space in the rear. He looked in a door window and spied white paint peelings on the floor just before a flight of stairs. Being a lawyer, he knew the consequences of breaking and entering. He paused to think, but his conscience was subdued enough for him to take off one shoe to smash in the tiny window which perhaps guarded a secret on the upstairs level. Before breaking the window, Albert was careful to take off a sock and wrap it around the heel. Any noise might attract someone. Possibly the police could hear and he'd be arrested. He drew his arm back and aimed the heel of his shoe against the tiny glass. Success! The muffled sound could only be heard by him or someone very close inside or outside the building. The opening was wide enough for his whole arm to reach in and feel for a key. He prayed that someone had honored the tradition of hanging the door key on a nail just inside the door knob or on the wood facing near the window. His spreading fingers felt every inch of the door facing that he could reach. After several tries, he felt something cold. A nail. The thought of lifting and dropping the key temporarily petrified the intruding attorney. He already felt guilty for breaking.

For a moment it was a struggle for control, which finally came after some effort. Gradually his fingers inched down the nail to the slender leg of a key. With a slow gentle pull he slid the key off the nail. A moment of small triumph lit his eyes when he held the key in his hands. He prayed that the key would unlock the door. He inserted it in the open hole and held his breath. One turn, one click and the door unlocked. He sighed.

Every step on the rickety stairs was so audible that Albert thought someone might hear him. Foolishly he thought if he crept lightly, his body would be lighter and the squeaking would stop. The creaks continued to cry out until he reached the second floor.

Fortunately all the doors on the second floor were unlocked. Albert sneaked into the first room. To his surprise it was a kitchenette. The room across the hall was a bathroom. A bedroom was attached to a small door in the bathroom. There was barely enough light to see the beds, couch, closet and chest. "*Where would a man keep a drawing?*" he asked himself as he strained to see in the dim outlines. "*Of course. The chest.*" It was an ancient locker crowned with a heavy lid. It was locked. He chuckled to himself, straining his arm muscles to the limit. With great effort the lid popped open.

When the lid creaked open, Albert heard lumbering footsteps down the hall. Quickly he shut and locked the lid and hid behind the old sofa to wait. Heavy footsteps of someone resounded down the hall to the room that seemed to end where Albert was hiding. The door opened slowly with a screech that made his flesh crawl. Albert throttled the sound trying to push itself out of his voice box. "*By God! It's Mort! I can't wait to tell Dennis about this!*"

At the McDill home, Helen lit a candle and prayed for Albert Monroe. She rose from her knees when Dennis opened the front door. "Helen, I believe our church will be complete soon. Our men and townspeople have finished clearing some of the ground behind the church except for a few trees. It'll look better with green grass and flowers."

"Dennis, I saw some beautiful yellow flowers blooming upriver yesterday. Can you send someone to get some of these for the ladies who fed the men working on the chapel?"

"I'd better stay here. Albert might send me a message with good news, I hope. I'll ask Phillipe to get some for us. That's one of his favorite hunting spots."

As Dennis stepped out on the porch to check the weather, he caught sight of two familiar figures, Comer and Phillipe. "Over here, men. I want to give Phillipe a pleasant duty." Energized, they walked briskly toward the commander's voice.

"Yes, Sir. You have something for me to do?" Phillipe asked cheerfully.

"Phillipe, I want you to go upriver and pick some flowers for those nice women who fed us so well while we were building the chapel."

Phillipe's eyes stared at his boss for a few seconds. "Flowers, Sir?"

"Yes, the ladies deserve our thanks. Helen says there are some nice yellow blooms on the river's edge."

"Aye Sir." He saluted thinking it was the strangest order he had ever received.

Just as the lieutenant reached the river, Dennis placed his fingers against his head. *"My God, What have I done? Sent Phillipe to his death? That vicious woman will shoot him if she sees him!"*

Phillipe's canoe lay on its side as though begging for him to turn it over and slip it into the cooling water. Its paddle protruded out of one side of the little boat. The mariner slid the craft into the river current and paddled against its strong force that was determined to drive him downstream. Phillipe would have to paddle upstream near the place he saw the angry woman he admired so much. When he looked back, he could see McDill racing down to the pier, however the current demanded his full attention. A mile ahead he could barely see a yellow blanket spreading its wings on the left bank of the waterway. And there was another color midst the flowers. A tanned buckskin moved. It bent down among the sunny plants. Two hands were breaking off stems and dropping flowers in a crude basket. His jaws opened and his eyes were all pupils. It was the little native. His oar dropped making a clunking noise inside the shell of the boat. Startled, she looked up from her chores.

The sun blinded her from seeing the noise maker. She shielded her eyes in vain. Phillipe snatched up the paddle and humped like a rower in a racing shell toward the blind maiden. Ten seconds passed and Phillipe was alongside the buckskinned beauty. She recognized him and waded as fast as she could for the shore. He caught her foot just as she landed. "I want to talk to you for a minute." She pulled away so hard, her deerskin moccasin came off in his hand. She got to her feet and ran. He was faster and caught her by the waist. The little woman shouted and screamed, but no one came to her rescue. She clawed the blood out of his hand. She bit his arm and kicked him in the stomach. Phillipe tried to hold her arms to her side to keep from hurting her and being hurt. Their little war continued for several minutes until both flopped over on their backs exhausted.

"I...I don't want to talk to you," she panted. "You and your kind want to hunt my land."

"If I promise never to hunt again, will you at least talk to me?" Phillipe promised.

She fought again until she was totally exhausted, and heaved air in gulps. "I have no choice. You're too strong." Her surrendered eyes looked into his eyeballs. "You promise not to hurt me?"

"I promise. I swear." He held up his right hand.

"My father told me not to trust white men." She continued to swallow air.

"I swear I won't hurt you. I just want to talk."

With great effort, she pulled her body further up on the ground and turned over in a sitting position. "Now what do you want to say?"

For a moment he choked. In a low voice it came out. "You are the prettiest woman I have ever seen."

Believing that he wanted to bargain for her land or something, she stood up astonished at such a frank admission."

"You haven't seen many women, have you?"

"Oh, yes I have, and I have seen beautiful women, but none as beautiful as you."

Her blush turned her skin dark crimson. She gazed into his pale hazel eyes to see if he was truthful. Finally, she noticed his square chin and mouth supported a thin moustache below his nose. His thick blond hair was almost as light as her raven pigtails were black. She had to look up at the man who was a head taller than the top of her head. Still blushing, she checked to see if anyone else saw them together. When he locked his eyes on her, she dropped her flowers. Her eyes fastened on his as if she were hypnotized. Several flowers fell into a feeder stream and floated gently out into the river. When he touched her hand, she wanted to retrieve it, but something compelled her to hold still. She told him about her powerful grandfather, Powhatan, her parents, and her little brother. He related that his grandparents fled France to escape the great purge. The Huguenots were slaughtered by the dozens. They moved to Pennsylvania and later southward."

"Where is Pennsylvania?"

"It's a land far north of here. It's one of our states."

"Yes, I've heard of United States. My people say there are many states for white men." She wasn't ashamed to show her ignorance. Her curiosity filled the voids.

"Yes, many and still growing," he answered. "By the way, what do they call you?"

"They call me 'Little Moon.' My mother said I was born when the moon was in its smallest." Little Moon liked her native name better than her white man's name.

"Do you have an English name?"

"It's Angelia Onneechee. I sign my name that way, but you call me Little Moon."

He smiled. "My mother's name was Angelique."

A little hand found his arm. Little Moon recognized the sadness in his voice. "Is it lonely not to have a mother?" Her sympathetic eyes portrayed the dark feathers of a cormorant. The little woman stretched her neck to see into the fair eyes of the officer. "By the way, what is your name?"

"Phillipe DuBois. Sometimes my friends call me Phil."

"Phillipe DuBois, it's getting late. I must take my flowers and go home." She gathered the remaining flowers she had picked.

"When can I see you again, Little Moon?"

"I often come down here to hunt, or just sit on the bank to enjoy the view and think."

"May I see you tomorrow? It'll be Sunday and I don't have to work," he proffered.

"I will be here tomorrow when the sun is the highest in the sky." She pointed straight overhead to make sure he knew her meaning.

DuBois ached to kiss the little buck-skinned woman, but he repelled his emotions until she knew him better. Her head barely reached his shoulder. When she loosened her pigtails, her shoulders supported jet black locks that bloomed out to her waist. Little Moon's reddish tan skin was smoother than a child's. At an early age, she had learned the white man's English and her father taught her how to figure as well as a store keeper. Her hunting skills were unparalleled, better than most braves.

Lieutenant DuBois gathered flowers and rowed home with a warm smile on his face. He knew he had found his woman.

It was dark when Phillipe's boots landed on the front steps of the McDills' front porch. A large candle was burning over the fireplace. Helen and Dennis sat in front of the fire discussing how the church should be dedicated. Helen turned when Phillipe knocked. "Ah, Lieutenant, those are beautiful flowers. I know the women will be glad to have them. Let me get some pots and put them in water. You and Dennis can figure out how to plant these in a garden at the chapel so they will bloom next summer."

"Comer promised some seeds, including vegetable seeds." Phillipe handed the flowers to Helen as she filled five pots.

"Gentlemen, do you think we can dedicate the church by Thanksgiving? We are most thankful for the opportunity we can build a church of our own." Helen wiped water from her hands and sat on the sofa with Dennis.

"Phillipe and I have already discussed it. We think we can."

"Praise the Lord! That would be wonderful!" She clapped.

The three friends talked for hours until Phillipe thought it time to go to the barn for a good night's sleep and dream about his newfound love. He dreamed about the little human flower he found near the river. But McDill's sleep

119

became a nightmare. He found himself in a dark dungeon chained to the wall. Periodically, some evil creatures would come by with whips and strike blood from his arms, torso and legs. He felt he was slowly bleeding to death. Dennis sat up suddenly around midnight in a cold sweat. He was shivering. Helen sprang up. "What's wrong, Dennis?"

"Just had a bad dream. Go back to sleep, Helen." Dennis could not sleep. He stayed awake until dawn.

Helen and Dennis said very little at breakfast. He sat staring out the window. "What are you thinking?" Helen asked.

"I hope Albert has found some evidence that will get me out of this mess."

"Dennis, I believe he will. He's a fine, seasoned lawyer if Miss Josephine's cousin recommended him."

"I hope he finds something before my time runs out." Dennis winced.

Neither could know what was happening.

Albert Monroe knew vividly what was happening. The night of Dennis' nightmare, Albert saw Captain Mort open a trunk, pull out a large rolled-up object, and spread it out on a table in the far corner of the room. Albert could barely hear the mumble. Mort whispered to himself, "This will bring a very good price. I'll be rich!"

When Mort took his hand away, the paper slid down to the side of the table. Albert could vaguely see the schematic of a large ship. "*I've struck pay dirt,*" he patted himself silently. "*I'll follow this villain and see where he goes.*"

Mort rolled up the document, tucked it under his arm and rumbled down the steps.

In the dark, Albert braced himself and guessed each step until he reached ground level. He rushed around the building as quietly as he could. At a distance he could spy Mort walking down the street to the train station. Albert saw him buy a ticket and board the first car. The lawyer sped to the counter, bought a ticket and boarded a car directly behind Captain Mort's. In five minutes the train slowly chugged out of the terminal. At every stop Monroe would step outside to see if Mort dismounted. After three stops, Mort got off at the D.C. main station. Mort hailed a taxi carriage and headed north. Albert hailed another one. "Follow that taxi!" He ordered with a shouting command. As Albert looked outside, it appeared they were leaving the heart of the city. Then he recognized something that he had seen when he was a boy. His parents took him to see the Capitol and many other places. Unbelieving, he looked three times. They were approaching Embassy Row.

"Where in the world is this hoodlum going?" Albert asked himself. In a flash he knew. In front of the embassy the spread-eagled flag flopped lazily in the breeze. It was the Kaiser's favorite flag. Captain Mort showed his credentials and disappeared inside the large red doors. Outside Albert caught the next taxi. "Take me to the nearest police precinct."

Inside, Captain Mort was escorted down a hallway decorated by large ornate pictures of men on horses battling each other with swords and spears. He could see the paint shining as though it was recently dipped and traced on canvases. His escorts stopped him at a huge door with two enormous swords crossing over it. Behind a big teak desk sat the figure of an admiral with a large red sash circling his shoulder and a chest completely filled with medals. "Come in, Captain. I hear you have something you want me to see."

Out of courtesy, Mort saluted the admiral. "Yes, Sir. I have something great to show you." He took the large roll from under his arm and spread it out on the desk. "I have here a drawing of the most modern military ship that anyone could invent."

Admiral Molotz stood erect as a seasoned cadet and studied the drawing for several minutes. "Is this to scale, Captain?"

"Yes, Sir. And she's designed to steam more than thirty-five knots," he uttered with pride.

Admiral Molotz adjusted his sash and leaned over to take a closer look at the design. Mort watched the admiral's eyes glitter as he inspected the schematic. "You say it's for sale, Captain?"

"Yes, Sir, it's for sale." Mentally, Mort crossed his fingers.

The admiral asked. "How did you get it in your possession?"

"I smuggled it from the Naval Maintenance Terminal."

"That is risky. You must want a high price."

"Well, Sir. The U.S. Navy won't sell anything like that to another country."

Molotz sat down, still erect, and folded his hands. "If we obtained such as prize as this, I know the Tsar will be most pleased. How much are you asking, Captain?"

"Two million in American money, Sir."

"That's a lot. Will you take gold bullion? We have it stored in a Swiss bank, but I will have to get permission from our chief attaché. He will be here tomorrow. Can you return with the drawing tomorrow?"

"Most certainly. I know it will please you and your Tsar."

Leaving, Captain Mort grabbed a taxi and instructed the driver to take him to his apartment on 31st Street in the District.

Three blocks away from the Embassy, Albert lit from his carriage in front of an old police station. The first policeman he saw was riding horseback back to the station. "Officer, where can I find a detective?"

"Take the next left," he pointed with his billy stick.

At the police station, crowds of people crammed the hallway. Albert had to muscle his way, saying many "Excuse me's." The door was in sight, but he still had to nudge his body between tight groups of citizens. He actually drew a breath of relief when he planted one foot inside the room. A sergeant sat hawkishly on a high stool overlooking the room and the hall. He looked down at Albert Monroe who felt like a dwarf under his reptilian eyes.

"Yes, you're next."

Albert carefully explained that he had chased a crook who needed to be arrested for grand larceny. "You need to go to the Detective Division. It's directly across the hall."

Albert had made the wrong turn so he had to plow through the mob once again. After a struggle, he found himself in a dark room with two men in civilian clothes leaning on a small desk. One man gnawed on the remains of a cigar and the other man, slightly shorter, knocked tobacco from his pipe bowl. They paid no attention to the attorney until Albert cleared his throat with a loud dissonant noise that got their attention.

"May we help you?" the cigar smoker asked a little irritated.

Albert moved closer to the desk which was hovered over by a cloud of smoke. Albert could not restrain his coughing. "I'm a lawyer and I need you to investigate a case of grand larceny." He presented his credentials to the pipe smoker.

"So, you're a lawyer from Fredericksburg." The pipe smoker handed Monroe's card to his partner.

"We work with lawyers all the time." The cigar smoker struck a match. "What's your story, Mr. Monroe?"

"A ranking officer of the Navy has stolen a schematic of a new ship that the shipyard hasn't built yet."

"Is it a secret?" the pipe smoker asked and relit his tobacco.

"I don't know, but I consider it a very important document. I'm informed that an officer named Captain Mort walked out of the maintenance terminal with it rolled up under his arm. I followed Mort this far. I saw him with the document."

"Wait a minute." The older detective raised his hand. "How did you know it was what you were trying to find?"

"It unrolled and I got a glance."

"That's not much, my friend. That could have been a map with some creases." The cigar smoker puffed rings at the ceiling.

"Detectives, I am sure it's the plans for a powerful, modern ship, and, what's more I believe he's planning to sell it to another country."

"How do you know that?" The smoker lit his stubby cigar.

"I saw him go into an embassy—the Russian Embassy."

"Barrister, you have a great story there. You plan to have it published?" the pipe smoker derided, and dumped ashes in a bowl.

Both lawmen focused their eyes on each other. "Maybe this guy's dreaming, but it won't hurt to investigate. We're not busy here now," the pipe smoker reasoned. He could think better when his tobacco was burning. "Okay, what's the next move, Mr. Monroe from Fredericksburg?"

"I want us to go where Mort is staying. He'll come out sooner or later, maybe after breakfast. If you have a paddy wagon you can spare, we can park near the thug's home, watch until he comes out and nab him. My bet is he'll head for the Embassy."

Reluctantly, the two detectives agreed to check the suspected thievery. The paddy wagon was available so they drove it across the street in front of the place where Captain Mort entered. The men took turns, so one at a time could sleep in the wagon. The air was chilled. Albert shivered as he stood leaning on a lamp post waiting. Each minute seemed to last an hour. Dawn came. They saw one woman come out and take in a bottle of milk. An hour passed. As he was about to fall asleep, Albert heard some boots hit stone steps across the street. Captain Mort emerged pushing his hat down to avoid a strong breeze. Under his arm was a large object, round like a loaf of bread. "Nab him!" Albert shouted as he ran toward Mort.

Mort recognized the lawyer and darted down the street. Albert galloped behind him. Distance between them shortened with every step. Albert lunged as far as he could, grabbing the officer's leg. Mort groped forward attempting to shake Albert's grip. The captain dragged the attorney almost eight feet. Albert's knees scraped against the hard pavement, leaving blood spots. He ignored his injuries and clutched both of the seaman's legs until Mort tumbled face down to the sidewalk. "Cuff him, men!" Albert yelled and straddled Mort's back.

During the scuffle, the drawings rolled into a street gutter. Albert could see his efforts float into the yawning cavity and plunge into a cesspool. "Cuff him. Quick!"

With a synchronized motion, Albert and the pipe-smoking detective immobilized the suspect. Then the attorney lunged for the schematic coursing its way down a little stream of water created by a nightime shower. With his fingernails, he snatched the drawings. In a wide sling he threw the schematics on the sidewalk.

In the meantime, the cigar man clasped his hands behind Mort's neck and forced him into the paddy cell inside the wagon. Captain Mort shook the door so hard the paddy wagon shook like an earthquake.

While the detective managed to drive the wagon to the police station, Albert held the ship design plans under his arm until the paddy stopped at the precinct. He unrolled them and sighed. "Thank God for indelible ink."

It took only minutes for Albert Monroe to file charges against Captain Norman Mort at Police Precinct 109. Before he left, Albert requested that the suspect be extradited to Naval Headquarters as soon as possible. The attorney said goodbye to his smoking partners and shouted for transportation.

A taxi carried Albert to a busy hotel in the center of the city. The driver was instructed to take him to a telegraph office. Albert's neck rolled right and left. He clutched the design to protect it. "Driver, this isn't a telegraph office."

"Sir, there's one inside. Just go in and turn to your right."

Still clutching the rolled-up plans, Albert followed the cabby's orders. At the entrance stood a large burly man with a Middle Eastern tan. His huge black hat was pulled down so far that Albert could not see his eyes. Purposefully, his gross body bumped into Albert's side, seized the plans and fled down the street. "Stop!" Monroe shouted. The thief's body knocked over two men and one boy. An old lady with shopping bags immediately assessed the situation. As the felon raced by, she calmly kicked her foot out in front of the villain's path. He fell tumbling to the ground in front of the store and lost his grip on the drawings. A nearby city policeman arrived, clubbed the attacker with a billy stick, and chained him to a lamp post.

"This yours?" The old lady held up a roll of paper and smiled.

"Thank you. Ma'am, you have done the government a great service. Take this money for your trouble."

"Young man, I don't want your money. I hate robbers, and I hope he gets his tail thrown into jail for many years."

Albert told the policeman about the carriage driver, believing him to be part of some plan to sell the schematics to a foreign country. Soon, another policeman walked up, uncuffed the robber and pushed him inside a carriage. "We will make a full report of this. Mister, be very careful around here."

"Thanks, officer. Tell me where I can find the nearest telegraph office."

"It's on our way. We'll drive you there and show you a safe place to stay."

With tired legs, Alfred Monroe dragged himself into the telegraph room and sent this message to McDill:

CAUGHT MORT. HE WILL BE SENT TO HEADQUARTERS BRIG. SCHEMATICS ARE IN MY POSSESSION.

⚓

It took Comer a few seconds to scribble the message. He jerked the paper off his desk and scurried to find McDill. He bumped into a bush, nearly crashing into the grass, and continued until he saw O'Malley. "Where's the Commander?" Comer screamed.

"I saw him at the chapel site. What do you have?"

"A message with good news! A telegram for the Commander. Excuse me. I've gotta run."

Comer traveled so fast his breath heaved in staccato spurts. McDill was supervising MacEaton and Sullivan who were digging bent shovels into the hard clay at the chapel site. An old man with a divining rod pronounced a square yard of land behind the church to be an excellent place to dig a well. "Commander. I've got a telegram you'll want to read!" Comer handed Dennis the message. Dennis read the message twice, looked up at the sky and began to sing. MacEaton and Sullivan read the telegram and joined McDill in singing an old hymn. "Men, let's quit for today. I can see you've finished the well. Let's go home, tell our families and celebrate."

Dennis McDill sent Sullivan to the barn to invite DuBois and Rogers. Rogers was outside washing his clothes when Sullivan arrived. "Chief, the Skipper wants you and the Lieutenant to come by his house and celebrate the good news."

"What good news?" Rogers dropped his clothes back in the tub.

"They've nabbed Captain Mort and recovered the ship designs the Commander created."

"That's the best news I've heard in the last two months!" The Chief smiled and bit off a chew of tobacco."

"Where's Lieutenant DuBois?" Sullivan queried looking in the barn.

"Not here. Guess he's gone to see that little gal again." The Chief rolled the quid around in his mouth. "I told that boy she's goin' to cause himself a heap of misery."

"You think he'll be back soon?" Sullivan asked.

"He left before quittin' time, and I don't know when he'll be back. But you can count me in. I'll be there even though the Lieutenant is absent."

Lieutenant DuBois' absence carried him to the meeting place of his lover. Little Moon was late, so he sat on the bank and watched the birds dive for bass and trout. A long-legged blue heron cautiously walked past him looking and listening for the slightest noise that might bring him his next meal.

Phillipe fished out his watch and thought to himself, "*She's late. I hope she's all right.*" Just then an oar splashed. The front of Little Moon's dugout nosed ashore. Little Moon couldn't wait for her vessel to stop before she jumped into his arms. She kissed every inch of his face and embraced him for a long time. For an era, they could not speak. It was the sweetest silence Phillipe ever knew. He explored her baby skin and caressed her raven hair which was loosened from her pigtails. She felt every molecule of his face and his sandy van dyke. Her fingernails squeezed into the muscles of his shoulders and arms. Their passion shut out the world. The two lovers were creating a world of their own, exploring every atom of their bodies until after dark. They stopped only once to build a little campfire in a small place cleared away by hunters.

Phillipe's urge was sudden, perhaps premature. He swallowed hard to summon his courage. Phillipe held both of his lover's hands, fastening his eyes on her. It was the most important question of his life. Finally he spoke. "Little Moon, will you marry me?"

A little shocked, she looked up at the face of the one white man she did not fear or despise. Fire flames seemed to dance into her wide-open eyes. She took hold of his hands. The little woman said nothing for what seemed infinity to him. "Phillipe. Yes, yes, I will marry you. You're the only man I've ever really loved. I want to be your wife."

Elation propelled his heart ten feet into the air. "I'm the happiest man alive! I'll do everything to make you happy forever!" He clapped and whirled around her.

Little Moon fastened her arms around his waist as he twirled. Her body gained enough force to extend her legs out into the air. Two happy people laughed and giggled for an hour.

Later the embers' glow changed from yellow to red. Little Moon became mute and pensive. Her wrinkled forehead exposed her anxiety. He could tell her mood changed, even feel her mood change. "What's wrong? Aren't you happy?"

"My father won't be happy. He will know about us and you know he hates white men."

"If he knew how much I love you and how well I will take care of you, he'd have no fear or concern."

"It's not that. He's hated white people ever since they took his grandfather's hunting ground. I know he will do all he can to prevent us from marrying. I was late because I had a long talk with my mother. We talked about the possibility of marriage. She agrees with me, but she will not oppose my father in this matter. Father wants me to marry another man."

"Things have changed in this country, Little Moon. Men and women are free to choose their own mates without arrangements or blessings, if they wish." Phillipe hoped he made a strong case.

"I know, but that doesn't change some of my people. My father has already chosen a mate for me and wants me to marry after the next twelve moons." She sniffed a teardrop and wiped her nose.

"Do you love his choice?"

"No, he's not a nice man. I don't love him. I love you, Phillipe DuBois."

Deep down, Phillip recalled the advice of Commander McDill and the Chief Rogers. They sensed a problem and gave him their best advice. DuBois' passion overpowered their concern. Phillipe kept thinking that love will somehow conquer any adversity. "Little Moon, we'll run away."

"Won't you be in trouble? Your Navy will catch you and punish you if you run away."

"I know I should get permission to marry and I shouldn't go AWOL. But I love you so much, I'm willing to take any chance. We could hide high in the mountains where no one will find us."

"Phillipe, I'd love that, but will it work?"

"Little Moon, I'd do anything to have you. My commander will try to persuade me not to marry, but I think he'll give permission. I'll find a priest who will marry us. Even though it is not completely finished, I think he'll come over to our chapel to perform the service."

She put her hands on her hips in a scolding position. "Phillipe DuBois, you had this planned all along, didn't you?"

"Yes," he responded sheepishly.

Her hands left her hips and rested on his shoulders. "My love, you are a brave man. I love you for it. Now we have some people to convince."

A bright moonlight replaced the dying firelight while Little Moon and Phillipe kissed a long goodbye and paddled to their separate homes.

When Phillipe tied his boat along the end of the boat landing, he stopped short. It hit him in the solar plexis. He realized what happened. Mixed feeling of joy, coupled with a rush of anxiety, swept over his heart and plunged his mind into a dilemma. DuBois plainly understood he was compelled to tell everybody the good news. But protocol dictated, loud and clear, that he should get his commander's permission. And that would not be good news to Little Moon's father. DuBois, a decisive man, garnered enough nerve to cut across two lawns to reach the McDills' home as quickly as possible. After two knocks, a shaft of light landed on the floor of the porch. Dennis looked furtively through the crack and smiled.

"Lieutenant, we missed you. Come in." Phillipe walked into the living room ahead of Dennis. "My friend, what got hold of you?"

"Some hounds. I was in a hurry to tell you something. I took a shortcut across a couple of yards. Two dogs chased me and one gnawed a rip in my trousers."

"You must have something very important to take a chance like that at night." McDill inspected the hole. "I'll get a robe. You take off your britches. I'll ask Helen to repair them. I know you are good at most things, but sewing? No." Dennis fetched his robe, told Phillipe to use the first bedroom and informed Helen they had a visitor. After Phillipe undressed, Dennis took Phillpe's pants into the small room behind the kitchen where his wife sewed. The host lit another candle while his second-in-command pranced into the living room to tell him about the flower that blossomed in the most important drama of his life.

"Commander, I…I…."

"Calm down, Lieutenant and tell me."

"I'm getting married, Sir?"

"Why Phillipe, that's the best news I've heard since they arrested Captain Mort. Who's the lucky lassie?"

"Little Moon."

Dennis mused. "Sounds familiar. Is she the little native woman you met one day hunting in the woods? And you asked my advice, I believe?" Dennis' eyes blinked as though they were sending a coded message. His eyelids stopped. Commander McDill looked squarely into Phillipe's mind. "You're begging for trouble, Lieutenant."

"But, Sir, I love her very much."

"My boy, sometimes love causes some people to make unwise decisions."

Helen burst into the room holding the damaged trouser leg. "Did I hear you're going to get married, Phillipe? How wonderful! Do I know the young lady?"

"You probably don't, Ma'am. She's a beautiful woman called Little Moon."

Helen dropped the britches, ran over to Phillipe and hugged him as if he were her own son. "Phillipe, I know you and I know this is serious. I wish you both great happiness!"

McDill couldn't share Helen's enthusiasm. He walked to the window to glare into the black evening. His thoughts were just as dark. "Phillipe, you really think this is right? You have the mettle to ask her father for his blessing?"

"Yes, Sir. I will try. However, first, I would like to have your permission. I will need a few days leave of absence after the wedding."

At first Dennis couldn't answer. Another dilemma. He moved from the window. His chest heaved in surrender. "With great reluctance, I'll give you permission, but you and Little Moon may cause trouble for others. You know there is much prejudice between both races."

"Sir, I already know. Little Moon said her father hates white men."

"Then, young man, I KNOW you have a problem."

Helen's fingers flew up to her open mouth. "Oh my Lord, Phillipe. Do you think she will accept our faith?"

"Ma'am, I'm sure she loves me enough to learn and abide by our faith."

Helen counseled Phillipe. "There are many rites that only a priest can explain. She'll need information and instruction."

Phillipe's discomforts attacked him like hot pepper. The young man actually squirmed from mental heat. "Well, we will have to face it and solve it."

Helen's fears began to surface. "Are you sure you can handle this, Phillipe? We can help you all we can, but this marriage could shatter our community into little bits."

Dennis' robe dragged the floor when Phillipe tried to walk. One time he almost tripped on the hem. The young lover boiled inside. Conflict or not, his mind told him to stand firm. "I know there will be difficult problems. You two know this, but we will bear the pressure, just as you fine people have these last several months."

Dennis McDill turned his head and rubbed the back of his neck. "At least we have something in common, my friend. We both have our share of problems." Three people in the living room began to joke about their predicaments. They consumed an entire bottle of wine. Helen and Dennis went to bed after Phillipe fell asleep on the sofa.

⚓

While they slept, Albert Monroe was busy in the records room at Headquarters. Large tombs of written documents were filled with thousands of entries. Flickering gas lights were dim causing him eye strain. For hours Albert looked for written orders and documents, hoping that McDill's ship designs contained Mort's fingerprints. Odds told him it was a slim chance he could find something that Mort had signed. Albert recently learned that Washington and other city police discovered how to use the new technique of fingerprinting. Some fingerprints might be accepted in evidence. He knew he could compare sets to see if they matched. Many judges had already acknowledged this process as proof, but others harbored doubts.

A church clock in the next building struck midnight. He could hear it through the thick walls of the room. The searcher stretched and rolled his shoulders, fighting oncoming slumber. The room was dusty and smelled like a muskrat had perished in between the pages of the records. He finally reached an obscure pile of books in the end of a dusty row and found a paper signed by Norman Mort. It was an order for a load of iron ingots to be sent from the shipyard dated two years ago. Albert ripped out the page and ran for the door. When he leaped for the door, it was locked. He knocked hard. Then knocked harder, yelling as loud as his lungs could endure. No one answered.

⚓

Back in the Point, three headaches woke under a brilliant sunlight that pounded through McDill's windows. Helen frowned, covered her eyes, and looked at her husband's lump on the other side of the bed. "Wake up, Dennis. It's morning. You get Phillipe up while I finish his pants. You'll have to cook the eggs and bacon."

Groggy throbs beat like kettle drums in Dennis' head, but he managed to crawl out of bed, get dressed and wake the sleeping lover who was slowly struggling back to consciousness.

After breakfast the torpid duo ambled to the building site. Their legs felt as though they were pulling a battleship out of quicksand. O'Connell and O'Leary were nailing the end panels on the pews while Sullivan and MacEaton were digging halfway down to an expectant water level for a well. To get back in shape, McDill took hold of a hammer and banged a nail into a pew panel. Lieutenant DuBois spoke to the others with a tongue that felt like cotton. "What the heck, I'll take turns with Sullivan and MacEaton. Digging will get me back in shape."

McDill's sixth sense alerted him. Someone or something was behind him.

"Commander, don't stop. It's nice to see a good man working to get our little chapel in shape for the dedication." Bishop King sat down beside Dennis in a finished pew. "Your crew and the townspeople have done a fine job on this little church."

"Bishop, thank you for coming. May we go outside and talk privately?"

"Of course. We can sit in my carriage. That should be private enough."

Dennis' kettle drums retarded a few beats. His head cleared enough to converse with the aging prelate.

Dennis settled next to the intrigued prelate. "What's on your mind, Commander?"

"Bishop, do you know any priests who will marry couples of different races?"

Dennis expected a surprised look, but the bishop's peaceful expression did not reveal astonishment. "Yes, but with provisions."

"Helen and I have discussed them with one of the betrothed and he's aware of the provisions. He is of the same faith as ours."

Curious, King asked. "Dennis, tell me more about this."

"It's Lieutenant DuBois. He wants to marry an Indian maiden."

"She'll need counseling first. You know the Pope is very strict about this." King's age and experience seemed to be the cause of his humped shoulders and onset deafness. But the old sage always listened and gave good advice.

"Yes, Sir. I know. But we need to find a priest who will conduct the wedding ceremony."

"Well, my good man, that's the easy part. Do you think the young maiden will agree to worship our God and accept our faith?" Bishop King became deadly serious and looked at the river currents.

"Phillipe thinks she loves him so much she will agree."

"Couples love each other, but sometimes they have difficulties when members of their families are of different races. I believe DuBois is an intelligent man and he will make a good husband, but I wonder if he's weighed all the consequences."

"Helen and I have tried to explain. I believe he knows the problems, but his emotions are in control now."

"To answer your question, Dennis, I know a young priest in Maryland who has instructed people of different races and has performed the correct rites for honorable marriages. His is Father Alfred Proctor, and has a church just across the border."

"Maryland." Dennis leaned back and held up one finger. "A day and night's ride by train."

"Yes, he can be here by then, but get him lodging for two or more days after that to talk with the young woman." King placed his hand on the commander's arm. "Dennis, can you arrange that?"

"Yes. But, again, I'll let Phillipe know that I think it's ill-advised to marry Little Moon."

The Bishop nodded. "Little Moon. What a nice name. She must be as beautiful as her name."

"Phillip says she is."

"Commander, I advise you and Helen meet her soon. You can also be your lieutenant's parents for a while. He needs the help."

"We will, but I'm not sure we want to meet her father."

"Understandable. That might be the worst obstacle." Bishop King expressed concern. Dennis agreed. King continued "I came here for another reason. What have you heard from your lawyer?"

Dennis grinned. "Good news. Captain Mort has been arrested for stealing and trying to sell my ship diagrams to another country. I was told he's in the Headquarters' brig. We are sure that the U.S. Government will want to try him. If they find him guilty, he could be out of sight for years."

"I am relieved for your sake, my son. The Lord has blessed you this time."

"Thank you for that thought. I know Albert Monroe has more work to do before I return for the trial."

Albert slammed his whole body at the door like a butting ram.

"He's locked up tight. Shall we take him now?"

"Might as well. I have my little derringer. We'll shoot him and snatch whatever evidence he's found. If he has the schematics, we'll get them to the Embassy before they change their minds."

"Fritzgerald, we can't forget Mort, can we?"

"Yeah. We can. We can split the money two ways instead of three." I.G. Fritzgerald jammed his hand in his coat pocket for a key. "You shoot him and I'll get his evidence."

Albert calculated at least two hostiles parked outside the door. He crouched in a sprinter's position as soon as he heard the key click inside the lock. Before Fritzgerald opened the door wide enough for him to enter, Albert tucked the document under his arm. He lurched headfirst like a snorting bull. Becoming a fleeing fugitive, he crashed between his adversaries, dashed outside the building and flew down a narrow alley. Twice he bumped his elbows on the sides of buildings as he ran. After ten minutes of sprinting, both pursuers crumpled in exhaustion. When he thought he was not being chased, Albert looked for the nearest police precinct. He spotted a policeman riding a prancing chestnut stallion. In return, the cop spotted Albert bending over to catch his breath. "You need some help, Mister?"

Between gasps, Albert was able to issue a feeble sound. "Am I glad to see you, officer. I've been locked up in a room by some enemies of the State."

Hastily, Albert gave the law enforcer the reason why he was running. The accommodating cop reached down for Albert's hand. "Hop on behind me. We can run fingerprints at our station."

The police stallion was a strong beast. He carried both men with ease. Soon, his hoof clops produced their familiar sounds outside the precinct door. The closer the horse reached home, the louder and quicker his clops. There, Albert was introduced to the fingerprinter. "Printer, I want you to get a good picture. Check and determine if this is good enough so I can compare the prints I secured in Navy Headquarters."

The policeman carefully dusted the document Albert handed him. Then he took a tintype of the prints. In an hour, Albert got a certified copy of the prints and asked how he could get to the train station the quickest way. "We'll take you in our paddy," the officers offered. Their horses galloped so fast Albert closed his eyes, hoping the carriage wheels would stay on at such a speed. Every time they dodged another vehicle or a pedestrian, Albert held his breath and clutched the evidence. Reaching the station, he climbed out of the wagon onto the platform, breathing easier with relief, and rushed to the ticket window. The train was scheduled to depart in seconds. Albert stuffed his money in the ticket window. With a ticket in hand, the attorney raced. No time to waste, for the next train would arrive one hour later.

"All aboard," the conductor boomed with a voice of thunder. Albert handed him his ticket, climbed inside the car and took the nearest empty seat. A sigh floated up from the bottom of his chest. Albert Monroe clutched two important documents, the drawings and the fingerprints on validated photographs. The locomotive rolled on a short hop to Headquarters.

Fritzgerald decided to visit Captain Mort in the brig. He wanted absolute secrecy, except for Mort's jailer, who was bribed considerably by the I.G.

Naval Headquarters' brig was still the same…cramped quarters, bad food and little sunlight. Fritzgerald waited until dark. With the stealth of a weasel looking for dinner, he sneaked to the front door of the brig. Recognizing a senior officer, the marines saluted and let the short-haired ermine enter. Down the hall Fritzgerald could hear keys rattling like out-of-tune chimes. They announced the jailer coming to meet the I.G. "Follow me, Sir. His cell is three down and to the left. I'll let you in."

Mort's hands clutched two bars while his chin protruded through the space just large enough for one cheek. "Thought you'd forgotten me." Mort continued to peer through the bars. "Any way you can get me out of this disgusting place? You have a law degree, don't you?"

"Yeah, but my job is to inspect for the prosecution." This irritated the I.G. He knew Mort should have known that.

"We're in this mess together and we both need a good lawyer. Surely you know some," Mort asked scornfully.

A loud squeak had whistled down the hall when the jailer opened the cell door to let Fritzgerald in to see his partner in crime. Slammed doors made Fritzgerald's back muscles stiffen. The effect created such a cool-down he had never experienced. He had visited the brig many times, but this was different. It had the tinge of something sinister. The I.G. could feel the shark's teeth gnawing him from behind bars. "You know I'll tell everybody if you let me hang alone with this litter of worms."

"You know I won't let you down. I'll find a way. We've got time. They'll take McDill's case first. If he's found guilty, we'll have a good chance." Somehow Mort found that hard to believe.

"And if he's acquitted?" Mort countered.

"Look, I've gotta go. I'll keep you posted." The I.G. summoned the jailer.

Fritzgerald could breathe better when his foot plopped down on the main entrance steps. He hailed the next carriage. "Naval Headquarters. Driver, hurry."

When the I.G. dismounted in front of Headquarters, Albert Monroe's carriage halted directly behind his. Albert recognized the I.G. immediately. "Captain Fritzgerald. What a coincidence, our arriving at the same time. I've got some more evidence on Captain Mort."

The I.G. reeled around to find the voice. "Oh. It's you, Monroe. I'm surprised to see you back this soon. We thought you had gone overseas or somewhere." Fritzgerald's mind, fired by curiosity, requested, "What kind of evidence?"

"I want to see Admiral Hicks first." Albert held his hand over a small bulge inside his coat holding a photograph of Mort's fingerprints. He stepped away from Fritzgerald, hoping to avoid a confrontation. "Excuse me. I'm in a bit of a hurry." Albert began to double-step down the hall.

"Hey! Wait! I want to talk to you. If you have any evidence, I should know about it." Fritzgerald gave chase, but Monroe was too fast.

"You'll know soon. I've got to see the Admiral Hicks first," Albert shouted back to the I.G.

Monroe bolted past the guard before the guard could react, then he plunged his body through Hicks' office door. An orderly stepped in front of Albert to block him. "May I help you, Sir?"

"I must see the admiral right now!" he ordered.

"He's busy at the moment." The orderly moved slightly to the right to check the office door to see. That slight movement was just enough for Albert to bend down, slide by and land in front of the desk.

"What in tarnation…?" Hicks shouted. "Orderly, how did you let this man by?"

Albert stood up like a cork. "Sir, it's me, Albert Monroe. You remember, McDill's defense attorney."

"Oh, it's you. Why'd you come crashing into my office like that?"

Puffing to grasp his breath, Albert could utter only one word. "Evidence."

"All right, Mr. Attorney. What's so all-fired important to burst into my office?" Hicks dropped his pen and leaned back.

"Can we talk alone, Sir?"

"Okay, Orderly, go out, close and guard the door."

Gingerly, Monroe lifted out the tin-typed photograph of the fingerprints on Captain Mort's document and held it up for Hicks to see. "These fingerprints match the fingerprints of McDill's ship design that I have tucked inside my coat. I plan to offer this into evidence to acquit my client."

"So, what does that prove, young man?"

"Captain Mort is implicated in a plan to sell our design to another country. I'm sure these fingerprints will match those on this order that Captain Mort signed."

"Then you will admit both in evidence," the admiral noted.

"Precisely, Admiral. These are the only prints, except for a delivery boy's. "Captain Fritzgerald might also be involved if I can find the connection. My guess is he wants some of the money of the illegal sale to the Russians."

Admiral Hicks whipped back and forth in his swivel chair and lit a cigar—his habit when facing a problem. "You can't possibly mean that Captain Fritzgerald had any part in this, can you?"

"Yes, Sir. He might have a major role. Somebody may have enticed him with some financial reward."

"Monroe, do you have any idea what the Russians will pay for McDill's designs?"

"The vessel McDill conceived is supposed to be the fastest military ship in the Navy today. They claim it will exceed 35 knots."

"That would be faster than anything in our present fleet." Then Hicks flicked cigar ashes in a large bowl-like tray and looked at the ceiling. "Attorney, if what you are saying is true, I have to confess that I didn't screen Mort enough before I had him appointed to the Inquiry Panel."

"Unfortunately, Admiral, we all make mistakes." Albert noticed the agony in Hicks' eyes. "Of course, I want to get my client acquitted."

"Young man, you must do your duty. As unpleasant as it is for the others and me, justice must be accomplished."

"If I understand it, being a traitor is a CAPITAL crime." Albert Monroe emphasized "capital."

"All right, Mr. Defender, we will compare the fingerprints on the telegram, the note ordering the telegram, and the prints on the schematic and see."

"Yes, Sir. Here's the photograph of Mort's fingerprints. I had the police print and verify. Notice it has the Chief of Police's seal on the bottom. He signed it underneath."

"Young man, meet me here at 9:00 tomorrow. You are excused."

For billeting, Albert was directed to an old tarnished one-story building.

Fading letters above the front entrance read "Officers' Club."

"*Something left over from the Civil War*," he thought. A corporal stood behind a dark brown desk which groaned under the weight of pamphlets and pictures of the great City. Just above the clerk, the statue of the giant eagle looked down with discriminating eyes, ready to sink its talons through the bodies of any unfortunate one who was not welcome in his cherished building. Albert could not avoid the great bird's attention, so he hurriedly registered. "Do you have a safe? I have two important documents to store."

"Yes Sir. Just behind me. One other clerk and I have the combination."

"Can I be sure it'll be secure for a few days?" Albert stretched his neck and peered around the clerk.

"We've had no robberies or thefts since we moved in here," the clerk vowed.

Albert rolled the ship plans tightly, handed them to the corporal and watched him carefully insert them in the safe. Albert couldn't avoid remembering the giant bird again, so he snapped up the key and scurried upstairs to his room. He was disappointed to see such small quarters for officers of the Navy and Marines. Dour drapes seem to stretch their fingers out to choke him. One small bed and one straight chair made it appear like a jail cell. The bed and chair were rock hard. Albert Monroe's fatigue superimposed itself over the bleak room. A pitcher of water and a basin were the only friendly items he could see. He poured out enough water to wash his face. As he wiped water from his face, a sharp knock from the door echoed around the room. A tiny opening in the door revealed a small slender sailor holding a piece of paper, "Telegram, Mr. Monroe."

"Yes, I'm Monroe. Here's a small tip."

"Sir, the Navy frowns on tips for my services. I'm glad to be of help."

Albert took the paper anxiously. "Well, thank you very much."

The telegram was from Dennis McDill giving vivid accounts of Lt. Phillipe DuBois' love affair with an Indian woman. He asked Monroe to give his lieutenant some legal advice. Albert sat down hard on the solidified bed that seemed to be composed of hardened concrete. He buried his face in his hands quietly muttering to himself. "*Dennis has enough troubles to rival the Book of Job. And here's another one*," he murmured. "*Dennis wants my advice. I'm not trained for this thicket of crooked thorns. Unfortunately I'll have to say, 'no.'*"

Chapter VI

"I don't care how pretty she is, that woman is trouble," Dennis said emphatically.

"Sir, let me bring her over tomorrow and you and Mrs. McDill can talk with her. Little Moon is willing to adopt our religion and obey our rules."

"You discussed this with her already?" Dennis asked, surprised.

"Yes, and I want her to talk with the priest that Bishop King recommended." Phillipe maintained a brave front.

"All right, Lieutenant, bring your bride-to-be over tomorrow afternoon. Actually, Helen really wants to meet her."

Phillipe, leaving with bundle of confidence, was assured that McDill would like her. DuBois stopped with a slam, like running into a wall. *"I've got to remember she's not the problem. Her father is. He'll want me drawn and quartered with the strongest saplings in the forest. But, I'm sure my love will overcome the terror my soul feels right now. If this means life or death for her, I will have to let her go. I love her too much to risk her life."* Reality of life or death was hanging in the core of his soul. Phillipe could feel unlimited torment that such a dilemma could be inflicted on him. *"Love is supposed to be happy and fulfilling, not filled with fear and dominating anxiety."* His heart was torn as much as his mind. Lt. DuBois' brain became meat melting from the bone. Without realizing it, Phillipe was inches from his canoe. The oar was in his hands and he was propelling upstream toward their clandestine rendezvous. Shortly, he found his pretty maiden sitting on the bank holding her knees and looking for her man.

"You're late, Phillipe."

"Sorry, Little Moon. I had to ask my boss for permission to marry you and for consent to bring you down to meet him and his wife."

"Phillipe, I will come to your town, but I cannot ask my father to see you.

At least, not yet. I am waiting for my mother to tell him."

"Then, meet me here tomorrow?" Phillipe hoped.

"Yes, my lover. I will go with you anywhere." She held his hand to her breast.

A screech owl's shrill call at midnight warned Phillipe and Little Moon to separate. Shortly her boat slid on the narrow beach near the Indian village. Darkness hid her from the two sentinels who could see a berry seed twenty feet away. Her soft moccasins could blunt any sound from her silent trek into the settlement, but she accidentally stepped on a twig. Two heads rotated toward the sound. Chilling sweat down her back, made her shiver. She had to hide somewhere, but where? No lights in the huts meant that everyone was asleep. She took a deep breath and plunged into the nearest hut. She nearly stumbled over a prone body snoring as loudly as a wounded bison. Little Moon squatted near the entrance and waited. She could hear the foot steps of the guards as they searched down each row of huts. One mumbled about seeing something that looked like a woman. At that, her throat became dry sand, and her body shook out of control. It took all her strength to keep quiet. An eon passed before she could no longer hear the searchers. Her body bent over so she could crawl down the next row to her parents' hut. When she stepped inside their hut, she heard heavy breathing, a sure sign of deep sleep. With the stealth of a hunting animal, Little Moon found her pallet. She dreamed about going to town with Phillipe and meeting his people.

"Mr. Monroe, come in. I've been expecting you. We're glad to get a real project this time."

Monroe was surprised to see a tired, old salt dressed in a white coat. He expected a uniform with an ink pad ready to take imprints. Instead, the lab cop started by inspecting Albert's photographs. "Looks like a nice job."

Albert pointed. "Yes, see the seal at the bottom of the picture?"

"Oh, yes. It looks legal enough." The technician continued to inspect the seal.

"May I see some identification?" He looked at Albert's coat.

"What? Identification? Admiral Hicks knows me and allowed me to bring this to you to check the prints against each other."

"Mr. Monroe, we can't be too careful."

Albert fumbled in each pocket for his card. He was getting frustrated by the minute. "I have it somewhere. Oh, here it is." He grimaced. "Satisfied?"

"We must be careful. Criminals can be very clever." The skeptical lab operator paused and offered his hospitality. "Have a seat. I need to make a copy of your fingerprints."

"Why?"

"Well, Mr. Monroe your fingerprints are on both sheets now. I'm instructed to single out any others that match. I presume that'll be your man?" He pointed to a smudge in the picture.

After agreeing to be fingerprinted, Albert abhorred the sight of the ink pad and the black goo sticking to his fingertips.

"Here, wipe with this wet towel. I believe I have a good print. Now let me check again."

Albert Monroe sat on the edge of his seat like a child unwrapping presents. He was tempted twice to look over the shoulder of the lab man.

"Sir, in my right hand is the print from the police station and in my left hand is the one that I showed the Admiral."

"Yes, I brought the one from the police and the barracks clerk gave me the other one."

Holding both prints over a lighted glass, the lab technician turned both copies several ways and looked at Albert. "Are you sure you got this one from the officer's barracks safe?"

"I'm rather sure." Albert nodded and looked again at the print. "I have the drawings of the fastest ship you've ever seen. I hope you can find they match."

Drawings were compared to the fingerprints of both. "It looks like you have a match between the drawings and one set of prints, but I hate to tell you, Mr. Monroe, the others do not match. You have less evidence than you thought."

"For heaven's sake. I observed the police and got their seal. Both were returned to me by an orderly in the barracks." Albert, thwarted by this, repeated his statement.

"Whose orderly?"

"Maybe someone tampered with it?"

Speculating, the fingerprinter asked. "Can you describe him?"

"Yes. He is about average height, probably weighs 160 pounds, light skin, brown eyes, sandy hair." Monroe felt like a detective.

"How old would you say?"

"Maybe twenty-two or twenty-three. A Marine private."

"Sir, that could match a dozen marines. Did you notice anything else?" he asked.

Albert placed a hand on the side of his head with his thumb under his chin. Then he looked down at the glass table. "I do remember something else. When he gave me the photo, I noticed he had a scar on his right hand."

"Mr. Monroe, you and I have a job to do. We've got to check every private aboard."

"How many?"

"I don't know, maybe twenty or more," he guessed.

"Won't we need to get permission?" Albert asked.

"Yes, from Admiral Hicks, since this is a matter for the court."

Albert nearly kicked over his chair when he got up. "Well, let's see him as soon as possible."

Both men crashed down the hall as though they thought the "suspect" would get away. They slowed down when they met the admiral's secretary.

"We need to see the boss right away," Albert puffed.

"Wait here," she said.

In a minute Admiral Hicks stepped from his office. "Got a match, I hope?"

"Just one set," Monroe answered.

"Explain."

Albert thought he had better stand at attention with the laboratory technician. In fact, he was tempted to salute. Hicks clenched his cigar between his teeth without lighting it. Albert noticed the senior officer's confusion was turning into fuel for his fierce temper. In alternating sentences, both men explained what happened. Hicks scowled at every word, wondering what kind of mistake either or both had fathered. Albert swallowed hard. "Sir, we'd like to check every Marine private in Headquarters. I'm sure we can identify him by his scar."

"What? Inspect every Marine private?" He steamed and walked close enough to inspect the ears of each man to see if they were clean.

"Yes, Sir," Albert answered timidly.

Hicks clutched his cigar in one hand and held a lit match in his other hand. After two ringed clouds drifted ceilingward, he mellowed slightly. "All right. I'll order a full inspection this afternoon. We'll have them pass in review with the band. It'll look like a monthly examination. Then we'll check every man in ranks. If we don't find a scar on the right hand of any marine, I'll have you both march around the field one hundred times."

Little Moon jumped into Phillipe's canoe and kissed him with wet lips. Her caress made him drop his oar. Arms tangled for several moments while his canoe turned sideways and floated by itself. They were halfway to City Point before they realized where they were.

Phillipe's paddle lay inside the boat while the two lovers clinched each other, what seemed to be an unending passion. Fortunately, he was able to find his oar and glide to shore. His little craft bumping hard on the landing ramp nearly tossed the two ashore on the narrow beach. The couple forgot Little Moon's canoe. They really didn't care. They got to their feet, held hands and dashed headlong up the lane to the home of Dennis and Helen McDill. Just before they reached the porch steps, Little Moon jerked back. It pulled her partner to a standstill. "Phillipe, I'm afraid. What if they won't like me?"

"Oh, my little one. They'll love you." He pulled her to his side, kissing her on her forehead.

"Phillipe, let's stand here a while. I want to think. Are we doing the right thing?"

"Of course we are. Why do you doubt it?" Phillipe looked unbelieving.

"My father. If your people accept and bless our marriage, I feel my father will cause trouble with his terrible disposition."

"He won't kill us. Will he, Little Moon?"

"He might be angry enough. Who knows? Phillipe, we must warn your people."

"Aw, we have nothing to fear. My crew'll handle anyone who gets mad and tries to make trouble."

"Yes, I know. You call it 'war,' don't you?"

Phillipe was forced to remain silent. He had no answer for war, realizing it to be a cruel thing that military hated the most. Phillipe was dumbfounded for a few seconds. He restrained his voice because he disliked controversy. But, determined, he cleared his throat and found his voice. "Let's go in."

"Let's wait one more minute," Little Moon implored.

"You know our love is deep enough to tackle the worst problems of life, Little Moon. Let's go in," he begged, and pulled her toward the house.

DuBois took his bride-to-be by the hand and proudly rapped on the McDills' front door. Dennis parted the door and looked down at an attractive Indian maiden. His eyes widened like two full moons. Her beauty astonished the seasoned commander. For seconds he could only gawk at the small, dark-haired princess standing at his door. "Please come in. I'm Dennis McDill and this is my wife, Helen."

"Folks, this is my precious gem, Little Moon."

Helen was quick to respond. She shook Little Moon's hand immediately, and stood back to admire her. "You ARE as attractive as Phillipe said you were. Welcome to our home. Please sit and chat with us"

Both lovers sat on the sofa with arms around each other while Helen offered tea and cookies. Somehow she could feel vibrating tenseness radiating from the betrothed woman. Helen and Dennis had agreed to tell her about their lives first to make her feel more at ease. Dennis and Helen expounded for almost an hour telling about how they met and married.

Albert stood with several top brass when the marines marched by in formation. Salutes were given by each leader as the U.S. flag floated by. Headwinds pushed against every one of its threads. Out of respect, Albert Monroe stood at attention and crossed his chest with his right arm. All companies turned at the end of the field, marched back toward the parade stand and halted.

Albert followed Admiral Hicks and the small collection of officers between the files of about eighty marines standing at attention. When Hicks faced each man, the leatherneck saluted crisply.

Before returning salutes, Hicks would inspect the saluting hand of each man, and not to be too obvious, he would check every uniform and every pair of shoes and notice each hand. By the time they finished, he turned to the parade marshal and ordered, "Lieutenant, I want the third man on the second row in my office."

Both companies were dismissed. One private was escorted between two shore patrol behind the inspection team.

Hicks dismissed the inspection team. Soon, three men stood at attention in front of Admiral Hicks' desk with Albert Monroe standing beside the large flag posted behind the Commandant of the U.S. Judge Advocate General. "State your name, private," Hicks ordered so loud the private blinked twice.

"Private Wilmer Rucker, Sir."

"Private Rucker, let me see your right hand." Rucker held out his hand, palm skyward, as commanded. "Turn your hand over," he ordered.

A large crescent shaped scar wrapped around the back of the private's hand, which shook. Private Rucker stood petrified, hoping this would not lead to a court-martial.

Hicks asked and pointed. "Have you ever seen this gentleman standing in front of the flag?"

Shaking, Rucker turned slightly and looked at Monroe. "Yes Sir, I saw him today. Sir, I delivered a package to him."

"Who gave you the package, Private Rucker?"

"Captain Fritzgerald, the Inspector General, Sir." He stopped shivering.

"That is all, Private Rucker. You're dismissed."

A most relieved marine gave the officer a salute, turned and marched out of the office. "Lawyer, what are you thinking?" Hicks' head leaned sideways.

Remembering the lab person's findings, Albert ventured, "Fritzgerald could have worn gloves, or Mort may have eliminated or faked the evidence somehow."

"That's a bit far-fetched," the admiral concluded. "Even if we suspect Mort was trying to sell our ship plans to another country, we'll hold him for questioning and continue to check all details." Hicks rose from his chair and smiled. "Monroe, you are your own witness."

"Yes, I believe I am. It may help clear my client."

"Look Monroe, I've got to be scarce at this point and be neutral. Remember, I'm President of a U.S. Navy Court-Martial Panel."

Albert thought he had lost a friend, but he understood. His mood curled into a sinkhole. He had to go to court with a bowl of doubtful evidence.

⚓

It was easy for the McDills to have parental feelings toward Little Moon and Lieutenant Dubois, after hearing them chatter about their future plans. Phillipe planned to build a home at the end of the street where the McDills resided. Little Moon's face enkindled her broadest smile.

"You two have our most sincere approval and blessing." Dennis placed his hands on their shoulders and nodded.

"Yes, and we wish you a very happy long life together," Helen added with a glistening cheek.

"Little Moon, do you know anything about our religion?" Dennis asked.

"A little. Just what Phillipe told me."

Helen offered more cookies. "Little Moon, I'm not familiar how your people marry. Is there some kind of ceremony?"

"Our Chief, Running Cloud, holds our hands and prays to our Great Spirit. The bridegroom, as you call him, gives the bride's father a present, usually a horse, a cow, or something valuable. The bride's father gives the bride to the groom, a little like your own custom."

"Just like we do?" Helen questioned.

"Not exactly. In our tribe sometimes a father promises his girl to a boy's father long before they wed."

Helen sat on the sofa near the native girl. "Tell me more about your Great Spirit, Little Moon." Helen offered another round of tea.

"He has big power and looks after us. We pray to the Great Spirit in many powwows."

Helen pulled up a chair, sat in front of Little Moon and took her hand. "Much like our God, I believe. You will have little trouble understanding our priest. A priest is like your Great Chief. He prays a lot to our Great Power we call God."

Dennis explained. "Tomorrow, Priest Proctor will come and explore our beliefs and discuss your wedding. Also, he will review our customs with you. Don't be afraid. He will ask you questions after he explains. Is that all right with you, Little Moon?"

She fastened her eyes on Phillipe's. "I will do anything to marry Phillipe DuBois."

Phillipe reached over and kissed his lover reverently. "I'll do anything to have you as my wife."

Dennis stretched and yawned. "Helen, it's time for bed. We've talked all day long."

"Yes, so it is. It's late for us. Little Moon, you take the other bedroom. Phillipe, we'll ask you to sleep on the couch."

"Ma'am, I'd sleep on a bed of rocks for Little Moon."

After the McDills retired, the soul-mates sat on the porch steps and talked about their future. One time Little Moon pushed Phillipe away from her. "Phillipe, I never asked you whether you wanted children or not."

"What a question. Of course I want children. I like children." He twisted around to gaze in her face to make his point understood.

"Phillipe, they'd be mixed. Will your people make fun of them?"

"I never thought of that. Perhaps some would, but when they really got to know them, they'd like them, I believe."

"Phillipe, you're dodging my point. There will be some problems. Some of my own people might have trouble accepting them—even our marriage."

"Little one, perhaps you're right. We must love and protect our children at all costs, and we may have to move away where they will be accepted."

"We agree on that, Phillipe?"

"Yes, my love, I agree. If it must be done, so be it."

Soon the entire house folded into a blanked of seclusion.

⚓

At dawn, Phillipe jumped out from under his cover. A fist was raised to knock again when Phillipe opened the door. "I am Father Proctor from Maryland. I take it you must be the groom?"

"I am, Sir. Please come in." Phillipe turned and yelled loud enough to open every eyelid in the house. "Wake up! The priest is here."

Dennis and Helen tumbled out of bed and threw on their robes. "Please pardon our dress, Reverend. We didn't expect you this soon. You must have arrived before dawn. Excuse us. We'll get dressed and get you some breakfast." Later, Dennis inspected the kitchen to see if Helen had the stove fire burning. By the time the priest scrambled to get his luggage, bacon was sizzling and the boiling kettle whistled its C# tune. Proctor's neck was so skinny his priestly collar propped one half inch away from his skin. His hollow cheeks created protruding bones, but he was handsome nonetheless, and stood almost as tall as Dennis McDill. His resonant voice could reach all ears in the back of a large cathedral. His smile was so infectious, it emitted light.

"Thank you for coming, Reverend," Dennis said, and offered him the end seat in the dining room. "You rode the train all night, didn't you?"

"Yes, but I slept some and I was able to prepare two sermons before I went to sleep."

"We suppose Bishop King told you why he wanted you to come here." Helen poured a round of coffee for everyone and offered more bacon.

"Yes, I have two tasks: First, to instruct this beautiful young woman about our faith, and second, marry her to this fine young man."

"We'd be most honored and thankful." Phillipe nodded to the slender clergyman sitting slightly bent over the table.

"Well, let us get started now," Proctor urged. "I have only a few days, then I must return to my parish before next Sunday."

The clergyman pulled a book from his suitcase. "Little Moon, you might recognize this."

"Yes, Sir. I guess it's your Holy Book."

"Right. It is our Holy Bible and it is divided in two parts. We have an Old Testament and a New Testament. We use this for instruction so that we may attain better lives. This book was written mostly by people known as Hebrews, holy men and women who lived long ago. The New Testament describes a man called Jesus Christ and that is why we are called Christians. We follow His teachings."

"Reverend, I heard of your Christ, but I know little about that man. I was taught to honor the Great Spirit."

"Little Moon, we have something in common. Your Great Spirit is somewhat like our God. If you believe in the Great Spirit, you may find it possible to believe in our God. Christ is His spiritual son who represents our God." Proctor handed her his Bible. "Can you read English?"

"Yes, my mother taught me some English and I learn more English when I hunt and trade with white people. I did not go to the white man's school, so I had to learn to read and figure on my own."

"Little Moon, we have what we call the Holy Trinity."

Little Moon sat on the front of her chair. "I have also heard of that, but I know very little about it."

Father Proctor opened the Bible before her and pointed to a passage. "We have a three-in-one God. We have God, the Father; God, the Son, Jesus Christ; and God, the Holy Spirit."

Little Moon was amazed as though she'd found some hidden treasure. "You have three gods? We have only one."

Reverend Proctor rubbed his chin and thought to himself, "*I'm going to have a hard time with this.*" He looked at her with fixed eyes. "Let us start with what we both know, the Great Spirit. This is the ghost who is invisible and walks with us."

"Yes, our chief thinks the Great Spirit lives somewhere invisible in the sky."

"We think that, too. We also think the all-powerful Father is invisible and lives in a place we call heaven."

"Father Proctor, would you explain heaven to her?" Phillipe requested.

"Yes it is a magnificent place we hope to live in when we die and forever live with our Father who made us."

"Sir, my people believe our Great Spirit is powerful and will gather us after death."

"*This is getting easier.*" Father Proctor relaxed.

"Yes, now I want to discuss His Son. His Son is the man-god who lived in our world long ago. He can connect us from this world to the world of our Father. God, the Father; God, the Son; and God, the Holy Spirit are combined into one, so we worship that one."

She looked at the priest with a puzzled frown. "You have three gods. I counted."

"No, little one. We have a three-in-one God."

"Reverend, you will have a tough time with this. It may take her a long time to grasp this," Dennis said.

"It isn't absolutely necessary in her case, Commander. We can make exceptions." The priest handed the Indian Princess several tracts to read and rites to memorize. "Little Moon, we will leave you alone to study these. If you can answer my questions satisfactorily, we will deem you to become a Catholic like Commander and Mrs. McDill and Lieutenant DuBois." He turned to Dennis. "I'd like to look at your chapel. Commander, may I?"

"Yes. It's not completely finished, but we think you can have a wedding ceremony in it, even if it isn't dedicated yet."

"Do not worry, Commander. I have married people out of doors under the beautiful trees."

Natives were already gossiping about the private meetings that Phillipe and Little Moon were having. Someone in the village accidentally saw them in a passionate clinch beside the river. He described it in detail to his friends. Some laughed and some frowned.

Little Moon's mother, Clear Sky, had to screw up her courage to tell her husband, Brave Running Elk about their engagement. Since Running Elk had already promised her to another man, Clear Sky knew this would erupt into an onslaught of curses. She dreaded this more than any other thing she had to do in her life. To ease the situation, she cooked her husband his favorite beef stew. *"I'll tell him after he has a good meal,"* she reasoned with a tinge of doubt

Arriving at his hut, Running Elk and his friend proudly displayed the large buck they had killed. "This'll be many meals for our families. You take half and I'll take the other," Running Elk suggested. After they divided their meat, Running Elk heaved his half through the hut door. Half a buck filled a large space in the hut. Clear Sky congratulated her husband and offered him a large bowl of hot beef stew. The hungry hunter swallowed the entire bowl of stew and asked for more. She served him four helpings until he rubbed his full stomach. Running Elk reached for his long pipe, crammed in some tobacco, and lit it with a quick burning straw. Clear Sky knew she had to tell him soon.

"May I come over and sit with you?" she asked.

"Sure, I'll move and give you some room."

"Running Elk, I must tell you something." She swallowed twice. "Little Moon is engaged to get married."

"That is good news! I thought they'd never find the time after I promised her to him."

"It's not like that." She hesitated and braced for a verbal blitz.

"What do you mean?" Running Elk twisted to see her face.

"She wants to marry another man, a white man." Clear Sky drew her body in a tight ball.

Running Elk leaped up and stomped the floor like a horse kicking dirt. His curses scorched the ceiling of his hut. Wind from his lungs made the walls bulge. He broke his pipe stem over his knee. Everybody in the village heard him bellow like a fighting bull pawing to charge. "I will not let my daughter marry another man, especially a white man. I gave a promise. My honor will be tarnished forever!" he screamed to the sky.

Running Elk's tirade lasted several minutes until he settled down to a cynical growl. "Wife, do you know where she is now?"

"I saw her paddle down the river, but I cannot tell you exactly where she went. It was early yesterday. She spent the night here and left at dawn."

"She's been gone all day?"

"Yes. And all night. I was worried, but I couldn't find you while you were out hunting for two days and nights."

"Wife, why didn't you tell the others. They could help you search." His chiding elevated.

"Something tells me she's safe. She probably ran into the arms of the man she loves. Little Moon told me about the engagement and left. I believe she went to her man and she is all right."

"She may be safe, but that white man's not safe," he snarled.

"You know and I know, promising a daughter to someone is an old and unfair custom. We must let our children decide for themselves." Clear Sky's face flashed from tan red to dark red and her eyes blazed.

"Woman, I'll take this into my own hands. She'll not marry a white man. Remember, whites took some of our hunting territory from us. Their reservations for us are nothing more than outdoor prisons." He pulled her by her shoulders. "Woman, you seem to be taking Little Moon's side."

"Running Elk, You know I do not agree with arranged marriages, no matter what race she chooses to live with the rest of her life."

"But I promised, and I intend to keep that promise." Elk's grinding teeth showed his persistence.

"Then what will you intend to do?"

"I don't know, yet. I will powwow with my friends." Running Elk huffed out of his tent, looked straight ahead, passed three huts and halted in front of the village hogan. Inside, two men huddled over a warming fire and lit their pipes. Others sat cross-legged in clouds of tobacco smoke.

"Friends, I need your help. My daughter is marrying a white eyes. You know I promised her to one of our own."

The men nodded in agreement.

"Have you seen Cougar Mountain? He's entitled to my daughter. He's the son of my best friend."

Two fire warmers pointed to the second hut across from their hut. Running Elk spun to face the other side of the path.

In five giant strides, he was at the bachelor's hogan. "Cougar Mountain, we need talk. You and I have much trouble."

The muscular Cougar Mountain bent down to keep from hitting the top of the entrance. Cougar positioned himself directly in front of Running Elk. "What kind of trouble?"

"Little Moon is trying to wed a white man. I willed her to you."

Cougar's huge brown eyes shot out balls of lightening. The giant howled like a volcano ready to vomit its hot lava over the entire settlement.

"No white eyes will marry my Little Moon. You and my father, you slit your wrists. You're blood brothers. I honor you as Little Moon's father. I'll kill that man." Cougar hissed and lunged toward his horse. Running Elk stepped directly in front of the titan, then dodged to avoid being trampled.

"Wait, I have a plan. We'll get rid of the white one and bring her back."

Cougar charged toward his horse, but Running Elk tripped him. The behemoth brute dropped like a pile of rocks sending clouds of dust everywhere. Running Elk helped Cougar stand and brushed him off.

"Will you listen? I have a plan to get every one of those white ones."

Cougar Mountain cooled down to a cinder. "All right, what do you have, my friend?"

"I want you to go into the white man's town, find Little Moon and her lover. Find out what they're doing. Then come back to see me soon."

"You are wise. Now can I get my horse?" He decided to mount quickly to avoid a longer conversation. Riding to town, Cougar Mountain mumbled, shook his fists, and cursed. In town, Cougar saw white men and women laughing and talking. He muttered, *"If I see Little Moon, I'll hide."*

Comer recognized the horse and rider instantly. "Cougar, what brings you to town? Need supplies?" Comer covered his eyes from the blinding rays to see the Goliath leaning over to answer him. "Yeah, I think I'll get some flour, if they got any left."

"Sure thing, There's enough flour to feed your whole tribe in the storage room back of the grocery store."

"Mr. Comer, Little Moon's family is worried. They don't know where she went. Is she in town?"

"Yes, I think Little Moon and Lieutenant DuBois went to the church to see the priest."

"Which one?" Cougar scanned the street.

"The one that's being built. Suppose you know about that."

"I heard. And I found out she's marrying someone," Cougar replied.

At that, Cougar wheeled his horse around and headed for the woods behind the chapel. Tree lines provided perfect cover, so he tied his horse and crept to it among the hardwoods. No one heard him. He crawled to the side of the chapel and looked around to see if anyone saw him. Outside he was alone. Inside he heard strange words. Little Moon was talking with two men. He made a vain attempt to understand what the strange words meant. Once in a while he understood their English, but Latin? Frustrated, he mounted and galloped back to his village.

Cougar's stallion snorted when he saw Running Elk. Cougar slid off his animal's back. "She's in little church with person who wears round collar. He talks in unknown tongue."

"You saw a priest. Do you think he was marrying them?"

"They were alone with the priest. There'd be more if they powwowed to marry, wouldn't they? The church'd be full." Cougar had one ingredient. He could reason as well as most.

"Cougar, they were just practicing for the real thing. I went to a white wedding where white people think their practices made weddings perfect."

"I know nothing about white man's practicing for a wedding," he admitted, and wanted to forget what Little Moon planned.

"My young friend, you have more to learn about white eyes. Now I know we have time to make my plan work."

"Phillipe, now that we have practiced your part and you know the rituals, please excuse Little Moon and me. I will need to instruct her more and have a prayer session. This will take some time."

"How long, Father?"

"Son, I want to be very sure. It will probably take two hours or more. There is much she needs to memorize on her own."

"That long, Reverend?" Phillipe hated to leave his bride-to-be.

"The Roman Church would not recognize her as the wife of a Catholic unless she learns our ways."

To occupy his mind, Phillipe decided to go down to the pier, take another look at the ships and apologize to each one of them for leaving them in worse shape. Phillipe looked around to see that no one was listening, so nobody would think he was mentally unstable if they heard him talking to ships. Seven ships' skeletons and one sailor were alone at the dock that day. Leland was the nearest. *"Little one, we truly regret that you were deserted after you gave your service to our country and...."*

Before the next phrase, two men jumped onto the pier from a canoe they had hidden under the landing. Both his arms were pinned behind his back and a strong hand covered his mouth. Phillipe could hardly breathe. He wrenched his body in both directions for freedom from four arms bulging with muscles. He tried to open his mouth enough to bite the hand that covered his lips. The hand clutched so hard, his mouth was clamped shut. Ropes looped over his wrists almost tight enough to stop his blood from circulating. More ropes were tied to his ankles until his muscles ceased to move. One arm picked up his shoulders while the huge hand still held his mouth. Two other arms picked up his legs. They tossed Phillipe into a waiting dugout. In the little boat, one knee pressed so hard against his chest he couldn't wiggle. When the hand released his mouth, a gag and blindfold were administered. Phillipe heard only the soft strokes of the oars. From the grunts, he realized they must be pushing upriver.

Cougar Mountain was so angry, he bent over the prone body and landed a blow to the side of his head. Phillipe's brain stopped, totally unconscious. How long, he couldn't calculate. When he awoke, he was tied to a tree trunk in the midst of dark, thick woods. "Whitey, that should hold you. You can forget Little Moon."

⚓

Down river at the chapel, Father Proctor finished his quiz, patted Little Moon on the back, and congratulated her. "You have done supremely well. It will be my pleasure to officiate at your wedding."

"Thank you, Father. May I go now?" She was anxious to see Phillipe.

"Certainly. Get your lover. I have two more days."

Little Moon burst out the front door expecting to see Phillipe. She saw no Phillipe. She darted down the street looking at every house and store. She ran down to the station to ask Comer. Comer couldn't help. She raced to the Ellis Manor. No one had seen Phillipe. Little Moon found Dennis McDill walking toward the dock. "Commander, have you seen Phillipe anywhere?"

"No, I thought he was with you."

"The priest wanted to see me alone for the test and to pray, so he excused Phillipe to wait until we finished."

"No, Little Moon. I haven't seen Phillipe for a while. Let's check all the houses and buildings. I don't believe he'd go somewhere and not return to you. I know he'll keep his promise. He's a loyal person."

McDill got word to his crew to quit work and help search for DuBois. Hearing their order, the crew's faces looked like tunnels of anxiety. Rogers feared more than anyone else for his roommate. "God, I hope he's not dead," he moaned. McDill aligned the men by twos and asked them to spread out for the search.

⚓

Still alive, Phillipe DuBois cocked his eyes at the sparkling point of a twelve-inch knife blade approaching his throat. Even though his mouth was free, he could only move his head slightly. None of his limbs could move under the grip of layers of rope. DuBois stared at the glistening blade. "What do you want?" he squealed as loud as he could.

"Little Moon," snapped Cougar Mountain. "She's mine, not yours."

"How she could love a savage like you?"

Cougar came into focus and touched the knife point to the skin of DuBois' neck. "She may be in love with a dead man."

"If you kill me, she certainly won't love you."

Cougar hissed and swiped the knife point across Phillipe's neck, barely touching the skin. "No matter. I want her. She's promised to me. I won't kill you. We'll just hold you in this place until she changes her mind. If she won't, we'll let Nature do the job. You can stay tied to this tree until you starve to death."

"You'd be guilty of kidnaping, blackmail and murder anyway." Phillipe strained to his limit against the ropes. His neck began to bleed.

Behind Cougar twigs were breaking fast. "Cougar, we'd better move him before they come to the village. You and I will be the first ones they'll look for." Running Elk began to remove several cords around the lieutenant's legs. "Remember our secret place up Snake Creek? They'll find it hard to find us there. I'll send a note to Little Moon in the white man's town. She'll have to change her mind or her white eyes is dead."

Phillipe's hands remained tied. Elk looped a rope around his neck and pulled hard, just hard enough to get him to move. "Come on, white man. Get in the wagon." An old horse, three men, and a squeaky wagon bumped along a narrow path, which was just wide enough for the vehicle. Weeds and briars scraped the sides of the wagon as it moved slowly down the winding road. Darkness and numerous thickets prevented Phillipe from recognizing the territory. He tried hard to memorize the trail, but failed. Soon, he heard water as it wiggled among the rocks. Faintly, he discerned the outline of an unpainted shack. He was yanked by the neck out of the wagon, dragged across the weeds, and tied to a heavy center post inside the dimly lit shanty. "You will get no food or water until Little Moon rejects you," Elk vowed.

Little Moon was frantic with swelling tears wetting her cheeks. The McDills tried to console the little bride-to-be. It was difficult, so they diverted her attention. "Little Moon, do you know anyone who would snatch Phillipe?" Dennis asked.

She sobbed more, then wiped her face. "I hate to believe it, but my father might be mad enough to do such a thing. His honor is at stake because he made a promise."

"You women stay here in the house. I'm going to find Deputy Seely. He's the only law man around since the sheriff got injured. And he has limited duty." Dennis scrambled to find Seely's hut.

Seely lived by himself in a shack outside of town. For a single man, he was very clean.

He kept an immaculate home. The lawman was stocky and strong as a bull. His hip bore a .45 and he always toted a double-barreled shotgun. Seely was cleaning his shotgun when McDill knocked. "Come in. The door's unlocked."

McDill peered in the open door. "Seely, we've got a problem."

Deputy Seely looked up. "What kind of problem?"

"We suspect Lt. DuBois may be kidnaped. We can't find him anywhere."

"Commander, you don't believe he got chicken and left town to avoid getting married, do you?"

"Now, Seely, you know better than that. He's a man of his word." McDill's rancor indicated he was mildly insulted.

"Any suspects?" Seely questioned.

"Yes, Little Moon figures her father's angry enough to abduct Phillipe."

Seely probed. "Why is that?"

"Her father promised her to another man called Cougar Mountain. He might be in on this."

"That giant that lives in the Indian village upriver?"

"Yeah, maybe he's the one." Dennis didn't really know, but he agreed anyway.

Seely drew in his belt and picked up his shotgun. "I'll round up a posse pronto." The deputy loaded his shotgun, invited McDill outside, and went behind the house to get to his horse. "Commander, meet me at the pier. I'll deputize some well-armed men. You and your boys get seven or eight boats and canoes ready to float."

Seven vessels were loaded with six sailors, eight citizens, and one deputy sheriff. Seely stood on the pier just before he got in his boat. "Raise your right hands." Every man swore with their right hands and held guns in their left hands. "You swear to uphold the laws of this state, so help you God?" Affirmations were unanimous.

Seely jumped in his canoe. "Follow me. Let's hurry."

Seven small crafts looked like one tiny armada. Oars strained against the relentless currents that could sometimes push a ship eighteen-knots-an-hour downstream. Determination kept each man's stamina flowing. When they saw empty dugouts resting on the bank, Seely signaled the posse to halt. "Stop. Wait here. The Commander and I will go in alone. I just want to question someone first."

The first native was an old man. His hat almost covered his eyes, and his fishing rod rested on the bow of his boat. Seely couldn't tell whether the old one was awake or asleep. "Hello, my friend," the deputy hollered.

The ancient one immediately recognized Seely. "Deputy, glad to see you again. Haven't seen you since you were hauling drunks to jail."

"No, Chief, it's been some weeks. I want to ask you something."

"Ask me anything." The chief pushed the brim of his hat backwards.

"Where's the hut of Running Elk?"

The old man leaned over and pointed to the shore. "See our little jetty? Look to your right. You'll see a row of huts. It's the third one."

"Thanks. Come to see me sometime. I'll be glad to see you and talk about the medical herbs you have," Seely offered.

"I'll be in town next week." The chief pulled his brim back down.

Deputy Seely and Dennis beached their little canoe onto the empty slip at the end of the jetty. One short man and one tall man strode side by side until they reached the third hut. Outside, a woman sat on the ground with her head in her hands. She was distraught and appeared weary from lack of sleep. "Clear Sky?" Seely bent over to ask the woman. She looked up with an expression of surprise.

"Deputy?"

"Yes, do you know where Running Elk is?"

"No, I'm worried. He left before I knew it, and he didn't leave a message. It's not like him. He always let's me know."

"Think hard." McDill took her hand.

"Well, if he didn't go to town, he may have gone to his hunting shack."

"Where?" McDill asked.

"About two miles up the James, north of your town."

"Tell us more," Seely requested.

"On the right you'll see two sycamores almost joined. The hut is directly behind them. It's close enough for our men to fish and hunt."

"I hate to tell you, Clear Sky, but your husband's our prime suspect."

"Oh no! What do you think he did?" she cried aloud.

"We don't know exactly, but he may have kidnaped Lieutenant DuBois." Seely frowned and turned away knowing there was no way he could console her. "Thanks for the information. I know our search will worry you more, but it's our job."

"Let's go, Seely," Dennis urged.

Both men jumped into their waiting canoe. The posse saw them pull out and followed them. Chief Rogers was puzzled. "We couldn't find Lieutenant DuBois nowhere in town. You think he's way upriver in the woods?" he shouted to his boss.

"Yes, Chief, we're going a mile or two farther to look for Running Elk's hunting shack."

Upstream was difficult. Hard strokes were needed for the little vessels to shoot into the center stream. Trees seemed to pass by slowly and they struggled. In an hour they spotted the twin woody perennials and coasted to the front of the Y-shape of the twin plants. The outline of a small shanty hidden among the woods was hard to spot at first. "Check your guns, men," Seely ordered. "Get low and crawl behind us."

Dennis parted some tall grass to see more clearly. Armed like a two-fisted gunman, Seely drew his pistol and raised his shotgun. Two men stood outside the hovel—a giant and a middle-aged man with long, straight hair down his shoulders. The giant's shoulders spread almost four feet.

"Let's take 'em alive if we can," Dennis whispered. "If Phillipe's there, they'll try to resist. I'll take the big one and you take the other one."

"Okay, let's go up and pretend we're hunting deer," whispered the deputy.

Dennis laid down his gun. Seely shouldered his shotgun and yelled, "Hey! You seen any deer?"

Startled, both men backed themselves to the cabin door. Seely and McDill slowed down. "We're hoping to bag some deer. Did you men get one yet?" Seely asked.

Running Elk and Cougar Mountain, unarmed, stood still. "No, we went earlier. We find no deer," Elk answered. "You're a little late; watering time is over now."

Cougar eyed Dennis curiously.

"Well, Elk, truth is we've been trying to find Lieutenant DuBois. Have you seen him?"

"We haven't seen him," Elk answered nervously with both eyes darting back and forth from the woods to the door.

"Can we go inside? We're getting cold." Dennis pretended to shiver.

Suddenly both kidnappers leaped on Seely and Dennis. Colossus's arms picked McDill up and threw him into a clump of bushes. Running Elk took hold of Seely's shotgun and wrestled him to the ground. Dennis jumped out of the bushes. His head butted the giant's stomach. Cougar Mountain caught Dennis with a sharp uppercut and sent him backward with blood gushing from his nose. Running Elk grabbed the shotgun from Seely and held it to his head. McDill got up again. "I'll blow the man's head off if you don't give up," Running Elk shouted. McDill and Seely froze.

Inside the hut, Phillipe could hear the ruckus outside. His mouth was gagged and his neck was still bleeding, but he managed to groan as loud as he could. That distracted Running Elk long enough for Dennis to bound across and snatch the shotgun from Running Elk's hand. He pointed the weapon skyward and pulled the trigger, hoping the posse would come running. "Grab that ox." He pointed to Cougar. In seconds the entire posse surrounded the cabin. Three caught Cougar just before his next attack. McDill ripped open the door and saw Phillipe wounded, gagged and bound to the center post.

Ungagged, Phillipe muffled, "Thank God you came, Sir. I thought I'd starve to death before anyone got here."

"You two are under arrest for kidnaping and attempted murder." Seely reached for his handcuffs. As soon as he said that, Cougar darted into the woods and disappeared. Four men chased him. For hours they ran through thickets, hardwoods, and briars. They finally gave up and paddled home. "At least we have Running Elk. When we get more men, we'll continue." Seely finished cuffing his attacker and shoved him in the boat.

Fatigued, Dennis McDill climbed on his front porch. Footsteps could be heard as he sat. "A telegram for you, Dennis." Comer handed him the paper to Dennis.

"I knew it was coming. The trial's convening in ten days. I hope my attorney is prepared."

Father Proctor saw Little Moon standing in front of the chapel. She gazed at the top of the newly formed roof. "My heart's aching, Father. I love Phillipe, but I love my father, too."

"Think of it this way. Of course your father may be in serious trouble, but I can't believe he would kill Phillipe. The deputy sheriff told me that your father admitted to the kidnaping, but Cougar Mountain actually threatened to slay your Phillipe. He will be tried for attempted murder."

"But my father?"

"Circumstances. He was doing what he thought was honorable. Not legal for us, but honorable for him. He may have to go to prison, but for a short time, I hope."

"I pray you're right, Father."

"Now the question is. Do you want to get married now? I can stay two more days if you want to get married soon."

"I've talked with Phillipe. We want to get married as soon as possible."

"You want Dennis McDill to be your temporary father and give you away to Phillipe, as is our custom?" Proctor already knew her answer.

"It will be an honor, Father. I'll talk with Phillipe. He should be rested by now. His wound won't show under his clean white collar. Miss Ellis let me borrow her mother's wedding dress that she had saved for herself. Father, you know I'm ready."

"Little Moon, you women have thought of everything. If everybody agrees, shall we have the ceremony tomorrow afternoon at 2:00 p.m.? I want you two married before Commander McDill has to leave for his trial."

Frantic preparations projected the wedding party into a frenzy. They buzzed around like angry bees after a hungry bear. Several ladies of the town baked bread, cooked chickens, and created delectable pies for the celebration. Even though the chapel was not finished, garlands of flowers were strung from ceiling to floor. Phillipe and Little Moon invited all the crew and several acquaintances. By midnight the couple flopped exhausted in their respective beds. At dawn they went back to the chapel to clean up debris created by the rushed wedding preparations. By 1:00 p.m., people began to occupy the pews. Shortly after, Chief Rogers, serving as best man, escorted Phillipe out of the barn, hefted him into a carriage and commanded the horse to gallop to church. Father Proctor, Rogers, and Phillipe were in place waiting for Dennis and Little Moon to appear down one of the narrow aisles. The chapel was so full, many guests had to stand. A violinist, hired by Comer, began to play the familiar march for the bride and her "father" to start down the aisle.

Dennis and Little Moon were halfway down to the priest when people inside turned their heads at a billowing alarm. "SMOKE!" someone yelled inside the front door. Black fingers of cloudy, dark mist coiled under the doors. Flames licked the outside walls. It was chaos. People stumbled over each other to get out. Disorganized shouting could be heard for two blocks. McDill called to his crew. "Man the well! I want every bucket moving. Form a line and start pouring water."

Father Proctor calmed people and herded them gently in line toward the front door so they could proceed quickly.

"MacEaton, you dip out the water. McConnell you start the bucket line. O'Malley, Sullivan, pour water on that fire. The rest of you get in the bucket line." Dennis took full charge. MacEaton dropped the roped bucket down to the bottom of the well. Half the water spilled before it reached the top. In a flash he poured the water in the first pail in the line. The young seaman moved so quickly he made up for the lost water. McDill had changed the chaos to a well-managed rescue. In fifteen minutes the fire smoldered into steaming cinders. The entire corner of the building was burned so badly it seemed ready to collapse. Little Moon almost collapsed from sobbing. "Who'd be so cruel?" she wailed. Phillipe ran over and drew her head to his chest.

McDill turned and answered, "I don't know."

Two riders' horses sloshed through swampy mud avoiding the quicksand. They almost broke their horses' ribs trying to garner every ounce of speed. Both animals lathered heavily with fatigue. The riders stopped and dismounted near an old sunken sloop. "Cougar Mountain," his friend panted. "You think you burned every man and woman in the church?" He looked back pretending he could see the embers.

"Yeah, I hope that white devil's dead."

"And Little Moon, too?" His partner displayed sorrow for the little woman.

Cougar Mountain threw both arms at the sky. "If I can't have her, this is the way it's going to end," he roared. "And I don't care how many others burned with 'em."

Cougar Mountain's comrade patted soothing mud on the horses. He dowsed their firebrands in the muddy water and buried them in the mud below the water level. "These could be evidence if they caught us."

"If I finished everybody in that church, I don't care." Cougar Mountain snapped.

"Well, Cougar. Want to surrender and take the consequences?"

"We'll hide here where they won't find us, at least for a while. Then we'll have time to think."

"You think Running Elk will report us, Cougar?"

"I don't know. One time he cared for his daughter. I don't know. We'll wait and see what happens. I'd be a fool to think Seely won't suspect it's me."

Rolled blankets from horses' backs were the only protection between the two arsonists and the sticky swamp mud. No fire could be lit for fear of being discovered, so jerky and canned beans became the night's meal. Each man had a blanket and a pistol to keep warm and to shoot any intruder that had the misfortune to stumble into their soggy bivouac. Night owls and stray dogs furnished a program filled with somber serenades. Several times Cougar stirred from his make-shift bed, growling in his sleep for revenge. Deep down he knew that Little Moon and her lover would survive the church fire, however he calculated that would make her reflect and reconsider. All he had left was a single thought that there was more to come. His uncontrolled blinding bitterness was forcing him to wish he could find a way to kill them both. The huge man pulled out his curved dagger, honed it to its sharpest, and inspected it over the brightness of the cinders. With the knife he purposely cut his arm. Cougar swore with each drop of blood that he would kill his adversaries. By the time his ritual stopped, sunshine had pushed through the swamp's underbrush. Breakfast was another round of jerky for the men and a few blades of marsh grass to satisfy their horses. Jumping on his horse, Cougar Mountain yelled to his companion, "Come on. Let's go. I've got some business to take care of." They raced at a full gallop until they reached the edge of the town that had awakened with the rising sun. Cougar pulled tight on his rein and held up his hand like a policeman's order to stop. Down the street, several feet away, Phillipe and Little Moon were strolling for a morning walk. His neck was still bandaged. Without hesitating, Cougar spurred his horse and charged in a direct line toward Phillipe's back. When the horse reared, its hoof caught Phillipe's shoulder throwing him down on his face.

Cougar slid from horseback with his knife slicing the midair. The dagger sank between Phillipe's shoulder blades. Phillipe screamed in utter agony. Cougar spun around, caught Little Moon by the waist and slung her over his horse. He mounted directly behind her, kicked his horse, and vanished into the woods below the city. Phillipe was bleeding to death. Little Moon was kidnaped.

"Come in, Monroe." Admiral Hicks had to see Albert. He pushed his chair back and stood to greet the anxious attorney. "You know we have less than ten days for the trial."

Albert stopped in front of the officer's desk, shaking from excessive fatigue. "Yes Sir, I know. We'll do our best to be ready."

"Young man, you'd better be ready. We replaced Captains Mort and Fritzgerald, and we've secured one of the best trial lawyers in the Navy. This case is going to be a sticky one, and I want everything done by the book."

"I know," Albert replied.

"I want you and McDill in court at 9:00 a.m. sharp, nine days from tomorrow. I cannot grant you any more time. Understand?"

"Yes, I'll get a message to the commander and we'll be there on time."

Out of habit, the admiral snapped, "Dismissed." Monroe almost saluted the four stars on the officer's uniform. When he turned to leave, Albert staggered. With a brief struggle, he reached the exit almost convulsive and nearly out of control. After working day and night, his tired muscles couldn't respond normally. He knew he needed rest. Holding a vivid grasp on the fact that he would face the best adversary that JAG could provide, he forced his ailing body into his quarters to script a message to McDill. He knew his best brief had to be prepared to perfection. And there were witnesses to summon. Revelation of the Trial Counselor Bailey's evidence was already established, but he would not know Bailey's strategies. He had to be ready for anything. Albert's thoughts ceased when he reached the door of his room. He had to rest. The worried man flopped into bed fully clothed.

Shortly before waking, the barrister's dream factory cranked at full speed. He saw a battlefield with a 20-foot judge's bench at one end and two men, one much larger than the other, throwing paper balls at each other. The bench lowered to the level of the battlefield. A large gavel pounded the ground until it shook like an earthquake. Scattered paper balls tumbled all over the ground. The enormous gavel pulverized the soil around its edges. Papers bounced with every strike of the gigantic hammer. Words boomed out like thunder— *Guilty! Guilty! GUILTY!*

Albert's bones locked into place in the middle of his bed. Sweat sprang in little rivers down his head, his forehead and his face. Albert lost control of his body movements. He could not quit shaking. Albert did manage to get dressed and make a cup of coffee, which shook nearly all the liquid out of his cup before he could drink the remainder. After coffee, bacon and two runny eggs, the young lawyer finally regained composure enough to scribble a few words. On a blank paper he scratched:

TO: COMMANDER DENNIS MCDILL, CITY POINT, VIRGINIA.: TRIAL IS SET NINE DAYS FROM TODAY. COME EARLIER. LET ME KNOW WHEN YOU WILL ARRIVE. WE NEED OUR BEST STRATEGY. WE HAVE A VERY COMPETENT FOE. I AM HOUSED IN HEADQUARTERS BARRACKS. FROM: ALBERT MONROE.

Sweat continued to stream down until his shirt was completely wet. Searing heat scorched his brain. Two blocks beyond Headquarters emerged a tiny telegraph office. Inside, a gaunt, straight-haired figure bent over a small desk behind a counter. He ignored Albert's entrance and continued to copy from the clicks of his machine as he hunched busily over his work. Clearing his throat loudly, Albert figured the man would notice him. The skinny figure with light brown thinning hair never looked up. Albert cleared his throat again, louder than before. Finally the bony fingers stopped and two dark brown eyes looked at Monroe over his half eyeglasses. "May I help you?"

"I want to send this message."

The clerk scanned the document, counted the words, took his pencil and figured the cost. Albert pulled out two silver dollars from his pocket. "Here, keep the rest. You see my address. I'll be there in a few minutes. You can deliver, can't you?"

"Yes, Sir. No need to tip. I'll give the rest of this to my delivery boy."

"I want to have the answer as soon as possible, even though it might take two days."

"Mister, we'll do that. Don't worry."

Attorney Monroe braced himself and ventured out to be scalded by the Indian summer's torrid light that seemed to unsheathe sharp fingernails to claw his head. Again, his perspiration streamed down his neck and back. "Someday I'm going to buy the biggest straw hat I can find," he told himself. The heat sucked his strength so much he lumbered like a drunken sailor down to Headquarters barracks. He decided not to stop to do anything else but plop on the top of his bed and get more sleep. In a few seconds Albert Monroe was sound asleep.

Next morning's temperature had already climbed to near ninety. Monroe was still in bed at 10:00 a.m. It was time for the cleaner to unlock the door and proceed to remove dirt and filth from the room. When he opened the door, he found the first room remained in neat condition. He hoped that other evidence would prove he didn't need to clean the rest of the little unit. Albert was still in bed when the cleaner opened the bedroom door. Being after 10:00 in the morning, the orderly wondered if he should gently awaken the mound in the cot. No sound nor motion issued from the lump. Bravely the cleaning man crept over to the bed and softly whispered, "It's after 10:00. Wake up, Sir." Albert's body was motionless. Then the cleaner gingerly shook the sleeper. Still no response. "Heavenly Mother, this man's dead or very sick," he shouted to himself and ran headlong through the door for help. Someone heard him and summoned an ambulance. The infirmary was three blocks from the barracks. One first class orderly sprinted into the mini hospital calling for assistance. A nurse and an intern bounced out of the ambulance. "What's wrong?" the doctor asked.

"In the barracks. A man. I can't wake him."

"Which room?" the nurse asked.

"Number 8," he replied as the medics rushed toward the barracks door.

Dr. Harris ripped the covers off Monroe's body and bent down to see if he was breathing. "This man's hardly breathing. He's barely alive."

"Thank God," the nurse prayed. "He had all the signs of death."

"I can smell what little breath this guy has. I think he's been poisoned," Harris diagnosed.

McDill and O'Connell dashed toward the Ellis Manor to ask permission to hold a reception in the great house on the Point. They halted, paralyzed to eye witness the attack on DuBois and the abduction of Little Moon. "O'Connell, take the Lieutenant to the doctor. You're strong enough to carry him. I'll confiscate that horse behind us." McDill rotated and leaped on the horse. Man and horse raced after the giant who fled into the brush with Little Moon.

DuBois slumped to the ground semi-conscious, bleeding between his shoulder blades. O'Connell ripped off his own shirt, wadded it in a ball and pressed it hard on the blood-spurting wound. Then he tore the arm of DuBois' shirt, secured the wad and tied it around the lieutenant's shoulders and waist. He bent down and hefted the officer on his own shoulder and jogged as fast as he could to Dr. Ellis' house.

McDill could not see the escaping villain who clutched the small woman with his right arm while he guided his horse with the other arm. Sun slits through the trees seemed to point due west. The woman was almost frozen from fear, but she was able to tear off a piece of her dress. In the heat of escaping, Cougar didn't notice. Even in the clutches of a giant gorilla, she flicked the tell-tale sign onto a briar bush. Cougar dug his heels in his horse and bent under tree limbs as they flew by. No matter how she strained at his grip, she could move very little. Her ribs felt like they might crack if he squeezed any tighter. Suddenly an idea popped into her head. She knew she had sharp teeth, so she lowered her head and opened her mouth wide. Her upper and lower jaws clamped down hard on the skin of his arm. Flinching with sudden pain, the abductor quickly let go of the brave little one. She fell to the ground and began to sprint back in the opposite direction. Cougar pulled on the reins so hard his horse bucked from pain and threw him to the ground, stunned. By the time he discovered Little Moon's escape, she had disappeared into the underbrush. His horse disappeared also. On foot, he trampled through the thick forest, thinking she would return to the town.

McDill calculated that since the pair fled into the woods at the edge of town, they headed west, so he spurred his horse in that direction. About twenty yards into the forest he spied a white object hanging on the limb of a bush. He quickly recognized it as Little Moon's and veered in the direction of the waving rag. Just then he heard a body crash through the thicket toward him. It was the frightened captive. Dennis dismounted to meet her. Just behind her was the large bulky figure of Cougar Mountain. Little Moon ducked behind Dennis for protection. Both men were unarmed. Cougar broke off a large limb and hurtled his huge frame toward his opponent. Dennis parried the blow and spun around kicking as hard as he could. His heel landed in the kidnapper's groin. Cougar doubled over and the officer chopped his neck with the side of his fist. The Goliath passed out and crumpled in a heap in front of Dennis. "Let's get out of here," Dennis shouted and pulled Little Moon toward his horse.

McDill and Little Moon mounted and sped off to town. The first sound Little Moon uttered was, "Is Phillipe all right?"

"I don't know. I ordered O'Connell to take him to the doctor."

Infirmary doctors laid Albert face down on a table, inserted a tube as far as possible and started to pump. The attorney's breath was almost gone when they started. They feared he would stop breathing entirely. Fluid splattered everywhere. Albert coughed and shook violently. With the poison outside his stomach, he felt somewhat relieved and awake. "That was close," one of the doctors sighed. "You're lucky you got here in time. If enough of that poison got in your blood, you'd be dead one."

"I've eaten nothing but some runny eggs and bacon for breakfast," Albert responded feebly.

"Did they taste okay?" a second doctor asked.

"They were soft boiled as I ordered, but I salt and pepper my food a great deal."

"Venom." One doctor looked at a sample he wiped off Albert's lips.

"Venom?" Albert screeched.

"Somebody may have slipped the poison in your soft eggs. With that much seasoning you probably couldn't detect it. It takes a while to kill."

"For God's sake, I wonder who'd want me dead," Albert wailed.

"Where did you eat breakfast?" The doctor helped the patient sit up.

"Headquarters barracks, my room. An orderly brought it."

"Sir, you rest. We'll get the authorities. You're right. Someone wants to slay you to get you out of the way for some reason."

Albert was bedded in one of the infirmary cots while a nurse was assigned to check on him every half hour. After he had rested for an hour, two patrol lieutenants walked over to his bed and asked him to describe everything that happened to him during the last twenty-four hours. Further, they asked if he knew anyone who would want him dead. Albert told them about Captain Mort and the Headquarters' I.G. But he discounted them, because they were in custody. Both officers soon concluded that these high-ranking officers might have had outside help. Albert couldn't think of any.

On a hunch, the lieutenants left to check if anyone, military or civilian, had a pet snake or snakes for any reason. They also knew potent venom could be purchased on the black market because venom was used to make anti-toxin for snake bites. Also, there are venomoids who keep dangerous snakes. It became a three-pronged investigation. More agents were called in to help. One agent scoured the area and asked if anyone had snakes for pets. He came up empty handed. One agent asked his informers about venom trading. This was foreign to his sources. They could only express indifference. One agent found a laboratory in D.C. that prepared anti-venom. Agent Cline got the address and hailed a carriage across town to a small brick building painted white, except for black wooden panels. Large cedars lined its wide path to the entrance. He was invited inside and began to question the white-coated attendant. "You people make anti-venom, do you not?"

"Yes. We make it for snake-bitten patients. We milk snake fangs every day."

"Milk? How?"

"From their fangs into little vials. We hold their heads over the vials until their fangs show and we press their heads until the venom flows out. Then, we mix the venom with hemoglobin from horses. The attendant showed them a row of vials on the first shelf.

"Hold it right there. You missed any vials lately?"

"Yeah, we did yesterday. A vial of copperhead venom. We believed it to be around here somewhere, but we couldn't find it."

"Did you report it?"

"Immediately."

All three agents gathered and started a complete search of the premises. For hours each man looked in every corner, on every inch of cabinet space, on every foot of the floor. They almost quit until one shouted. "I see it right here in the corner. It's empty."

"Don't touch it. Pick it up with your knife blade. It may have fingerprints."

It did. There were two sets. After checking and fingerprinting the lab workers, they found one that did not match with the lab specialists. "We need to see the lawyer," the older lieutenant decided.

Monroe was half awake when the two lieutenants arrived. "Mister, could you recognize the orderly who brought you your breakfast?"

"I think so. He was small, dark and walked with a kind of skipping motion."

With their help, the wobbly lawyer was carried to a lineup of six food service personnel.

Albert had to sit in front of the lineup and pointed to the shortest one. "That's him."

The orderly was fingerprinted right away. "It matches the vial." One lieutenant observed and checked the vial again. "Let's get him over to our office and ask him some questions."

Interrogation lights glared in the face of the orderly until salty beads of sweat bubbled up on his forehead. They heard an expected flow of denials. "Young man, you're in trouble up to your neck. We might give you a break if you tell us who're your working for."

More denials blew out of his mouth. The suspect decided not to cooperate.

"Fellow, do you realize we can hold you for attempted murder? That'll get you at least fifty in prison."

Large blobs of perspiration rolled down the face of the accused while he sat under the hot, steady lamp. He squirmed and looked all around for an escape.

The questioning lasted for two more hours. Being grilled hard for this length of time grated on the man's mind. "Please don't ask me any more questions. I'll tell you what happened. When I was going to mess the other day, two big gents took hold of my arms and blindfolded me. They shoved me into a wagon. We rode for what seemed like an hour. Things got dark like I was carried into a cave. I could smell vodka. When I was forced into a chair, the blindfold came off. A man with top heavy shoulders and lots of ribbons on a red uniform, moved over me. I asked him to tell me why I was there. He told me I was in the Russian Embassy. 'You want a lot of money, sailor?' I answered, 'Of course.' 'How about a thousand?' He asked kind of seriously."

The sailor paused to catch his breath.

"Go on," the older man ordered.

"Without hesitation, the Russian man told me about some new plans for a gigantic battleship that his country wanted. He said they were probably somewhere near the barracks. I could get paid $5,000 if I found them and bring them to him even if I had to kill to get 'em."

The younger patrol swung his chair around. "How did you know how to find those plans?"

"Well, I was in the lobby of the barracks when a civilian—that man in the chair—came in to register. I could see something rolled up under his arm. He asked the clerk to store it in our safe. When he went upstairs, the clerk asked me to put them in the safe because he was in a hurry to get home. I was curious, so I unrolled the bundle. There it was, a design of the largest ship I'd ever seen. So, I stuffed them in the safe and locked it right away. That's how I knew about the plans and the person who brought 'em into the barracks. I thought I'd better get rid of him, so I stole the venom from the lab and slipped it in his eggs."

"All right, put this skunk in the worst hole in the jail. Attorney, I believe we have your man. You can rest easier now."

"Thanks. I can sleep better tonight."

He ambled slowly up to his room and slid down on his bed. For a moment he glanced at his clock. "I should have heard from Dennis McDill by now. Wonder what's wrong."

⚓

"Seely, get a posse and go after Cougar Mountain. I think he may still be around, but I wouldn't count on it. Go about a mile in that southwestern direction. If he's not there, I want you to search for him somewhere else. He's guilty of kidnaping Little Moon and attempting to murder Phillipe DuBois."

Arriving, McDill slipped down from his horse and helped the exhausted native woman down. "How is Phillipe?" she cried, pulling on McDill's shirt sleeve.

"I don't know," Dennis responded. "I think the doctor is working on him now."

Little Moon scampered up the lane to the doctor's office. She stumbled up the steps of the porch and flung open the door. "How is he, Doc?"

"Pretty bad, I'm afraid. He's lost a lot of blood."

Little Moon sucked in a gasp when she saw her lover's chalk white face.

Doctor Ellis held her shoulders. "I don't want to give you too much hope. There's a new process. It might save him."

She gave a faint smile through glistening tears. "Anything, Doc. Save my Phillipe if you can. Do anything. I want my man to live."

"What kind of process, Doctor?" McDill asked.

"It's known as transfusion. I know a little about it. We take blood from one person to another, but we must be careful. The blood must match, or it won't help the patient. He could die from a mismatch."

"How can you prevent a mismatch?" McDill pried.

"By typing the blood."

"I've never heard of that." Dennis admitted.

"It's like the alphabet," the doctor explained. "Well, almost. I can check the blood under a microscope. I will draw Phillipe's blood and check his type, then I'll sample others for the same type. Then with a syringe on each end of a small tube I can pump the good blood into the patient. The good blood should save the patient."

"Type mine," Dennis offered.

"Thanks, Commander. Roll up your sleeve. I'll just need a little amount." He aimed the syringe at the inside center of Dennis forearm. Dennis flinched.

Dennis McDill felt like a medical experiment. None of the Navy doctors ever mentioned transfusing or typing blood. Dennis watched even the slightest moves the physician made to draw blood from his arm. When he got his sample, the doctor carried it to his little corner near the sterilization kettle. He slid the sample under his microscope. Prior to this, Dr. Ellis had sampled DuBois' blood. "Dennis, Phillipe's blood type is 'O.' It's very common. Give me a minute."

"Type 'O,' you say. I hope mine will be the same." Commander McDill examined the tiny hole in his forearm.

"If not, try mine next," Little Moon volunteered.

Doctor Ellis focused on Dennis' sample and shook his head slowly. "I can't use yours, Dennis. You have a rare type, 'AB,' but I'll make a record of this in case we need yours for someone else."

Little Moon stepped up to the doctor. "Here, take my blood," she urged.

Doctor Ellis nodded politely to Little Moon, who immediately thrust her entire arm in front of the physician. She winced and gritted her teeth when he punctured her skin.

"Want me to stop?" he asked with a hurt look on his face.

"No, I want my man to get well. Go on."

Again, Ellis retired to his small laboratory in the corner. In a few minutes he turned around with a smile. "You're okay, my little lady. Now, the hard part comes. I've got to hook this tube to a long needle in your vein and the other in Phillipe's vein. I'll elevate your cot. You're a heathy young woman, so I know my patient will get some good blood."

Little Moon tried in vain to look passive, but she was trembling scared as she lay in the make-shift bed beside Phillipe. She almost shouted in pain when the syringe poked her vein, but her jaws tightened with determination. She forced herself to remain absolutely still. Then she looked at her lover lying unconscious beside her. After a while it was over. She was relieved.

"We'll just have to wait and see what happens. It might take hours before the Lieutenant responds." Ellis wiped his instruments in alcohol and carefully placed them in a cabinet just above his corner laboratory.

McDill, O'Connell, Little Moon and the medical staff sat in the room watching Phillipe. No one said a word. It was like a funeral wake. Phillipe was alive, but seemed to be in a deep trance with his eyes closed and his breathing shallow. Each person offered a silent prayer for the young man lying in the bed.

Four hours dragged on into eternity. O'Connell jerked his head to keep awake. McDill paced the floor like an expectant father. The doctor felt the patient's pulse every few minutes while Mrs. Ellis kept adjusting the covers on the bed.

A lilliputian flutter from his eyelashes announced that Phillipe DuBois was regaining consciousness. Instinctively his hand reached back toward his wound. Pain hit him like the plunge of an arrow.

"Nurse, give this man some of that new medicine. It'll ease the pain."

Little Moon rushed over and pulled his hand toward her. "Phillipe, you're better. I gave you my blood."

At that Phillipe was confused. "I've got your blood?"

"It's all right, my dearest. We'll explain later. Just get well enough so we can get married."

A slender face peeked in the door. "May I come in?" Father Proctor asked. "How is he?"   "He's better. I gave him a transfusion." Doctor Ellis

170

answered. "Phillipe is alive because his betrothed volunteered a pint of her blood to her man."

Father Proctor bent over Phillipe and gave a prayer to God to help Phillipe recover.

DuBois tried to sit up on his own, but Mrs. Ellis helped him elevate his head. "There. You can see everyone in this room."

"Are we looking at hours and days to recover, Doctor? I can stay one or two more days, if you think he'll be strong enough to marry this nice young lassie," Father Proctor asked.

Dr. Ellis donned his stethoscope and examined his patient again. "If he recovers this fast and if Little Moon will take him in this shape, I would guess day after tomorrow afternoon."

Overhearing the conversation, Little Moon released Phillipe's hand and hugged him until he cringed in agony and groaned.

"I'll take him in any shape as long as we can wed. Should anybody ask, day after tomorrow will be fine, even if I have to support his whole frame to the altar." Little Moon smiled and took her arms away from her lover. Phillipe was able to produce a weak smile in spite of his pain which was slowly abating. "I want to marry this lady as soon as I can. I'd even crawl to church to do it."

"I'd haul you to the altar, Phillipe," she joked.

"I'm too heavy. I'll manage." Phillipe wobbled to his feet to prove his point.

"Why can't I get an answer from Dennis? Something's wrong, I know it." Every three hours Albert would drop in on the telegrapher even though the man agreed to send a boy with the answer. Somehow it made Albert feel some progress and helped him get a little stronger. He frequently asked, "Are you sure there's no word from Commander McDill?" He'd get a helpless shrug. Once the admiral warned the attorney to be ready, time would be a premium. Depression dropped on Albert like a ton of river jacks. He had to set strategy with Dennis, but Dennis seemed absent without leave. "God, I hope he won't skip out on us." Monroe moaned and stared out his window.

Regardless of no word from the commander, Albert proceeded to telegraph his witnesses to tell them to be in D.C. at least two days before the trial.

Albert plodded to his room and had slipped into bed when his door squeaked. *"Some ghost is coming in to haunt me, as if I don't have enough already,"* he wailed silently to himself.

A gentle knock on his door. No response. The door was unlocked.

"May I come in, Sir?" A white capped head leaned in the narrow opening. It was followed by a man in a clean white uniform and a clean-shaven face. Albert did not recognize the face, but he knew a medic's uniform.

"Yes, come in. I bet you're wanting to see if I died of poisoning."

"No, Sir. We're hoping you are recovering."

"I was able to go and send a telegram." Monroe said.

"Mr. Monroe, in your condition you need plenty of rest. When I saw you in bed, I thought that's what you were doing."

"Satisfied? I'm back in bed." Albert's edgy tone seemed to drip the smelly odor of hostility. "All right, I won't move out of this cot until tomorrow morning."

"A wise idea. But while you're resting, can we get you something?"

"Some food. I'm starving."

"I'll check the kitchen and return soon. You'll have to eat what we find."

"I know it won't be a T-Bone steak, but you'll find something that will be good for me, won't you?"

"Yes."

Albert noticed an odd smile on the medic's face. Paranoia seeped into his emotional complex. He could trust no one, and wondered if he could trust even his own ability to function. He raced across the room almost stumbling over a chair and reached for the bolt lock. *"That should be safer,"* he thought and covered himself. Before he dozed, another knock roused him. "Who is it?" His body felt like an ice pond.

"A telegram for you, Sir."

"Push it under the door," he yelled across the room, and started for the door.

"Sir, you'll have to sign this cover sheet for me, since this is a delivery."

"All right, jam the paper under the door. I'll sign."

Fumbling for a pen was a task. Where was it? "Just a minute until I find a pen." Albert's pen was in his coat pocket. His name was reduced to a few scribbles on the paper which traveled again under the door.

"Sir, is this your signature? You are Mr. Albert Monroe, aren't you?"

In a fit of irritation, he blurted, "You expected a forger?" Albert grumbled.

"No, Sir. I couldn't read your signature very well."

"Look, I'm ill. I'm not opening this door. I assure you that I am none other than Albert Monroe, Attorney from Fredericksburg. Now give me the cotton picking telegram!"

Slowly the delivery boy eased the telegram through Albert's established channel. Eagerly, the lawyer from Fredericksburg ripped open the envelope. The words were clear to his eyes, but their meaning merely bounced around his brain in an incoherent fury. It had to be from McDill, but he could not decipher its meaning. *"Did the poison affect my brain?"* he gasped. *"Dear God, what'll I do?"* He could not control his quaking mind. Courage was the only advocate he had, so he momentarily dismissed his fears and decided to ask for help, at least read the message to him. A mature thirty-one-year-old felt like a four-year-old learning the alphabet. Trying the door bolt was difficult. He seemed to loose most of his strength. The bolt yielded the door.

Albert staggered down the path to Headquarters. "Halt! State your name and your business," the loud voice of a marine yelled in his ear.

"I am an attorney from Fredricksburg. I am defending one of your Navy's officers in an impending court-martial. Admiral Hicks knows me. My name is Albert Monroe."

"Sir, wait here. We'll check."

While waiting, Albert had to brace against a wall to steady his shaking limbs. He wondered if Admiral Hicks would even speak to him in his present condition. Fact is, Hick's yeoman could read the message to him, he calculated.

"Come in now, Mr. Monroe." His eyes searched Albert's hands as they braced against the wall. "You need some help, Sir?"

"No, I can find my way to the Admiral Hick's office."

The marine motioned for another marine to follow the unsteady man weaving down the long corridor. Letters and numbers became strange to him. In fact the entire area was unknown as though his memory had abandoned him. Albert ducked into the nearest office. A table stood squarely in front inside the door. "Another recruit? You are the tenth one today." The recruiter scrutinized Monroe's whole body. "You seem to be a little old to join the Navy, aren't you?"

"I just want someone to read this to me. I can't understand the words. Yeah, I know it's in English, but I think I have a mental block or something. Here, will you read it to me?"

"Yes, but will you sit down? Your legs seem to be getting wobbly. Take this chair beside the table."

As he sat, Albert Monroe implored, "Please, for God's sake, read it to me."

"All right, I'll read it now." The recruiter unfolded the message and read aloud:

I AM DELAYED. DUBOIS WANTS TO GET MARRIED. HE HAS BEEN WOUNDED. NEEDS TIME TO HEAL. I AM GIVING THE BRIDE AWAY. I OWE IT TO THE COUPLE. I WILL COME AS SOON AS POSSIBLE. DENNIS MCDILL, U.S. NAVY LIEUTENANT COMMANDER.

Albert's whole frame weighed two tons. "My, Lord. What else?

Little Moon gently rolled back the covers on Phillipe's bed and kissed his forehead. "Wake up. Tell me how you're feeling."

His dormant eye opened slowly, but when he saw his gorgeous bride, he smiled and sat up cautiously. When he moved, pain reminded him of his injury. To his surprise it wasn't as intense. "I'm better. And I'm hungry. Can you find me something to eat?"

"Good. Some food will make you stronger." She pressed her finger against his right biceps and pinched slightly.

DuBois' quick recovery was a miracle, according to Dr. Ellis who entered to check. "I never saw a man heal so fast. You're a tough young man."

"Doctor, give the credit to this beauty sitting beside me. She could cure a dying man if he thought she'd marry him."

"Phillipe, let's not delay. You're well enough to marry. I'll fetch Father Proctor. You get dressed." Little Moon commanded like a general. "Your best suit is pressed. We kept it clean. If you noticed, I have borrowed a wedding dress. It's hanging on the door behind you."

"A wedding dress? Where did you get such a fine wedding gown?" DuBois asked, still disoriented.

"From Miss Josephine. She told me it was in her family for years. She said her mother fitted it for her wedding."

Proctor's light footfall could barely be heard when he stepped inside. Little Moon turned in surprise. "I was just leaving to get you, Father."

"I came to see how Phillipe is feeling." Proctor approached like he wanted to feel his pulse.

"Phillipe and I are ready to get married NOW!" Little Moon exclaimed and hugged her man.

"Are you sure?" Proctor looked at Phillipe for a sign.

"Absolutely," Phillipe answered and took Little Moon's hand.

"Our chapel is not completely repaired from the fire, but we'll use it anyway. We want it dedicated by Thanksgiving,"Phillipe replied.

"Little Moon, I'll give you away to this man. It's our custom. Of course, it's your decision." McDill entered and offered, hoping she would say yes.

"What a nice custom. I'd be honored to have you give me to this wonderful sailor."

"That's all settled," Proctor observed. "Commander, will you have someone get the wedding party and announce the wedding to the people?"

Dennis caught the first man coming toward his house. It was Dr. Ellis who wanted to check the patient. "Doctor, could you have someone get the entire wedding party?"

"Is the Lieutenant well already?"

"Not entirely, but well enough to marry that young lady."

Walking away, Ellis shouted back, "I'll get my everybody I can. You get your crew."

Preparation sped at a blinding pace. In two hours, all the wedding party was assembled and some people of the town went in and occupied all the seats. McDill and DuBois were dressed in their best whites. Little Moon's white gown glowed brighter than the uniforms. Father Proctor, dressed in a high priest's gold and purple robe, stood behind the altar. Chief Rogers stood beside Phillipe as best man and as a prop if he staggered or fell. No piano or harpsichord was installed. The only music was a plump soprano who sang a hymn in Latin. Her tones were so perfect and she expressed so much feeling that many women cried. Father Proctor gave prayers and invited all to join him.

Commander McDill and Little Moon marched proudly with the music until they reached the altar. "Who gives this woman to be this man's wife?" Proctor asked ceremoniously.

"I do," Dennis responded firmly. The couple knelt before the altar and Father Proctor continued to pray. He asked them to stand and give their pledges. Still feeling pain, Phillipe hesitated but bravely stood in front of his lady.

"I now pronounce you man and wife." The priest lifted his hand in blessing.

The whole assembly congratulated the couple, or so it seemed. Commander McDill was the first to kiss the bride after the groom sealed their vows with a kiss. Miss Josephine invited everyone to her manor for wine and a little celebration, which lasted until midnight.

Walking home, the McDills were silent. Dennis knew the next morning he would have to catch the first train to Washington."

⚓

Dennis rode alone on the early morning passenger car. It was planned that Helen would come later. Trying to sleep was impossible. It was not the noise of the train, it was the noise of his brain. His mind saw Lizzy standing with a smoking shotgun over a dead body while the acrid smoke flooded McDill's nostrils. He could feel hard metal crush her husband's head by an escapee turned killer, and Gaith's dead body thrown in the swamp for whatever wanted to eat it. Not that the convict did not deserve to die, but disposal of his remains was barbaric.

Dennis could see his enemies parading in front of him and mocking him with sardonic laughs. His muscles tensed when he remembered his own perilous predicament. For the first time in his life, the brave seaman faced the potent god of fear. He knew when Helen joined him at the trial, he would be less afraid. But for now, he was petrified.

Dennis' train slowed to a halt. A few passengers got off from the other cars. Many people stamped onto the train and pushed Dennis back while he tried to dismount. One bump almost caused him to lose his little suitcase. He held on tight and dodged the human traffic. He hoped perhaps Albert was in the train station to meet him. He searched the station twice. Albert was not there. Maybe Albert did not know exactly which train Dennis would take, but Dennis remembered that Monroe told him once about the barracks. "That's it, Headquarters Barracks."

Several taxi carriages were all filled. He had to step out in the street to be noticed. A large stallion reared, just missing McDill's head. "Mister, if you want us that bad, I'll stop and open the door for you."

"Take me to the United States Navy Headquarters. Here's your fare in advance with a tip if you hurry."

The horse stood on hind legs at the crack of the driver's whip and bolted forward. Dennis' head flew back, hitting the hard carriage wall. He was dazed, but managed to grip the sides of the seat to steady himself as the coach crashed through dozens of vehicles and pedestrians. For a moment McDill regretted he gave a reward for speed. "*Was it worth a bump on the head?*" he wondered. Minutes later, he wheeled out of the carriage and reached in to grab his luggage. "*Whew! That was one of the roughest rides I've ever had.*"

Sailors walked in quick-step as though a war had hit the city. The building he was directed to looked like a house of ghouls, but he went in anyway.

"Is this the barracks?" Monroe asked.

The man at the desk was probably retired and earning a meager wage. "Can I help you, Mister?"

"Yeah, what room's Albert Monroe's?"

"Number 8. Down the hall. He's just back from the infirmary." He pointed with a crooked finger that ended with a nail as long as the fingernail of a witch.

Number 8 was four doors down, odd numbers on one side, even on the other. Dennis knocked directly on the figure 8. No answer. He knocked again, a little louder.

"Who is it?" a soft voice verbalized weakly.

"It's me. Dennis McDill."

Albert pulled back the deadbolt and cracked the door to see if there was a Dennis McDill at his door. "Thank goodness. Come in. I have been expecting you for a long time."

"Sorry, I had some delays." He looked down at the man in the doorway that he thought was Albert Monroe. "What happened to you? You look awful. You on a drinking binge or something?"

"Long story, Dennis. Don't worry about me. Let's concentrate on the trial. Sit over there and have some coffee."

Dennis pulled in his traveling bag, plopped it down, and rested his chin in his hands. "My trip here was not so good. I kept remembering some of the horrors of my past year."

"Dennis, we're in trouble. Headquarters has appointed their best lawyer to prosecute. I have some fingerprints on documents, enough to have Captain Mort in the brig waiting for trial. The I.G. is a prime suspect, also. And I have one or two witnesses. You'd think we had a strong case, but I'm not sure, and to make matters worse—look at me, I'm sick."

"Man, you look like a corpse already. Really, what's wrong with you?" Dennis was aghast.

"Poison, I think. It left me in this condition."

"What can we do, Albert?" Dennis asked with a helpless expression.
"Get them to appoint one of their defense attorneys, I guess."

⚓

While Monroe prepped for a trial, another trial in Richmond had been postponed for almost one year. It was Lizzy's. Her trial was entrapped in political debate. Half the Commonwealth thought she should go to trial and be punished. Half the Commonwealth believed the whole incident should be dismissed summarily. The Commonwealth's Court had great difficulty obtaining an unbiased jury. Some citizens marched in front of the Capitol with signs reading "No Trial for Lizzy." The scene became nasty. Criminal court turned into the vortex of a small-scaled civil war.

When the debate paused with a jittery peace, the trial was set and a jury was appointed. All of the jurors were taken from the far western section of the state to insure at least a minimum of objectivity.

Lizzy readily admitted shooting the escaped con, but there was the matter of a non existent corpse. Where was it and how did it get there? Since it was evident that Lizzy couldn't tote such a heavy body, she certainly could not carry it away to some hideaway. Marshal Moore was called in since the escaped victim fled U.S. Navy Prison. Prosecutors thoroughly questioned Moore. He was still looking for a body or a grave in the swamp. From memory, he could recollect some of the people he questioned at City Point and what they told him. Jonathan Moore was grilled for a whole day on the stand. Prosecutors were nonproductive and deeply frustrated.

Lizzy's lawyer moved that the case be dismissed for justifiable homicide and a body that could not be found. The motion was accepted and Lizzy was freed. Lizzy was in the clear, but she still longed for her Clyde, one of the country's best locomotive engineers.

Among Lizzy's sympathizers were five sailors from the town, a short sail of 23 miles to Richmond. The entire population seemed to sway to her side and newspapers wrote pages of praise for the little lady with the big shotgun. Many firms offered her good jobs.

As Lizzy's case was closed, a man sent her flowers. The card read, "From: Chief Petty Officer, Sam Rogers."

Chapter VII

Albert Monroe felt he had no legs. He doubted that a substitute defender would have the energetic loyalty and dedication to his case as he did. His eyes looked like sinkholes, he had lost hair on several parts of his body, and some days he shook like dried leaves in a tornado. "Dennis, I'm afraid I have to bow out. My doctors say I have complications, maybe pneumonia and God knows what else. I'll have to be hospitalized."

"For heaven's sake, keep trying to get well," Dennis pled.

"I'll have to tell the Panel that I'm unable to attend court. The best I can do is to stay in bed and help the appointed attorney all I can."

"I'll go to the Headquarters' Legal Department and request when they select someone, have him come over to check your brief with him." Dennis looked away, wondering what kind of help he would get.

"Dennis, I'm really sorry I have to do it this way. My condition is much worse than I believed it could be. Just think, a lousy little bit of snake venom…and this."

"You know who might want you dead?"

"My hunch is someone working with Mort. I know you're not a detective, Dennis, but could you help the police investigate?" Albert stopped to cough.

"If they'll put up with a military officer."

Albert scribbled some words on a piece of paper lying on his bed table. The sick attorney was so nervous, he spilled two blotches of ink on the page. "Here, take this. It's my request for an attorney and a request for them to arrange for you to work with him and the military police in my stead. Also, here's another note for the clerk downstairs. Your schematics and fingerprint documents are in there. The Admiral's office let me have both of them back for evidence. Take them to Headquarters and have them keep them in their

179

vault. I don't trust the safe here. It's not secure."

"I will if you'll keep doing what the doctors ordered. You promise?"

"Yes, I promise." He swore with his right hand and coughed until his lungs ached.

"Albert, I'll leave now. Promise you will get some rest."

Downstairs, Dennis presented the permission note to the clerk and asked for the contents of the safe. The clerk hesitated. "You're not the one who checked into room 8. I remember him. He was shorter than you."

"Yes, I know. Check your register and check the signature on this note. See, it is the same."

The clerk rapidly compared both notes. "Sir, I can't tell."

"All right, let's go up to the room and ask your resident if did he give the permission. Will you at least do that?" Dennis asked impatiently.

Rather than have a confrontation, the clerk acquiesced and turned around to open the squat safe just inside a small closet. "Is this what you want, Sir?"

Albert took the documents to a corner of the room. Finding them in order he approached the clerk.

"Yes. Thank you. I'll be on my way."

"You're welcome, Sir."

⚓

The legal office was in an imposing building on the other side of the jail. Suddenly, Dennis spied a form shooting from the brig as though someone or something was ready to pounce. The form swooped directly toward him closing fast with a crescent dagger in its right hand. A dark stranger lunged toward him. Dennis caught the assailant's wrist to avoid his murderous thrust, but the attacker pushed him to the dirt holding a shiny dagger inches from McDill's throat. The attacker's arm kept pushing the dagger downward in spite of what Dennis could do. Sweat swam down his neck as he prepared a spot on Dennis' neck for the sharp tip of the glistening instrument. McDill could see death at the end of a crooked knife. One inch more would slit his throat. With all his strength, Dennis twisted his body just in time. The dagger plunged into the dirt beside the would-be victim's throat. Again, the aggressor pulled the weapon from the soil and tried again, but this time Dennis was ready. He rolled over quickly and kicked the man's chest. His enemy doubled over, then Dennis caught the assailant just under the chin, forcing him to careen backwards. With a tight arm lock around the man's neck, McDill was able to render his opponent semi-conscious.

From a distance, two shore patrols saw the melee. One whistle brought two more police.

"Take this scum in for questioning." Dennis wiped the soil from his britches. "I'll be back as soon as I deliver this message."

Military police did not look with admiration on anyone who would attack one of their men or officers. They dragged the groggy scoundrel across the roughest part of the road, pushed him inside the jail, and threw him in the nearest empty cell. "Jump one of our commanders, will you? We ought to kick your guts out right here," the younger seaman growled.

"Hold on," the older seaman shouted. "He's in plenty of trouble. And we're eye witnesses. Let him stay in that cell until the commander comes."

"I hope he rots in jail."

"I'm sure he'll get what he deserves. Come on, fella. Let's get some food."

McDill brushed off more dirt from his uniform and recovered his evidence and Albert's note. He hoped when JAG learned what happened and read the message, they would ignore a dirty uniform. One marine guarding the door to the building drew back in surprise to see the disheveled senior officer. "Sir, if you pardon me, aren't you a little out of uniform?"

"Corporal, you might say that. A few minutes ago I was attacked by a knife-stabbing enemy who tried to kill me. If you want to know more, ask the shore patrols near the jail."

"Whom do you want to see, Sir?"

"Your officer in charge." Dennis tried to adjust his uniform.

"Come with me, Sir. You can talk to his assistant."

"Anybody, just let me in to see him."

On their way down the hall, several sailors' necks craned around to see a dirty commander still wiping some portions of the earth's surface from his chin following a marine. They debated whether to salute or not, but most of them did out of respect for the circles of gold.

High-ranking attorneys had rows of volumes that stood in lofty cabinets in the office. It looked like a library, only most of the volumes were stacked in uniform size. Two large table tops were invisible with papers and books scattered in some kind of logical fashion. Two officers sat at each table and one bent over an oversized desk at the far end of the office. "Which one's the Skipper, Corporal?"

"Behind that big desk, Sir." He pointed.

Dennis cleared his throat. The officer kept writing, never looking at his visitor, dipped his pen in ink again. Dennis walked closer. "May I see you? You are the C.O., I believe."

Two gray eyes focused over thick glasses. Irritated, the eyelids narrowed and the gentleman behind the desk grumbled in a raspy voice. "Yes, you're looking at him. What do you want?"

"Here, read this note, please Sir," Dennis answered in a half-diplomatic voice.

Sitting behind the desk seemed to protect Dennis from lashing out at the old grouch. The irate "Sitting Tom" snatched Albert's note and read it twice. "I can hardly make out what this says."

"Sir, it requests that you assign a defending officer to help me at my court-martial."

"Commander, er...."

"Lt. Commander Dennis McDill, Sir."

The grouch removed his glasses and looked at Commander McDill. "The way you look and dress, you ought to be court-martialed."

"Some villain attacked me with a knife, but I got the best of him."

"I hope for your sake he looks worse than you do."

"Sir, about the note...."

He adjusted his glasses. "Oh, the note. Well, I have one officer unassigned at the moment."

"Mr. Monroe, my civilian lawyer, says he'll help him. He is very ill and is unable to attend the trial, but he is willing to divulge all the evidence he has and he'll work from his bed if necessary."

"Commander McDill, how commendable. Irregular, but commendable," he commented with an obvious expression of resentment "The only counselor we have available is Captain Ripple. He's about to retire. He's a little rusty."

Surprised, Dennis blurted out, "Is that the best you have?"

"That's all I have. The rest are tied up with cases, and I'm up to my hips as you can see."

"When can I see him?" Dennis asked.

"Tomorrow. He'll be in my office at 9:00 a.m. You can take him to see Mr. Monroe if you wish."

"It's a start anyway. Thanks for your time." Dennis saluted.

The man behind the half-glasses grunted and leaned over the mountain of paperwork.

Anxiety welled up in Dennis like a volcano ready to blast off and send him riding downstream on a river of lava. *"Why did he and Albert have to draw an old man? Why can't the doctors cure Albert?"* he pondered to himself repeatedly.

Next day, Dennis met "Old Man Ripple." Ripple looked old, too. His voice quivered a little, as is common with aged people. On their way, Dennis tried to describe his plight to the officer who planned to retire in a few months. When they arrived at the officers' barracks, Albert gave Ripple a cordial welcome and his thanks for substituting.

"It will be my pleasure. I will do my best," Ripple replied.

⚓

Albert's fever shot him into the middle of what would have been a long discussion. "Dennis, you can't go to the Russian Embassy and ask them to turn over their conspirator. He has diplomatic immunity even if he paid this man to obtain the plans." Albert drew back in his bed and took a long breath of dejection.

"I can try. There must be some justice somewhere for such a crime," Dennis hoped.

"Dennis, I'm telling you. It won't be worth your effort. All we can do is try our own creep and hope he stays in prison for the rest of his life."

"I'm going to take my witnesses with me and talk to the person in charge of the Russian Embassy."

Albert dropped in his bed and heaved a sigh. "All right, Dennis. Go. I wish you well."

McDill went to the door and walked outside to the patrol station. It was hot when he started to jog double time. His hands were so wet from sweat he hardly could turn the doorknob. A marine sitting near the door gawked at the panting commander approaching in a trot. He always thought officers, unless in battle, remained calm and cool. "Sir, may I help you?"

"Yes, I'm looking for two shore patrols that were on duty near the entrance to the jail yesterday."

"Do you remember the time or the approximate time, Sir? Then, I can check my roster."

"Around 10:30," Dennis estimated.

The marine bent around to view a large white calendar with black ink marks that scribbled a dozen names, dates and times.

"That would be Spires and James. They're in mess hall now. That's down this hall and to the right."

With a quick "Thank you," Dennis jolted down the corridor. At least twenty seamen and a few marines chewed and chattered like a dozen children at a birthday party. Dennis McDill had to shout to be heard. "ATTENTION!" A louder noise ensued. Forks bounced on tables and dishes, then absolute silence followed. Everyone stood at attention. "Spires, James, come forward." At that command, two men marched up to Commander McDill and saluted. Returning their salutes, McDill ordered, "Come with me. We're going to take a little trip to the Russian Embassy. I need you two for witnesses of what you saw earlier."

"Sir, we'd be glad to go with you." The second class shore patrol moved up in step with his superior.

Lt. Commander McDill stopped and turned to the third class sailor. "Get your patrol wagon. Hurry."

"Aye, Sir." The patrol ran and saluted at the same time.

D.C. traffic, heavy at lunch time, choked travel to a turtle pace, but the two horses had learned how to maneuver. Soon Embassy Row produced a neat and well-kept line of buildings. Each building's national flag flew straight east, driven by a strong west wind. Both horses stopped politely in front of the Embassy. "Wait here, men. I'll go up and state our purpose."

Through the trees, the sailors spotted a red coat with gold trim answering the door. They could see the commander as he spoke with the doorman. Shortly, the doorman disappeared, leaving McDill alone on the porch. "You think they'll let us in?" the younger sailor asked.

"Don't know, but I bet that commander can get in if anybody can."

Two red coats appeared. A short pause. The witnesses waited. McDill's right arm waved his informants to join him. "The ambassador will see us for a few minutes After I give him the situation, both of you get ready to testify to what you saw. Be brief but accurate. You understand?"

Both sailors nodded.

The three were guided to a large office where everything was red—the walls, the floor, even the furniture. Inside, when the temperature climbed over 60, to the inhabitants it would feel like Hades on Earth. In stark contrast, a calm white-haired man stood behind a desk which was placed directly in front of a national flag. The distinguished man looked older than anyone Dennis McDill had imagined, but his greeting sounded much younger. In accented English, the ancient person invited the seamen to sit in front of him.

"I hear you have news of the utmost importance. Please describe."

Dennis gave a terse account of his bout with his attacker. Both observers gave the ambassador a complete description of McDill's assailant and what had happened.

"Did your attacker describe the person who hired him?" the elder diplomat probed, folding his arms.

"Yes, Sir. The knifer feared he'd have to face charges alone, so after the questioning he was ready to cooperate. He said that the man—your man—offered him five thousand dollars to get some important schematics of a ship I designed for our Navy. He described him as being around middle age, average height and weight. He was balding with black hair sprinkled with white. So far Sir, this could be anybody, but our prisoner said the man had a birthmark from the back of his left jaw to the left side of his neck."

The white-haired embassador rose slowly. Frowns plowed from his forehead to his cheeks. "That sounds like one of my assistants. I shall call him in, but you must know he has diplomatic immunity."

"Yes, my attorney told me." McDill sat erect with hands on his knees, hoping he could bargain with the old one. "But we would like to try him in our courts."

"Hold for a moment. I want our person to come before his accusers. You do that in your country, don't you?"

Dennis was taken aback thinking that courts were different. "Why, yes we do."

"Commander, we will record from this point on. Agreed?"

"Agreed, Sir."

In a louder voice, the Russian ordered his secretary. "Come in. I want you to take down everything that is said until I tell you to stop."

A young Russian entered the room, saluted and sat in a corner with his pen and pad.

"Ready with your pad? Start when I call in my assistant."

In one motion, agile as a cadet, the ancient official dashed to the door and yelled at the guard. "Bring in Switz." Then his voice mellowed to demonstrate his hospitality. "Relax, gentlemen. While we wait, will you have some vodka?"

"That's kind of you, Sir, but we're on duty. If you have some tea or coffee?" Dennis asked.

"We're always prepared for Americans. There's a pitcher of tea and some glasses in that corner. Have your men serve us."

As they drank, a bear-like man appeared and stopped abruptly at seeing U.S. Navy servicemen.

"Switz, these men are here to accuse you of a serious crime. They say you hired one of their men to rob the United States and get some plans for a great ship. He was told to get them even if he had to kill for them. Is that true?"

"No, Sir. It is not true," Switz swore.

"Then, let me question these men in front of you and give you a chance to ask them questions."

The old Russian had often wondered about the honesty of his assistant because he had received complaints about Switz's behavior from several of his own embassy personnel.

Switz was baffled. "Is this a trial or something?"

"I want the truth," Ambassador Molotz asserted. "Commander, will you and your men tell your story one more time?"

McDill and his witnesses presented a more complete description.

They delineated every detail of the interrogation of their own sailor who had admitted he had been hired by someone from the Embassy to obtain the schematics. The sailor described his "employer."

Near the end of the questioning, Switz concluded, "I'm not the man you want. That description can fit almost anyone."

Molotz's eyes burrowed into Switz's brain. "Commander McDill and his witnesses described a certain birthmark that was seen. There's no one here who has a birthmark like yours, you imbecile. All of us can see it easily. You have immunity, but you're forgetting one thing. You only have immunity against the Americans, not with me." Molotz folded his arms and sat down quietly. "My clerk has recorded all of this verbatim." The old one unfolded his arms and pointed his index finger. "Switz, you're going back home on the next ship. I'll recommend that you be tried for larceny and attempted murder. You are restricted to this building and you will not leave until you get aboard the next vessel to our homeland."

"But Sir, you can't...."

"Oh, yes I can. As of now, you're under house arrest. And you know back home you could be hanged."

Two towering guards marched in and clicked their heels. Switz was lifted by his arms and hauled out without hesitation.

"Sir, we are most grateful to you for your cooperation. We didn't know whether we could get any kind of justice with immunity on the side of the accused." McDill gratefully shook hands and saluted the distinguished Russian.

Ambassador Molotz seem relieved. "Commander, I have suspected this poor excuse for a Russian for a long time. Now I'm glad we have a reason to place him in custody."

Dennis back-pedaled and whispered to his men, "Let's get out of before our luck runs out." Aloud, Dennis addressed the admiral. "Sir, it is good to know that our countries can cooperate in peace."

"Glad to be of service to your U.S. Navy. You leave with our best regards."

Mounting the carriage, the older patrol asked, "Commander, do you really believe they will try that crook?"

"Hard to tell, but I certainly hope so. It's my guess that he'll never be able to get back into the United States again, at least."

"Good riddance," the younger patrol added.

Going back to Headquarters, McDill waded into a hot bed of mixed emotions. He was glad that one problem was solved, but massive problems continued their onslaught. Dennis felt an anaconda was squeezing his entire being.

⚓

"Captain Ripple, this is a surprise. I'm supposed to meet you in the Admiral Hicks' office tomorrow." Dennis tried to hide his shock.

"I thought I'd get started earlier. The Court's President, Admiral Hicks, knows I'm here and I have learned a lot from Mr. Monroe already."

"Have you defended criminal cases?" Dennis looked at a long nose between two small brown eyes he thought might be untrustworthy.

"Yes, but it's been a long time ago. Mr. Monroe is a very good attorney. You are fortunate to have him." Ripple's eyes seem to pat Albert on the back.

Dennis nodded slowly, feeling the bondage of anxiety crushing his ribs. "I hope you've learned enough to defend me in this trial. Albert says this is going to be a tough one because we'll have one of the government's best trial lawyers as our opponent."

"Commander, I will do my best." Ripple replied with a flair of pseudo confidence. His wrinkled face supplied proof his certain retirement, however, his eyes brightened with optimism.

"All right. Albert, what witnesses and pieces of evidence do you have so far?" Dennis asked.

"Sam Giles, two shore patrol guards, one more person that I haven't selected yet, and this legal fellow can put me on the stand. I have much to reveal. No doubt the trial counsel will put Captain Fritzgerald on the stand. He may call Captain Mort from the brig to testify. Those two will be great for the defense to cross examine. For evidence, I will present your telegraphed request to Mort about the mission, a police document giving the results of the fingerprints, and your schematics. It's risky, but I plan to put you on the stand, Dennis."

"But the trial officer will have evidence of the direct order and pictures of houses that Commander McDill and his crew built with Navy material and money," Ripple countered.

Encouraged, Dennis nodded. "This defense lawyer may be more able than I thought, Albert."

"The Navy is always selective. That's why we have a determined opponent who will try to get you in prison for a long, long time," Albert countered back.

"Where will the witnesses be when the trial starts?" McDill asked.

"They will be sequestered in the hotel down the street." Albert's shaky finger pointed west. "During the trial, they'll congregate outside the courtroom, so they can't hear any testimony before they're seated. The same will be true for the prosecution. No matter the outcome, Dennis, we will make sure that you get a fair court-martial."

"I've heard sailors say when a seaman is court-martialed, he's automatically guilty before he's tried." Dennis bent his head sideways and ran furrows with his fingers through his hair twice.

"Not true, Dennis," Albert parried. "Once in a while there's a mistake, but our military courts are usually fair."

"Yes, I believe Admiral Hicks will be fair, but he can't avoid testimonies and the evidence, can he?"

"No. And he should not." Albert looked down at his trembling legs. "By the way, Dennis, they're putting me in the Naval Hospital tomorrow."

"Won't that be awkward for Captain Ripple to operate without you?"

"I have insisted on having visitors almost any time, day or night."

"Al, that makes me feel a little better. I pray they'll cure your hideous disease. You have suffered too much." For a moment Dennis forgot his own troubles.

"Don't worry about me, Commander. I'll beat this. You concentrate on staying out of the brig."

"Tell me again, when does the trial begin?" Dennis asked.

"Day after tomorrow. One day after I'm hospitalized." Attacked by a dizzy spell, Monroe stumbled over to his bed.

"Not much time. Better prep your substitute so he can figure the strategy of the prosecution." Dennis hated to burden Monroe, but the trial was stalking him.

From his bunk, Albert swore, "Dennis, he'll be ready if I have to instruct him all night."

"Good. I'll leave you two alone to work." When he reached the door, Dennis gave his new defender one more look.

Crushing specters of uncertainty still haunted Dennis McDill. He accepted Albert's substitute, but he could not forget the captain was out of practice with no recent experience in criminology. In fact, serious doubts infected him like a plague. He began to have daytime nightmares about a dismal cell that would be too small for his size and he would be surrounded by hardened criminals for many years. Not an enjoyable future. Dennis McDill lumbered to his room in silence.

In deep concentration, Dennis stumbled into his room. The door was already open and gaslights flickered spontaneously, generating several contrasting moods. He stooped and crouched inside the door. He peeked cautiously. He could see no one. Dennis listened for a while. No sound gave him a clue. His curiosity was boiling, so he stepped further inside. Then he smelled something—a familiar aroma. "Helen, is that you? You're early. I was ready to pounce on a hiding attacker."

"Dennis, give me a hug. I couldn't wait any longer. I hope you don't mind. You smelled my favorite perfume, didn't you?" Helen was always a fastidious dresser and wore her perfume like a professional model. Dennis admired her light brown hair that floated when she walked.

"Of course, Helen, I don't mind. In fact, I'm happy. How did you get in?"

"After I told him who I was, the clerk let me in. I think he believed I was harmless."

"Helen, I really need some encouragement. This trial could go sour on me at any time. I hate to tell you, Albert Monroe will be admitted to the hospital tomorrow."

"What's wrong with him?" Helen plopped down on the bed.

"Poisoned with some terrible toxin. His doctors think the aftermath is serious. Whatever it is, it's making him weaker by the day."

"Then, who'll defend you?" Helen's voice cracked slightly. "Every accused has a right to a lawyer."

"Headquarters' Legal Department has appointed Captain Ralph Ripple to defend me."

Helen's small frame was a foot shorter than Dennis'. She had to look up to him. "Dennis, that's awful. Monroe has put so much time on your case."

"Ripple seems capable enough. He's conferring with Albert at this moment. However, we're not complacent. The Navy's trial lawyer is a very competent lawyer who will try to send me to federal prison."

Helen's eyes teared. "Now I feel very uneasy, Dennis. Any hope at all?"

Dennis felt the same as his wife, but he tried to cheer her by citing a slight advantage. "So far, we have more witnesses, if that helps."

"It'll reassure me if the U.S. Navy Court will listen your new lawyer."

"Well, we have some reliable witnesses. They'll have positive effects on our future."

"I pray you won't have to go, but you know I will wait for you no matter what."

Dennis and Helen held each other for a long time, silently thinking and listening to their hearts beat. Helen, nearly always brave, shivered as though the cold hand of fate had entrapped her. She snuggled in the arms of her lover and dreamed of hope for the future. Dennis rolled over, blew out the candles and shut down the gas. His eyes roamed the ceiling all night.

Fog and drizzle welled up in during the night. The weather dropped like a pall on Dennis. Somatic sensations crawled into his body like leeches each time he thought about the legal proceedings he would face soon. Neither he nor Helen could eat breakfast. Sadly, they poked along to court where Captain Ripple met them at the door. "Commander, everything is in order. Trial Counselor Bailey will give a summation of the charges. He will try to prove you're a very bad person. Brace yourself, Commander, he'll criminalize you and persuade the Panel to look upon you with their most utmost disfavor." Ripple wanted his clients to be prepared for the worst.

"I never thought he'd have any complimentary words for me." Dennis followed behind Ripple down to a short table directly in front of a longer table.

"Mrs. McDill, you may sit behind us, if you wish."

"Thanks, Captain." She placed herself exactly behind her husband. "I want to get as close to him as possible."

A starch-like uniformed commander walked in and sat at a table about ten feet to the left of Dennis. His brown hair was cropped so short it looked as if he had shaved his head. Bailey sat as straight as a Prussian soldier and laid his briefcase squarely on his table. When he pulled out several papers, Dennis began to feel his muscles tense. Five top-ranking officers marched in and settled behind the long table. Admiral Hicks occupied the middle chair with three captains and a Marine general. Lt. Commander McDill and Captain Ripple stood at attention when the court arrived, then sat at a nod from Hicks. Admiral Hicks looked at Commander Bailey. "Is the prosecution ready?" he asked.

"Counsel is ready, your Honor," Commander Baily responded.

"Proceed," Hicks ordered.

"Members of the Panel, I want to call your attention to the defendant sitting at the table before you. Please note that he is a Lieutenant Commander in the U.S. Navy. I do not have to remind the Court that ranking officers and all military personnel must obey their superiors. I will prove that this man disobeyed a direct order, and furthermore he misused government property and money. To top it, he aborted his mission. Therefore, he is a disobedient thief."

At "disobedient thief," Dennis jumped from his seat. Ripple gently pulled his client's elbow. "Please. We'll prove him wrong."

Commander Bailey continued. "Gentlemen, I will show you proof that this man blatantly rejected a direct order. I present Exhibit 1, the telegram sent to the Commander refusing his request and ordering him to continue with his mission. This telegram is certified in writing by the telegrapher who sent it to Commander McDill." Bailey handed Exhibit 1 to the Panel to inspect. He privately gloated to see them scowl.

Hicks read the evidence and interrupted. "Before you continue, Counsel, I want to ask the defendant how he pleads." He looked at McDill. "Lt. Commander Dennis McDill, how do you plead?"

"Not guilty, your Honor," Dennis answered without hesitating.

The panel members looked at each other and mumbled, surprised that any officer, when confronted by such obvious proof, would not admit guilt and plead for mercy from the Court.

"Do I understand correctly?" Admiral Hicks pressed. "You plead not guilty?"

"Yes, your Honor." Dennis braced for repercussions that would drop like bombs.

"Clerk, note the response of the accused." The admiral looked at the far corner of the room at a small yeoman sitting at a table with a pen and pad.

Dennis murmured to himself, then whispered to Ripple. "It's really true. In military court a man is guilty before he is tried," Dennis grumbled.

Overhearing their conversation, Hicks banged his gavel hard against the top of the table. "Order in the Court," he demanded.

Ripple cued McDill. "Please. We've got to make a good impression or the court will rule against you for certain."

"Again," Hicks ordered. "Proceed, Counselor."

"Honor, I call my first witness, the yeoman who telegraphed the message to the defendant. Yeoman First Class McHenry, will you come forward?" As the sailor stood before the Navy Court-Martial Panel, the clerk held out a Bible. "Raise your right hand. Do you swear to tell the truth, so help you God?"

"I do."

"Sit, Yeoman McHenry." At the admiral's command, the young seaman nervously sat behind the witness stand that felt like a chair of stone.

"For the record, what is your job?" Bailey questioned.

"I write orders. I have learned the Morse Code so I am assigned to send and receive telegraphed messages, also."

"Yeoman McHenry, I show you this document. Do you recognize it?"

McHenry held the paper as steadily as his nerves permitted.

"Yes, Sir. That is a telegram I sent."

"Is that your signature at the bottom of this sheet?" Bailey pursued.

"Yes, it's my signature. It was requested as part of my sworn statement."

Bailey rotated to face the accused. "To whom did you send it, Yeoman McHenry?"

"To Lieutenant Commander Dennis McDill at City Point, Virginia."

"Do you see him in this court room?" Bailey continued to stare at McDill.

"Yes, Sir. That's him sitting behind that table in front of the admiral." He pointed and Dennis shrank into a tight ball.

"Yeoman, have you ever met him? How could you recognize him?"

"Sir, his picture was in all our newspapers. I recognize his face."

"Thank you. Defense, your witness." Bailey sat.

Captain Ripple stood up and pulled down his coat to straighten its wrinkles. "Yeoman, tell the Court who ordered you to send this message."

"Captain Norman Mort, Sir."

"And what capacity was Captain Mort in at that time?" Rippled asked.

"He was and is assigned to Headquarters in charge of ship maintenance and repair, Sir."

"Did the Captain dictate this message to you?" Ripple planted himself directly in front of the witness.

"No, Sir. He wrote it himself and I sent it."

"And it is addressed to Lt. Commander Dennis McDill, is it not?" Ripple left the witness to stand beside McDill.

"That is correct, Sir."

"Did you receive any telegraph messages from Commander McDill before you sent this telegram?" Ripple stepped over to face the Panel.

"Yes, Sir."

"Explain to the court the contents of Commander McDill's request."

McHenry cleared his throat. "He requested that the mission stop and that his crew be reassigned."

"May it please the Court, I submit Defense Exhibit A." Ripple had the clerk record the exhibit. Then he stepped over to the witness. "Do you recognize this document? Tell us who this is from."

"Yes. It's from Commander McDill."

Admiral Hicks, up all night, began to doze. Out of fear, no panel member dared to nudge him.

"This is all I have for this witness," Ripple told the admiral.

At that moment the admiral blinked when he realized what was happening. "Captain, you cannot present your exhibit at a cross examination. Not with this court. You know better. Recall this witness if you wish but use your exhibit with your own witness. Sit down and wait your turn." Hicks' temper swelled like a balloon

Dennis smelled something going bad, but it was too late to get his lawyer's attention. As soon as Ripple sat down beside McDill, Dennis pulled at his attorney's starched sleeve. "For St. Joseph's sake, man, call for a recess." Dennis' face launched several rocket glares at his defense attorney. "With all due respect, Captain, we need to get organized. Are you sure you remember the law? You butted in at the wrong time. Please ask for a recess and let's check with Monroe. I don't have a law degree, but I can tell when you skipped protocol. The Trial Counsel could let that error ride and smack you with it later when you least expect it. Maybe Monroe can find some way to get us out of this mess and we're making the admiral angry."

Ripple squeaked, "Yes, I hope we can pacify him." Slowly Ripple stood in front of the court. "Your Honors, I ask for a recess to talk with my client."

Hicks glowered at Ripple. "It's nearly lunch time. We'll recess for two hours."

Dennis realized his mistake. "Captain. I berated you—my superior. I apologize, Sir."

"No need. We are performing as client to lawyer. Be frank. It's the only honest way during a trial."

⚓

It took several minutes to walk to the Navy Hospital five blocks away. The little building was crowded with several patients bedded in the halls, the sad effect of some epidemic. McDill approached a busy nurse bustling to get some medicine. "Nurse, where is the room of Albert Monroe?"

"I don't know. Ask the orderly behind the desk over there." She pointed to a man dressed in white, thumbing pages in a thick book.

Dennis bounded across the lobby to the desk placed in front of the bleach-coated man. "Can you tell me where I can find a patient named Albert Monroe?"

"Let me see." The hospital orderly pulled out a large sheet of paper covered with names and numbers. "He's in room 118. Down the hall to your right."

"Captain, I hope Albert can straighten this out enough for me to have a chance."

McDill calmly cracked the door of room 118. Albert had fallen asleep on his side facing the window. A cover was wrapped tightly around his body and he was breathing erratically.

"Albert, I hate to wake you, but we need your help," Dennis whispered.

Monroe rolled over, yawned, and mumbled, "Oh, it's you Dennis."

"Yes, it's me. Your substitute may have made a mistake."

"What kind of mistake?" Albert, slowly recovering from a stupor, removed his covers.

"My defender, here, produced his own exhibit before his turn. I'm afraid the court will react against me. I'm certain that Prosecutor Bailey will take advantage and have the court think it's a grave error. On a technicality, he may try to get Admiral Hicks to make our exhibit invalid. I remember you informed me that Trial Counselor Bailey is quite good."

Albert lay without a word for a long time, staring at the lamp on the other side of his room. "First of all, stay calm. Let the president take the lead and you take notes. Ripple, bring up your witnesses and evidence when it's your turn to present. The Panel may already think you're 'over the hill.' Some of them probably know you'll retire soon. When and if the Panel reads your telegram, they may not notice the signature of Commander McDill. It's much better for the witness to verify everything. Bring in Mr. Comer to certify to his message if you need to. And you, Dennis, you're overreacting. If you continue that, you'll be your own enemy."

Dennis moped out of the hospital embarrassed as a freshly shorn sheep. "All right, Counselor, you do your job and I'll do mine," he concluded.

Both men snatched sandwiches and gobbled them on the way to the court. They came in just as the high-ranking officers entered. "Now we'll convene again."

McDill could tell the president of the Panel was still puffed with anger.

After "Order in the Court," Hicks hammered his gavel. "Continue, Prosecutor."

"Sir, I call to the stand Captain Rupert Fritzgerald." On either side of the bewildered I.G. marched two guards. Fritzgerald was released at the courtroom door so the crowd could not see the man in custody.

After the swearing in, Commander Bailey continued. "State your position, Captain."

"I work for the department of the Inspector General."

"Did you have an occasion to meet the defendant?" Bailey nodded at McDill and Ripple.

"Yes."

"If he is in the courtroom, will you point him out for us?"

Fritzgerald pointed directly at Commander McDill long enough for Dennis to feel the heat of the Inspector General's finger.

"Where did you meet him?" Bailey asked.

"At City Point, Virginia."

"And, Captain Fritzgerald, what was your purpose in going to City Point?"

"We received a tip that Commander McDill had abandoned his mission to repair ships and was misusing government funds." With a aura of confidence, Fritzgerald leaned back and placed his hand on the witness stand rail.

"Did you see anyone working on those ships?"

"No. No one was working, so I inquired where I could find the commander in charge. I was directed to a new house and discovered it was his home."

"Please explain," Bailey requested.

"Well, I found out that the home belonged to Lt. Commander Dennis McDill."

"Go on," Bailey encouraged.

"I learned that the house was recently built for him to live in."

"Then what did you do?" Bailey moved so that Fritzgerald could see McDill clearly.

"I knocked on the door and confronted him."

"And then?"

"Prior to that, I had noticed there were seven old ships tied up at the dock. They were stripped of some wood and metal. I asked him about that. He admitted that he and his men needed the material to build homes for himself and his crew." Fritzgerald leaned forward to face Dennis.

"Please continue," Baily asked.

"Well, I had all the information I needed at that time. I ordered Commander McDill to go with me to Headquarters."

"Can you tell us more?"

"Yes, we later learned that he took some of the money given to him for repairs and bought lumber and materials to build those homes. Commander McDill admitted he took the money to purchase more lumber."

Dennis jerked his attorney's sleeve again. "That's a lie! I never confessed anything to Fritzgerald. Can't you do something?"

Ripple had the talent of calming down people. "We will. Wait until later."

"You took that as a confession?" Bailey probed.

"Yes, I did."

"Did you find out more?"

"On another trip down to City Point to verify my information, I met an Indian named Running Elk. He told me he saw the houses being built, and that a Naval officer was in charge."

The Trial Counsel drew out a deposition from his case. "If it pleases the Court, I present Trial's Exhibit 2. It is a sworn statement signed by Running Elk."

Admiral Hicks received the document, read it and passed it around to the other members. Hicks decided to ask his own question. "Where does this Running Elk live?"

"In an Indian village near City Point about two miles up the river."

"You saw and questioned this man? You witnessed his signature on this deposition?" Bailey rested his arm on the witness stand.

"Yes, I did."

"Defense, do you want to cross?" Bailey returned to his seat.

Ripple stood upright. "If it please the Court, I would like to speak in private with my client."

Hicks scowled at Ripple. "Another delay? I want you to get organized, men. We don't have months to finish this case. All right, recess for thirty minutes."

Ripple and McDill sat alone in the corner of the room whispering. "Who is this Running Elk, Commander?" Ripple crooked his neck and stared at Dennis.

"He's the father of a woman who's married to my Lieutenant DuBois. Running Elk was furious that an Indian woman would marry a white man, especially his daughter marrying a white man."

Dennis described the entire episode that Running Elk attempted which ended with the murderous attack by Cougar Mountain. "Cougar is the man that Elk promised his daughter to for a bride." Dennis kept whispering. "You know, that old time custom."

Ripple spoke softly. "Then, Running Elk would go out of his way to tell anyone interested about the houses built by government material and money, right?"

"Precisely. I believe that Indian would be angry enough to tell that to the I.G. or any Navy official." Dennis stopped when the Panel returned.

Ripple stood. "Your Honors, we are ready to continue."

"Proceed," Admiral Hicks ordered, still looking at Ripple.

"May I ask the Trial Counsel's witness a question?" He stared straight at Bailey.

Bailey leaped. "Your Honor, my witness and I are being interrupted. My colleague here is pulling some kind of trick."

Ripple slid his chair back. "Your Honor, the Trial Counsel did not disclose this witness in the information he was to exchange with us. As a compromise, I would like to ask the witness some questions now."

"Commander Bailey, I know it's a bit unusual, but I want to know. Proceed, Defense." Hicks gave Bailey a suspicious glance.

"Captain, tell the Court what you know about this Running Elk," Ripple asked.

Fritzgerald blushed. "Only that I saw him one day and he told me he knew something about the case that I should know."

"Tell us exactly where you saw that man," Hicks asked.

Fritzgerald loosened his collar and stuttered. "In jail."

"For what?" Hicks prodded.

"Involved in a kidnaping."

"Did the jailer tell you why?" Ripple requested.

"He was mad because his daughter wanted to marry a white man and he had promised her to another." Fritzgerald leaned forward and shifted uneasily.

"Pardon me," the Marine general interrupted. "How did you know this man was in jail and wanted to tell you something?"

"Well, Sir. A man who didn't want to reveal his name told me to go to the jail and talk with Running Elk. He said Elk would have first hand information."

"I see. Did that man, who did not want you to know you his name, tell you anything else?" the general asked.

Fritzgerald hesitated. "Only he said he was a member of Running Elk's tribe."

"Why didn't he tell you himself?" the general probed further.

"I believe he thought Running Elk really wanted to be the one to tell me, and he would have some first hand knowledge."

"Admiral, this sounds like revenge, but evidence anyway," the general proffered.

"That's all for this witness," Bailey prompted. "I now call in Marshal Moore."

Admiral Hicks took out his pocket watch. "We will recess for an hour."

Staying in their seats, Ripple leaned over to whisper to Dennis. "What's the marshal going to say? Albert and I didn't get a chance to talk about him."

"He's been looking for a convict who shot and killed a woman's husband. I witnessed her shooting the man who murdered her husband."

Taken by surprise, Ripple swallowed. "Commander, tell me more."

"She's the wife of a man the murderer killed with a piece of iron railing. When she learned who the murderer was, she grabbed a shotgun and blew a hole in his chest. State Court tried her, but dismissed the case."

"McDill, did the marshal question you at any time?" Ripple regained control.

"Yes."

"Were you charged for not telling the marshal everything you knew about the case?" Ripple questioned.

"No. We did tell him that our men buried the convict in the swamp," Dennis revealed.

"What did the marshal do then?"

"Captain, he tried to find the body."

"Did he?" Ripple inquired.

"As far as I know, he didn't."

"For your sake, McDill, we'd better hope he didn't." Ripple paused. "Since he didn't have you charged you with anything, did he take any other action?"

"No. In fact, he offered immunity if we told him all we knew."

"Dennis, I'm still a little puzzled. Are you sure that's all you told the marshal?"

"Yes. That was all we told him."

Returning, Hicks looked at Bailey. "Counselor, you may continue with the witness."

"Yes, your Honor. I call to the stand U.S. Marshal Jonathan Moore." Bailey continued, looking worried.

After Moore was sworn in, Bailey asked. "State your name and position."

"I am Jonathan Moore, U.S. Marshal."

"Did you have an occasion to meet the accused?"

"Yes, I went to his city when I was tracking a convict named Gaith Johnson." Moore answered.

Moore testified for more than an hour, reiterating what McDill told him. Bailey struck a nerve by asking what role did the accused play during the shooting of the convict. He issued a sharp look at Lt. Commander McDill, worming in his seat. Ripple advised Dennis to remain mute and reminded him that he was not on the witness stand at the moment. Every panel member seemed unusually interested.

Quietly Ripple got back to Running Elk. Dennis repeated all he knew about Little Moon's father. "I believed the Indian was basically a good man. He had an oath to uphold. He's a deeply troubled man."

"Defense Counselor, if you continue to talk aside the testimony, I will hold you in contempt," Hick roared.

Bailey looked at Moore. "I have no further questions of this witness."

"Counselor Ripple, do you have any questions for this witness?"

"No, Sir. I would like to recall Captain Fritzgerald." Ripple reached for a note remembering too well the advice that Monroe gave him.

"Remember, you are still under oath," Hick stated.

"Captain, you say the accused admitted to disobeying orders and misusing Navy property and money. Is that correct?" Ripple placed both hands on the witness stand.

"That is correct," Fritzgerald stated, wondering what the next question would be.

"Did the Lt. Commander tell you why he disobeyed the order?" Ripple turned around to the audience.

"No, not in so many words. He only told me about needing to get housing for families of his crew," the I.G. answered.

Ripple suggested, "Then you would say it was for a good cause?"

Bailey jumped from his table. "Object. This is simply the opinion of the witness, not a fact."

"Objection sustained," Hicks grunted. "Barrister, we are here to obtain facts about the case and not seek advice or opinions." Admiral Hicks shoved his gavel to the table's edge in front of him. With his hand over his mouth, Hicks whispered to the general. "Where did JAG get such an old coot to defend a senior officer?"

The general's shoulders humped in bewilderment.

"Continue, but stick to the facts. Understand?" Hicks ordered.

Ripple's throat tightened. "I will, Sir." Ripple walked briskly from the witness chair. "Have you had occasion to talk with some of the crew about the condition of the ships and their need for housing their families?"

"No," Fritzgerald answered with a tense voice.

"Then you have talked about this only with this defendant, correct?"

"Yes." The I.G.'s body tensed.

"Gentlemen of the jury, I have no more questions of this witness."

Admiral Hicks leaned back and checked down each side of the table. He caught their thoughts immediately. "Prosecution, do you have any more witnesses?"

"No," the prosecution answered.

Admiral Hicks' gavel resounded throughout the building. "Time for another recess. We will reconvene in one hour."

Dennis looked at Ralph Ripple with mixed feelings. Sometimes Ripple seemed to be the Navy's most incompetent lawyer. Sometimes he saw tiny threads of success. Regardless, Dennis McDill prayed silently that Albert Monroe could be able to join him in the process of his court-martial—a fate almost as bad as death to a serviceman. "We better go see Albert. I pray he's getting well."

"So do I, McDill. I admit he knows much more than I do. Let's go to his room."

Albert Monroe reared up in bed when Dennis McDill cracked his hospital door. "You're up," he observed.

"Almost up." Albert checked his feet. "Still wobbly."

"Feeling better?" Ralph trusted his senses, for he had seen many military men recover from the worst of wounds.

"Yeah, I'm a little stronger and I feel much better." Monroe anticipated better things to come.

"Enough to go to court?" Dennis hoped.

"Maybe. You're out on recess. How long?" Albert knew he'd need time to recover.

Dennis looked at his watch. "One hour left for us to talk."

At that, Albert swung around and pulled up a chair. Ralph and Dennis recounted all the testimony and evidence the Trial Counsel and the Defense presented.

"Let's start at the beginning when you drew the schematics for the newest and best ships the Navy could have built, Dennis."

"I will testify to that right now," Dennis brightened.

"No. You won't," Albert fired back. "I want us to put Sam Giles on the stand first."

"Good. I've never known Sam to tell a lie."

"Ralph, for God's sake don't sound off about the jealousy angle that Mort harbored against Dennis for inventing such a prize vessel. Just ask Sam Giles tell what he saw, okay?"

"Okay, I'll just pull the facts from the witness. I want Commander McDill acquitted as much as you do."

"That's settled then." Albert continued to instruct Ripple. "I want you to get the plans from the vault at Headquarters and show them to the Panel as soon as you finish with Sam. At least the court will see how important that document is. You remember, it will be your Exhibit A."

Washington and Virginia citizens envied the chance to cultivate pity for an unfortunate innocent man or express disapproval for such a villain.

Again, popping tintypes blinded McDill and Ripple as reporters ambushed them at the entrance. When they asked, Lt. Commander McDill refused to speculate on his future. Some news media developed a thirst for justice for the Naval officer. Citizens from the Point, led by Helen, carried banners urging a fair trial. Uncertain destiny awaited Dennis McDill. Politics and justice became entwined like ivy. Even an interested senator could be seen in the crowd. Admiral Hicks wondered why, but he had no choice but to ignore him and proceed with the trial. Unknown to all, Bailey gave the lawmaker a slight nod as he sat five rows behind the Trial Counselor's table.

Going to Court, Ripple hoped aloud, "You think Mr. Monroe will be able to join us soon?" Ripple's voice elevated slightly.

"Lord knows I hope so. No offense to you, but Albert's been working on my case for months."

Leathernecks bolted the doors immediately when the Panel marched into the crowded room. All officers were in single file according to rank. Admiral Hicks led the Panel in file as though they were recently recruited cadets. As ordered, they all pulled out their chairs at the same time, and sat at the same time. "Court will come to order. Defense, you're up."

Ripple looked down the aisle. "Your Honors, I would like to call Sam Giles to testify."

A brawny tanned figure emerged and took a seat in the witness chair. Giles was duly sworn to tell the truth while Ripple approached. "Do you know the accused? If so, will you point him out in this room?"

Sam fingered Dennis without hesitation. "That's him, Lt. Commander Dennis McDill."

"How do you know him?" Ripple's head turned to Dennis.

"We worked together in the Navy's Maintenance and Repair Depot," he replied. "We've known each other for a long time."

"What were your jobs?"

"The Commander was a shipwright who led a large crew to repair military vessels. In his spare time, he designed ships. I was one of his floor foremen who supervised welders."

"Did you have occasion to see any designs of the accused?"

"Yes. Being a friend, the Commander McDill showed me most of his plans."

"Any particular plan?" Ripple's long experience required him to know what his witness would say.

"Yes. He designed one of the fastest and best battleships anyone could imagine." Sam smiled at Dennis.

"Please tell us more, Mr. Giles, about any particular incident regarding this design." Ripple noticed the smile, but kept a sober visage.

"Well, one day, I noticed the commander carefully roll up these plans and place them on his desk."

"I object. Where is this leading? Who cares whether or not someone carefully placed some plans on a desk?" Bailey begged.

Hicks bellowed. "Counselor Ripple, you'd better move on, or you'll be through with this witness."

Ripple's face flushed. "Aye, Sir." For a moment Lawyer Ripple was lost. "What happened next?"

Sam's voice became decisive and took careful aim. "After the commander left, I turned around and headed to the office. The office door was open. I saw Captain Mort take the roll from the commander's desk and leave."

"No further questions." Ripple reached for a glass of water.

Bailey straightened and walked over to the witness and parked his elbow on the edge of the stand. "You said Captain Mort picked up the plans and walked out. Is that correct?"

"Yes."

"Can you swear the rolled up paper was Lt. Commander McDill's work?" Bailey dug hard.

"I'm sure it was." Sam changed his position, searching for comfort.

"Any identifying markings?" Bailey's pick ax plunged again.

"Well, no, not that I know. But I'm certain they were the commander's plans," Sam blurted.

Bailey straightened up from the stand and looked at the Panel while speaking to the witness. "Then you cannot prove that was the work of the accused. No further questions."

Giles dismounted, giving Dennis a helpless gesture.

McDill leaned over his table with glazed eyes aimed at his attorney. "We're in trouble. For heaven's sake, call for another recess. We've got to talk with Albert and get him over here if we have to bring him on stretcher."

Ripple rubbed his neck anticipating a blitz from the court, but he managed to stand his ground. "Your Honors, may we have two hours recess?"

Hicks shouted and almost cursed. "This is getting ridiculous! This is the last time you're going to get a recess. Make it tomorrow at 9:00."

Albert Monroe was standing against the shaving bowl with foam and a straight razor. "Come in. I thought I would join you. I don't want to let you men have all the fun."

"Fun?" McDill snarled. "I certainly don't call it fun."

"Problem?" Albert flipped the foam from his king size razor.

"Yes. A big problem." McDill grimaced. "We might find it hard to prove that Mort stole my plans. You said our opponent was sharp. Now, I believe it."

"Keep calm. There's no law that says I can't be a witness. Remember, I found them in Mort's trunk and we have them in a safe at Headquarters."

"All right, then. This can help with the conviction of Mort, but what about my court-martial? To be sure, I want that rascal to get prison for this and other crimes." Dismay seemed to camp out in McDill's hide.

"As your lawyer knows, Bailey is trying to discredit your witness. If he's successful, it certainly will hurt you," Albert admitted.

"About the fingerprints? Can you testify to them?" McDill drifted over to the pitcher stand and poured a glass of water. "And since it's a new science, will they even believe you?"

"Whoa, Dennis! One question at a time. "I believe my answers can cover all of these. Just let my assistant ask the right questions."

"How will I know he'll ask the right questions?" Dennis swallowed the last drop and let go of the empty glass, shattering pieces on the floor. Both attorneys ignored the accident. "Sometimes I wonder if you've gone rusty." Instantly he knew he insulted a superior officer. "Oh, please, I beg your pardon again, Captain."

Ripple sank lower in his chair, not responding at first. "I admit I'm a bit lost at times. Comes with age, I guess."

Albert reached for a pen and paper on the table. "Hey, Dennis. I'll write out the questions and Ralph can look at each one before he asks, okay?"

Dennis squinted at Ralph as though Ralph Ripple was a demented clown. "I'll go with this idea, but I want to be able to see the questions before you get up and try to defend me."

Ralph looked up at Dennis. "I'll do my best."

Dennis caught sight of the large clock that was buried in the wall over the door. "We'd better get back. Our time is almost over. We don't want to keep that court waiting. We've probably used all the recesses available in this court. They will not grant any more. The Admiral can be one tough sailor when he gets angry."

⚓

Crowds surged as Dennis and his lawyers pushed through the mob. A noose of fear tightened around his throat. But win or lose, his courage brought him to the table of the accused. Helen marched in behind him and sat quietly while the officers processed as usual to their chairs behind the long table. Dennis turned around to see her. She seemed more beautiful than ever. *"I'd risk everything to stay with my beautiful lady."*

Ripple's clear voice announced. "Your Honors, I call Albert Monroe to the stand."

Albert held his hand in front of the clerk and swore to tell the whole truth. He uttered, "So help me God," and whispered the phrase again to himself as he sat down in the stony witness chair. He glanced at Hicks who sat stone-faced. His head turned to Ripple who stood directly in front of him. "State your name and your occupation," Ralph proceeded.

"Albert Monroe, Attorney at Law. I know the accused."

Bailey rolled his eyes at Dennis.

"Yes, as you know, I am the lawyer who is defending him."

Prosecutor Bailey popped. "Your Honors, we all know that the accused has two lawyers and they both know him. Can we proceed?"

Hicks glared at Ripple. "Proceed, and don't take all day."

"Aye, Sir." He continued. "Mr. Monroe, I ask you to examine this document that I submit as Exhibit A."

Albert carefully unrolled the plans. "Yes. In addition to the initials, I found a small smudge in the upper right-hand corner. I figured it was someone's fingerprint, so I got suspicious."

"What do you mean?" Ralph noticed that every eye was plastered on Albert.

"Well, I knew police can now identify a person by his fingerprints. So, I wondered whose prints might be on the schematics." He paused giving Ralph time to check his notes.

"Then, what did you do?" Ripple asked.

"In conversations with the accused, I had become suspicious of the Inspector General."

"Why?" Captain Ripple looked at the crowd behind McDill.

"It seemed odd to me that an Inspector General would drag off a suspect to Headquarters without hesitation. And the accused told me that Captain Mort was his immediate superior who was on his inquisition."

"Your Honors," Bailey implored, "isn't this bordering on hearsay?"

"I'll allow it this time, but Captain, be careful," Hicks warned with a frown.

Ripple focused his eyes on the instructions Monroe had dictated. "Do you know any relationship between Captain Mort and Captain Fritzgerald?"

Monroe supplied a quick answer. "Their offices were on the same hall in Headquarters at one time."

Ralph gave a respectful nod toward the Panel. "Tell us what you did about the fingerprints."

"First, I secured the plans in a safe place."

"And then?" Ripple proceeded.

"Then I went to Headquarters' Records Office to find anything that might have either or both of the captains' fingerprints. After searching for hours I got lucky and found an old order that had a name I wanted. It was Captain Norman Mort's. I had trouble getting out of there because someone locked the door while I was in the room. With the document under my arm, I tried to force my way out, but the door was bolted too securely. Finally, I realized that whoever was out there might decide to unlock and let me out in order to attack me. The door opened. I bolted between two men. I couldn't get a good look, but it appeared to me that Captain Fritzpatrick and a civilian wanted me and wanted what I had found. It was a track meet but I won. Later, I carried the evidence to the local police who had fingerprinting equipment."

Ralph expanded his chest. "What did they discover?"

"They were able to match the fingerprints of Captain Mort on both documents. I have a certified copy of these from the police department."

"I offer this police-certified letter and picture of the fingerprints as Exhibit B," Ripple said proudly.

Every soul in the courtroom sat motionless while each panel member examined the exhibit. McDill held his breath and rubbed a small crucifix he kept in his pocket. The general's icy owl eyes looked directly into the subtle brown eyes of the defending Captain Ripple. "This is a new process. Do you really think it's been proven to be reliable?"

"Sir, the police think so."

The general closed his eyes in heavy meditation. Ripple couldn't decipher the general's thoughts.

"Your witness," Ripple announced with confidence.

"All right. We'll recess for lunch," Hicks gaveled. "We'll reconvene in one hour."

Helen rushed over to Dennis and locked her fingers in his left hand. "Do you think we have a chance?"

"I hope so, but the prosecution hasn't cross examined Albert yet."

To forget their troubles for a while, the couple had an enjoyable lunch together. It was refreshing to have at least an ounce of relief from the barbs of the government's competent trial counselor. They had time to stroll down the street, enjoy fresh air, and take their time getting back to the courtroom. When they arrived, as usual, the massive crowd gathered to hear the fate of one man that some believed to be a hero.

"If it please the Court," Bailey stepped slowly toward Albert. "You testified that the two captains had offices on the same hall at Headquarters, correct?"

"Yes."

"Have you ever seen them together?" Bailey seemed to smirk.

"No, I haven't." Albert swallowed.

"I understand that you based your suspicion on what this defendant told you about them, correct?"

"Yes, I believed him. I really don't think he'd have any reason to lie." Albert's teeth cracked against each other.

Bailey turned to face the court. "Sirs, this witness is becoming hostile. May I ask leading questions?"

Hicks hesitated and looked at the crowd. "I'll allow it, but you might be stepping on eggshells."

"Thank you, Sir. Mr. Monroe, this accused might lie to save his neck. Did you sense some animosity between Commander McDill and the two captains?"

"No, not at first. I remembered what he told me. But, I did my own research."

"Your own research? Then please tell the Court the details of how you obtained those highly appraised drawings?" Bailey snipped.

Albert bowed his head and sighed so softly that the people could barely hear him. "I...I found Captain Mort's room. I hid and watched him open the chest and pull out the drawing These appeared to be the same drawings that the accused told me. After he left, I opened the chest, found the schematics and discovered they were the drawings."

"Then you stole the plans, didn't you?" Bailey grinned.

Like a firestorm, Albert leaped from his chair. "I stole the plans from a person who stole them in the first place!"

"Sit down," Hicks cried and struck his fist until the table shook.

Albert quickly realized he had confessed to a crime, but then he settled down. "You might charge me with illegal entry, but I was simply recovering stolen property which really belongs to the federal government anyway."

"Objection, your Honors. This kind of sophistry must cease," Bailey appealed.

Ralph countered. "Counselor, you're not questioning a hostile witness, you're badgering the witness."

"Order! Order!" the president shouted.

Two Marine guards planted their feet and stood on each end of the Panel's table. Their granite faces and bayonets quickly restored order.

"I'll take another approach," Bailey offered.

"Mr. Monroe, do you know about military orders?"

"Yes, I was in the Army for a while."

Bailey thought he had snared a prize. "Did you obey all your orders?"

"Yes."

"Were you instructed what would happen to you if you disobeyed orders?"

"Yes."

"At the least you'd be highly reprimanded and, at most, you'd be court-martialed. Right?"

"Yes. Your Honors, we stipulate that my client disobeyed the order. But we ask, was it a legal order?"

"I beg the Court," Bailey pleaded. "Is this man a witness or a defendant's lawyer? Is he some kind of schizophrenic?"

"Watch yourself, Mr. Monroe." Hicks leaned over to get a better view of the witness.

Albert leaped from his chair. "If this man is finished with me, may I be excused from the witness chair? I have an expert witness to offer. May I, your Honors?"

"Object, again," Bailey bellowed. "This is highly irregular. This was not revealed before the trial."

"Your Honor, this lawyer surprised us with a witness, too," Ripple griped.

"Wait," Hicks ordered, "the general has asked for a quick conference."

Four officers huddled around Admiral Hicks and whispered while people

208

strained to hear them. In a few minutes they returned to their assigned seats. Admiral Hicks stated in a clear voice, "Admittedly this is irregular, but we will allow this. Counselor, call in your expert."

"I call Justice Malcolm Tremain to the stand."

A man with bushy white hair appeared from the crowd at the back of the room. Every eye followed him as if they were gazing at a bride-to-be marching down the long aisle of a church. Most had never seen a U.S. Supreme Court Justice. Before the clerk could ask him, he raised his hand and said, "I swear to tell the truth, so help me God." He rested in the witness seat and looked up at Albert with a fatherly look.

"Sir, are you acquainted with the Code of Military Justice?"

"Quite well. I was a U.S. Navy attorney once and a circuit judge in Philadelphia before I was appointed to the Supreme Court," the stately man responded.

"Sir, will you define for the court the term, 'illegal order'?"

"Yes, an illegal order is an order that cannot be obeyed or one that is not acceptable."

"Have you heard the testimony here in this Court?" Albert asked while eyeing every panel member.

"Yes, I was here on vacation and acquired an interest in this case. I sought you out in private to discuss this case. We promised to be confidential until the proper time to testify."

"Justice Tremain, would you consider that order Captain Mort gave to Lt. Commander McDill to be an illegal order?"

"I would, and I am certain that other Supreme Justices would, also," he certified.

Bedlam broke like a tornado. Cheers and hand claps drowned out any further testimony. Only the court could hear the defense counsel say, "I have no further questions."

When the crowd quieted, routine summations followed, for everybody already knew what the lawyers would argue. The court was adjourned to allow the court to deliberate.

Dennis, Helen, Albert, and Ralph rested on a bench outside of Headquarters. "What do you think?" Dennis asked Albert.

"It could go either way. The Panel may discredit some of my testimony.

They may agree with the prosecution that I was a thief. But I hope they won't discount the evidence about the fingerprints. They probably respect the testimony of the Justice, but they have minds of their own. Frankly Dennis, you have a 50-50 chance of staying out of prison."

Dennis wiped his neck like he had a terrific pain. "Oh, well. I'll bear it as long as they give me a cell that's not too small for this frame of mine."

"Dennis, don't talk like that," Helen chided and gave his neck a rub down.

"Well, Helen, it's a possibility, we both know that."

For more than an hour, the four sat and speculated. They even prayed once. McDill could feel the jaws of justice clamping down on his mortal soul. Bravely, he hid his rabid fear from his wife and his lawyers. The waiting was stifling. Helen felt as though she would choke from anticipation while she tried to resist the awful fright that might overcome her. Fear was their most dreadful enemy at the moment. Suddenly, the flash of a rifle barrel got their attention. A Marine guard approached. "Gentlemen and Lady, the court will be in session in a few minutes. Will you follow me, please?"

When McDill entered the massive front entrance he could see gallows hanging from the ceiling. The audience was hushed as the Panel quietly entered and sat at attention behind the long table. "Will the defendant rise?" Admiral Hicks ordered.

Dennis' knees and legs were straight, but his body quivered inside. He held his breath for several seconds.

Hicks began. "Lieutenant Commander Dennis McDill, you realize that we must have strict discipline among our ranks, or we will have chaos."

"Yes, Sir. I know."

"We are commanded to obey orders."

"Yes, Sir."

"Further, you know that larceny is against the law."

"Yes, I do, Sir."

"Commander McDill, this is the decision of this tribunal: As to the larceny, we find you guilty. We sentence you to two years in jail."

Helen held Dennis' arm trying not to faint.

Hicks continued. "However, these years will be suspended provided that your future record remains unblemished."

"Thank God," Helen prayed.

"Commander, as to the charge of disobeying an order, we find that the order is an illegal one and find you not guilty. This court is adjourned."

Dennis' sympathizers actually danced in the aisles. Women kissed him and men shook his hand. The celebration poured out into the street. Dennis McDill was their hero.

Before Dennis went home, Albert drifted beside him. "Dennis, Admiral Hicks has just informed me that Captains Mort and Fritzgerald will be facing court-martials for conspiracy and probably other charges. And I heard that Cougar Mountain is in prison for attempted murder."

"Al, the credit goes to you. Without your gallant research and defense, I'd be in the brig."

"Dennis, this is a great celebration, but I'm worried and curious. I saw Bailey and the senator leave together. That makes me uneasy."

The End

EPILOGUE

"Boss, they christen ships. Shouldn't we christen this little house of worship?"

"Chief, I don't believe it is done that way for a chapel."

"How then, Sir?"

"We'll dedicate it. Bishop King will tell us how."

Another telegram was dispatched to Bishop King by Comer shortly before 8:00 a.m. The Bishop had paid two recent visits to City Point to supervise the erection of the little building and applauded the work both times. Dr. Ellis was elected to dictate a letter to Bishop King in these words:

> *Dear Bishop King,*
> *You are aware of our progress regarding the chapel at City Point. Since it is near my home, I have checked the work every day. I can assert that its construction is finished. We are ready for a proper dedication and respectfully request that you, the Bishop of the Richmond Diocese, oversee and conduct the dedication of our new House of God.*
> *Signed—Richard Ellis, M. D.*

In one day, Dr. Ellis received an affirmative reply. Bishop John J. King of the Diocese of Richmond announced that he would arrive by boat the next Monday afternoon. Miss Josephine Ellis of Appomattox Manor invited the prelate to spend several days and nights at her manor.

On the day of the Bishop's arrival, MacEaton was on watch at the pier. His spyglass scanned the river several times. It focused on a bright object sailing down the river. A regal pennant with a cross majestically floated above a crystal white ship. The young mariner cheered until his lungs almost collapsed. "The Bishop's here! The Bishop's here!"

Crowding feet pounded the boat dock until it began to squeak for mercy under the tonnage. Bishop King walked off the vessel like a revered hero. Quickly he was ushered up the hill to the imposing manor. After a short reception, King met with Lt. Commander McDill, Lieutenant DuBois, and Comer. "I understand you represent the Catholics here in town, am I right?"

McDill moved in front of King, extended his hand and nodded. "Sir, we haven't been elected, but our people want us to assist you in the planning, Bishop."

"Let us dedicate the chapel on Thanksgiving Day because we have a lot to be thankful for. By the way, what shall we name our little house of worship?"

"Bishop, may I speak?" Lt. Phillipe DuBois stood up and shifted into a beam of sunlight. "Some of the people and our crew met last night and we have a suggestion." He shot a nervous look at the commander who was not invited to the meeting. DuBois paused.

"Go ahead, son. Tell us," King insisted.

"We believe it should be named St. Dennis Chapel for two reasons."

"Proceed, young man."

"Years ago my ancestors practically worshiped a saint who lived in Paris. He was their patron saint and he was named St. Denis [sic]."

"Most impressive. A patron saint would be a great model. If I remember my history, he was very popular."

"Yes, Sir. With your blessing, we would like to name our church St. Dennis Chapel."

"You know I shall grant that and firmly support it." Bishop King turned his chair to see DuBois better. "You said, 'for two reasons,' is that correct?"

"Yes, Sir." DuBois shot another nervous look at his commanding officer. "We all voted that it should also be called St. Dennis Chapel in honor of our most revered Lt. Commander Dennis McDill, also."

"I heartily congratulate you and your committee. On behalf of the Diocese, I formally approve and plan to dedicate St. Dennis Chapel of Bermuda Cities in the Commonwealth of Virginia this year of our Lord 1887. If it is agreed, I will lead a delegation from Petersburg, Virginia, to St. Dennis at City Point. We will begin the dedication ceremonies immediately after an early Mass."

"Won't that be a long journey for the Petersburg congregation to march, Bishop?" Dr. Ellis questioned. "There may be some exhaustion."

"My dear doctor, the long march will be worth it. After all, some of you have walked that far to hear a homily of mine."

⚓

Thanksgiving morning ushered a brilliant sunrise. Scores of worshipers gathered.

Marchers, organized four abreast, filed down the road eastward to St. Dennis Chapel promptly. At 11:30 a.m. all marchers arrived, but the band was a few minutes late, so they caught the train. After Mass, an elegant ceremony lasted over an hour. According to the Progress Index of Petersburg, Virginia, a reporter concluded that "It was the equal of which was never heard in this sector. The bishop preached a most eloquent and forceful sermon. For more than an hour he held his hearers spellbound and many regrets were expressed that time would not allow the eloquent divine to entertain his hearers longer. The little chapel was compared to a mustard seed that would flourish and grow to greater dimensions."

At the end of the service, the bishop announced that Reverend John O'Farrell, Pastor of St. Joseph's Church in Petersburg, would run the mission.

Postscript: St. Dennis Chapel exists as a museum at this printing.
It is located in City Point, Hopewell, Virginia.